Because all is fair in love and football...and the past is just the beginning.

Other books by Katie Graykowski

Changing Lanes

By
Katie Graykowski

Dedication

For Robyn and Jax—two mothers who found their families in the foster care system. Motherhood is a gift and you've worked hard for it.

Acknowledgments

Books are like children, you plan for them, but in the end they surprise you. This was not an easy book to write. I cried more than my fair share of tears, but in the end, I'm happy. Thank you to Emily McKay and Jane Myers Perrine for allowing me to bounce ideas off of you. Thank you to Tracy Wolff who is my very own cheering section...all you need are some pom-poms. Thanks to Catherine Morris who inspires me as both a mother and a writer. Thank you to the Chez Zee crowd for providing stimulating conversation on topics that seem to make the other patrons at the surrounding tables leave abruptly. Thank you to Jessica LaMirand for so many things they are too numerous to count. Thanks to Austin RWA because without you, I'd still think GMC was a type of vehicle. Thank you to my husband and daughter who show me everyday that love is the only thing that matters. Thank you to my mother for showing me unconditional love.

Thanks to my 'reckless' sisters who were willing to share their own personal recklessness with me: Catherine Morris, Monika Cimolin, Sharon Harriger-Kraeling, Dawn Sullivan, Ella Quinn, Cheri Jennings-Wine, Jennifer

Pecoraro-Holmes, Renee Tschoepe-Havis, Jessica Sigur, Maryeah Kramer, Susan Pitman-Simpson, Kate Marchand, Amy Wilson, Laura Akers-Collins, Becky Darmogray. Ladies, you amaze me.

Thank you to my beta readers: Angel Buskey, Darla Pond, Amy Howard, Shanna Lubold, Katy Otter, Emily Maynard, Joy Carnation, Sherry Ness, Kathy Camp, Dawn Marie Blackmon, Joanne Pope, Cindy Lee, Stacy Sanders, Sandra Griffiths, Stephanie Zinnicker, and Jenny Kanagy. Ladies, you ROCK! I couldn't have done it without you.

A big thank you to my fans, your encouragement keeps me going.

Chapter 1

Pediatric Oncologist, Laney Nixon longed to do something reckless. With her left pinkie, she flicked on her blinker a good quarter of a mile before she needed to turn. Always the cautious one, she made sure to keep her Volvo sedan five miles under the speed limit, she never gunned it on a yellow, and she always stopped a good five seconds at a stop sign. Being careful was just as much a part of Laney's DNA as eye color or the ability to curl her tongue.

If only she could allow herself to skydive, but she couldn't even bring herself to rip the tag off the mattress she'd bought two years ago. It's not that she was too controlled to be reckless, it was just … well she was too controlled to be reckless.

The fact that she was aware of her controlling nature in itself should have helped her to change it, but recognizing it and fixing it were two different things.

In two days she'd turn thirty. It was a sad state of affairs that an almost-thirty something woman hadn't done anything she regretted. A woman should have at least a few regrets before she turned thirty, but sadly the closest thing she had to a bad decision was an impulse buy of a pair of purple platform heels. When she'd bought them, she'd envisioned herself club hopping like Paris Hilton or God forbid singing karaoke in a spandex mini, but the reality was, they didn't match anything she owned and squished her baby toes. Now, they sat unused in her closet taunting her with their blatant purple-ness and unrealized reckless potential.

She checked the clock on the dash—ten minutes until two. She was going to be early. Laney rolled her eyes. Early went along with the regret-free, boring package. She turned into the parking lot of the Austin Lone Stars football stadium.

Today, she and her fellow Tough Ladies, the triathlon team she'd joined three years ago, were giving a talk on teamwork to the Super Bowl defending champion football team. More than once, she'd wondered why her insignificant little triathlon team needed to talk to anyone about teamwork. True, they all got along, and they were a team, but for the most part, they didn't play together. It's not that they purposefully didn't work as a team, it's just that besides training together, swimming, running, and cycling were solitary sports.

Laney chewed on the inside of her cheek.

Every single Tough Lady was a risk-taker except her. Nina was a commercial airline pilot who was always flying off to some exotic destination. January owned a bar on Sixth Street and didn't take crap from anyone. Charisma, their fearless leader, had been known to talk perfectly sane people into running another ten miles for no good reason. And then there was Susie. If their team had a mom, she was it. She made homemade granola and taught eighth grade—if that wasn't fearless, then Laney didn't know what was.

Her teammates were always after her to break out of her shell.

Maybe today Laney would have raunchy sex with a steaming hot football player in the elevator of the stadium, or better yet, on the fifty-yard line. She glanced down at her serviceable beige pantsuit and matching beige pumps.

Underneath, she wore a comfortable beige cotton bra and panty set. Not exactly hot sex lingerie. What were the chances of her meeting a legally blind professional football player?

In great detail, she would describe the sexy bra and panty set she'd wished she were wearing. It would be red and lacy and tiny. How exactly did the sighted explain red to the blind? Okay, so he needed to have been sighted and then lost his vision. But how? Disease? If he played pro ball than he was too young for Cataracts, Glaucoma, Macular degeneration and the chances of an athlete having diabetic eye disease or a brain tumor was slim. It could happen, but it wasn't likely. For that matter, the chances were slim there would be a legally blind professional football player.

So ... there was zero chance of raunchy football player sex. She couldn't exactly be fearless in safe underwear.

She pulled into a parking space by the front gate, put the car in park, and turned off the engine.

That was it. She slapped the steering wheel for effect. After this meeting, she was heading straight to the closest Victoria Secret and buying them out of thongs—lacy ones that probably itched and would take a highly trained surgical staff to remove. By this time tomorrow, she'd have an underwear drawer full of regrets.

She stepped out of the car, clicked the fob to lock it, and walked toward the front gate.

"Lanes, over here," a high-pitched Betty-Boop voice called over her right shoulder.

She turned around. Nina Munoz waved from two rows over. She was petite, curvy, and had miles of thick black hair. Add in her fiery Latin attitude and Betty Boop voice— she was a walking, talking male fantasy. Laney imagined that every single man on board the plane she was piloting, paid close attention to the preflight announcements.

"We're supposed to meet them on the field or something." Nina made her way to Laney.

Why couldn't she be more like Nina? She scuba-dived, sky dived, and ate carbs at every meal. She drove a Corvette and routinely ran red lights. Nina probably had thousands of regrets.

"Ladies, wait for me." January Jenkowski called from the window of her Nissan Leaf. She pulled into the parking space close to Laney and got out of her car.

Laney's boxy beige Volvo looked like a square mushroom next to the baby blue car. And next to January who was a six-foot blonde surfer girl, Laney's dishwater brown bob and five foot six inch height might as well have been beige too.

Laney looked down. Her suit was the exact same color as her car. Was everything in her life beige? When she got home, she was burning everything beige. She sucked on her bottom lip. Now that she thought about it, her entire condo was beige.

"I just came from Susie's. She's up and walking around." January shook her head and artfully windblown blonde waves settled around her like a model in a shampoo commercial. "They remove the pins tomorrow."

"I know. My father does good work." Laney rolled her eyes. Her father, orthopedic surgeon Giles Nixon was the master of control. His God complex gave God a run for his money. But he knew how to fix bones, if not people, and he'd helped her friend. Not only would Susie be back on her feet soon, but she'd be running like nothing had ever happened.

"Okay, ladies," Charisma LeMair looped an arm around Laney and January. "Let's give this football team some hell."

Charisma was the most aptly named person that Laney had ever met. Add in her take-no-prisoners personality and she could talk a legion of couch potatoes into running ten miles uphill, in the rain. Her dirty blonde hair had streaks of purple this week. Last week it was red. Part manic cheerleader and part evil dictator, she got things done. And the fact that she was all of five foot tall, only made her more formidable. She was a walking-talking risk taker.

They marched arm-in-arm to the front gate. Laney was proud to be a Tough Lady, proud to be in the company of these dynamic women, and proud to have them as her close friends. If she couldn't manage reckless, then she would live vicariously through them.

Devon Harding rubbed his aching shoulder and told himself that exhaustion was just a state of mind. Practice had kicked his butt today. His back hurt from the last hit he'd taken, and his knees were killing him. As a ten-year veteran of the NFL, this would be his last year. It's not that he'd lost his edge, but rather football just wasn't fun anymore. He'd made plenty of money, and it was time for pursuing his true passion—food. First and Ten Barbecue had been his dream for as long as he could remember. He realized that most men dreamed of becoming a professional football player while he dreamed of smoked chicken and brisket. Yet another example of how he liked to march to a different drummer. Many times his mother had commented that she'd like to shoot that fucking drummer.

Right now, all he wanted to do was go home, soak his tired body in the hot tub for several hours, and check on the brisket he'd started smoking earlier this morning. The last thing he wanted to do was sit through some dull team meeting where the coach hammered home all the mistakes he'd made today. Not that Coach Robbins wasn't justified, but Devon realized he'd made mistakes, and he would run over them again and again in his head, beating himself up for the rest of the evening. Tomorrow, he wouldn't make the same mistake again.

"Hey big guy." Grace Robbins, the coach's new wife, touched his left arm. The moment he'd met Grace he'd known they would become friends. At one point, he'd been of a mind to ask her out, but she'd always had eyes for the coach. Now, she was one of his best friends.

"What's up?" He set his helmet on the table, grabbed a paper cup, and filled it with water from the large orange cooler always sitting on the sidelines.

"What did you think about Marla?" Grace was on a mission to find him a love connection.

He tried to explain to her that he'd already met the woman of his dreams and they'd lost touch. He'd purposefully left out the part about having met her at Camp Huawni when he was seventeen and that he couldn't remember her name. A long time ago, he'd learned two things—most people didn't believe in true love and those that did, didn't believe he'd met his at the age of seventeen.

But he had.

Even now when he dreamed of her, he still got that zip of a feeling. She'd had eyes the color of the Caribbean, hair the color of peanut butter, and wanted to be a painter instead of a doctor like both her parents. Back then it had been a lightning bolt to the heart.

Now, he was just waiting for The Universe to circle back around and reintroduce them, another fact which he left out.

"Marla?" He scratched the back of his head. "Was she the blonde or the brunette you set me up with last week?"

Grace rolled her eyes as she shifted her newborn son from her right arm to her left. "She was the redhead. She called last night to tell me she thinks she's in love with you even though you kept calling her Monica."

"Oh yeah … Monica." He nodded. "She had a whiny voice and kept flipping her hair. It was weird."

"You're so picky. She was nice … good marriage potential." Grace smiled kindly. "I know you've met Miss Right and that you lost touch. I wish you'd let me help you find her."

He shook his head. "You've been talking to my mother."

His mother was dying to hire a private detective to track down EJ—short for Elaine Janece—but he wouldn't let her. Unfortunately, Camp Huawni hadn't been big on last names so he only knew her first and middle names. They'd called each other by their initials—EJ and DJ.

Grace put her free hand up like a traffic cop. "We just want you to be happy. We love you and worry."

How could he argue with that? The women in his life wanted him to be happy. He just wished they'd dial it down a notch. Re-meeting EJ because his mother and his friend had signed him up on e-Harmony, Match.com, Christian Mingle, Jewish Singles, and Farmer's Only wasn't exactly the way he'd envisioned it. He imagined it would be something more organic, like the way his father had met his mother.

When his dad had met his mom at the grocery store pouring over the mangos, he'd taken one look at her and asked her to marry him. Devon smiled to himself. His mom had promptly slapped the crap out of his dad, turned around, and finished her shopping. They met again six months later at a Fourth of July barbecue and began dating.

Clearly God or The Universe was taking its own damn time directing him back to EJ, but he would wait because she was worth it.

He reached his hands out to the baby. "Give me my godson."

It was the proudest moment in his life when Coach Robbins and Grace had asked him and Clint Grayson to be co-godfathers to their son Luke.

"You're all sweaty and gross."

"Guys love sweat." He leaned over and kissed the top of Luke's precious little head. "It's manly."

Grace shrugged and handed him the baby. "He needs a bath anyway."

Carefully, he cuddled the little guy like a football. Not having been around babies much, he was a little intimidated at first, but all it had taken was one look into Luke's sweet and soulful eyes, and he was in love. Luke yawned with his whole body and his eyelids drooped. Devon couldn't help the grin. That was just about the cutest thing ever.

"He's getting tired." He rocked Luke back and forth. "Seth, get over here and sing this baby to sleep."

Devon winked at Grace. "Since he's the newest rookie, we make him do all sorts of crazy things. He likes it."

"I can't sing." Seth Charming ambled over. "I'm not singing the baby to sleep."

"Yes, you are." With his free hand, he pointed to the field. "Remember how those pesky defensive tackles want to kill you. Remember how I'm the only person standing between you and them?"

"Twinkle, twinkle little star…"

"That's what I thought."

Grace put her hands over her ears. Clearly, just because she was a singer with one platinum single and an album coming out, she couldn't appreciate some excellent humiliation singing. He glanced down at Luke. His eyes were closed, and his breathing was steady and shallow. The kid didn't mind that Seth was off key, hummed when he couldn't remember the words, and tapped his foot to some imagined rhythm that wasn't Twinkle, Twinkle Little Star.

Grace looked like she was about to cry. "Please stop. For the good of the hearing world, please stop singing."

Seth shot her a charming smile. "Told you I can't sing." His hips rocked from side-to-side. "But I sure can dance."

Grace held her arms out for the baby. "Let me put him back in his stroller for his nap."

Devon took a step back. "He's good. I don't mind holding him through the team meeting."

Plus, it would give him an excuse to duck into the locker room if the meeting ran too long.

A loud whistle blew, and he turned around.

Coach Robbins motioned them over to him. "Take a seat. Today we're talking about team work."

There were groans and moans and lots of eye rolling, but everyone took a seat in the front few rows of the stadium. Devon scanned his fellow teammates looking for a seat that would give him an easy out. He plopped down in front of Grace.

"While y'all are working much better as a team, I would like for you guys to meet some ladies who have taken team work to a new level. The Tough Ladies are a local triathlon team who just completed the Ironman Cozumel. When I heard their story, I knew I wanted you to meet them." Coach pointed to the four ladies walking around the backside of the track toward them.

Devon leaned closer trying to make out the four women laughing and talking as they walked. One was a tall blonde who looked like she could have just walked off a beach, there was another short blonde who talked animatedly with her hands, then a tiny, dark haired beauty, and a slightly taller than average sized brunette wearing the ugliest brown pant suit he'd ever seen. Sunlight skipped off her hair—it was the color of peanut butter.

He sat up.

As they got closer, the brunette looked up, and her Caribbean blue eyes made contact with his. His pulse skyrocketed. Could it be EJ?

Relief and nerves jangled through him. Finally. Thank you, God. He'd sent her back to him.

Devon's gaze never left her. Part of him couldn't believe that she was really here. She'd filled out in the last fourteen years. Gone was the skinny girl he'd known— she'd been replaced with a tall, lanky woman. Did she still have freckles on her nose? He strained to see, but couldn't tell from this distance.

It seemed as though a lifetime and no time at all had passed since the last night they'd snuck out of their cabins to meet by the lake.

And here she was again.

She smiled and waved to him, and he nearly dropped poor Luke.

EJ headed straight for him. She recognized him—of course she did. His heart rate skyrocketed. He turned on his most charming smile and waited for her. It seemed to take a lifetime. Had she thought about him every day too? Did she still have the leather bracelet with his initials he'd made for her? He still had the one she'd made for him.

Anticipation nearly choked the life out of him. He couldn't believe his luck. He'd been in love with her for almost half his life and here she was finally making her way to him. In a matter of milliseconds, she would jump up and down, screaming with joy and sobbing her heart out because she'd found him again.

She nodded in his direction and kept on walking. "Grace, what are you doing here?"

He waited for her to say something to him … and waited … and waited … and waited.

Nothing.

She didn't remember him. His heart fell out of his chest and rolled to her feet. He actually glanced down to see if it was under her ugly brown shoe.

How could she have forgotten him? He'd thought of her every day since her dad had picked her up two days early at the last session of Camp Huawni.

He craned his neck so he could keep watching her.

"Laney, I didn't know you were a Tough Lady." Grace said from one row behind him.

Laney? She didn't go by EJ anymore? Maybe this wasn't her. Then why did his gut twist up like a pretzel?

Hell, nervous excitement vibrated out of him. Maybe Laney was a nickname for Elaine?

"For three years now." She nodded as she turned to him. "May I hold my favorite baby?"

She was smiling directly at him. The radiance of it made him want to offer her marriage right on the spot. He chewed on his lower lip. He was ninety percent sure that was a bad idea.

What exactly was he supposed to say to her? At camp they'd talked about everything, but now it appeared she didn't remember him. The subject of lost love wasn't exactly small talk. He looked around. Did he mention the weather? He'd never had trouble talking to her before, but he was pretty sure his mouth was broken. Her gaze locked onto his, and he forgot how to breathe. He forced air into his lungs.

"The baby." She pointed to Luke. "May I hold him?"

Devon glanced down to find he was indeed holding baby Luke.

"Sorry about Devon. He's Luke's godfather, and he loves holding him." Grace smacked him on the back of the head. "Give her the baby."

"Sh-sh-sh-sh … sure." Now he was stammering. He'd never stammered in his life. He stood and gently passed Luke to her. As second-time first impressions went, this was a fumble of epic proportions.

When their hands made contact, he leaned forward wanting to be a little closer to her. Now, if he could only talk to her. Surely that would help to further their relationship … well to actually get her to remember him would be an excellent start.

"There's my sweet boy." She positioned Luke with his head on her shoulder and stuck out her hand to Devon. "I'm Laney Nixon."

Nixon. Now, he remembered. How many nights had he laid awake trying to recall that fact? And here she was.

He concentrated hard on saying his name, trying to keep the stammering away. "I love you. Will you marry me?"

Crap. This was bad.

Chapter 2

Laney handed the baby over to Grace. Clearly this guy had a head injury. Poor thing, it appeared that he didn't even know.

"Okay, big guy. Let's have a seat." She touched his arm meaning to help him into the chair and noticed that he was shaking ever so slightly. The temperature was in the low-eighties—not overly hot for October, but the sun was beating down. Perhaps it was heat stroke. She pulled the penlight she always carried out of her jacket pocket and clicked it on. She leaned down to him and flicked it back and forth checking for pupil response. "Besides the shaking, sweating, and light headedness, are you nauseated? Do you have a headache? Do you feel any tingling in your hands or feet?"

His pupil response was normal.

"Don't worry, Devon. She's a doctor." Grace patted his shoulder.

The dumbstruck look on his face was fading into something a little closer to normal. "I'm fine. I feel fine."

He stuck out his hand to her. "Devon Harding."

There was something about him ... something familiar. She felt like they'd met before, but she couldn't place him. It must be déjà vu, or as science explained, an anomaly of the brain in which it creates an impression that the experience has happened before. That made more sense. Her brain had misfired—that was completely understandable considering how magnificently he was built. He was a large, powerful man, but beautiful too.

"I'm fine." He smiled. "Really."

Laney wasn't convinced, but she shook his hand anyway. "Laney Nixon. Are you having any chest pain or numbness in your left arm?"

His smiled drooped like he was disappointed about something, and then he shook his head and smiled brightly. "No ma'am, I'm just about perfect, thank you. Will you have dinner with me tonight?"

"Um …" She looked to Grace for clarification. Was he for real? He still looked a little red in the face.

Grace shrugged.

"Why?" The question fell out of Laney's mouth. Strangers never asked her out, especially muscular and handsome strangers. Apart from an amazing body that she could clearly see because he wasn't wearing a shirt, he had kind brown eyes and a headful of thick red-gold hair. It was just long enough to run her fingers through but not too long that it could be pulled back. In her book, a man with a ponytail was someone too lazy to have his hair cut.

"I'd like to have dinner with you tonight because you look like an interesting person, and I want to get to know you better. It's just dinner. I'm harmless." He glanced at Grace. "Tell her that I'm harmless and that she should have dinner with me."

Grace shifted her sleeping baby to her shoulder. "He's harmless. He lives with his mom. If he does anything to make you angry, just tell his mother, Sweet Louise and she'll kill him."

He lived with his mother? He had to be in his early thirties. Why did someone that old still live at home? She'd already dated more than her fair share of dysfunctional men. Being reckless didn't involve dysfunctional.

"Thanks, Grace." He shot her a dirty look. "Now she thinks I'm a loser."

He turned back to Laney. "I don't live with my mother, she lives with me. Five years ago she came to Austin to take care of me after shoulder surgery, and she never left. I can't help that we share a house. She won't leave."

That sort of made sense.

His gaze turned hopeful. He really wanted to go out with her. It had been a long time since anyone but her patients had looked at her with hopeful eyes.

Laney wanted to do something reckless, well here was her chance.

"Okay. Dinner it is." Her tone was resolute like she'd just decided she needed to do surgery.

She debated about giving a stranger her home address. "You can pick me up at Dell Children's hospital. I need to see a patient. How about six o'clock?"

She'd have to buy some sexy underwear and a new dress—something that wasn't beige. Did she have time to shop this afternoon? If this didn't take more than an hour, she could stop off at Nordstrom before heading back to the hospital. Maybe Nina could go with her and keep her from buying something beige.

"That's perfect. I'll pick you up at six in the lobby." He cocked his head to the left and his smile turned plastic. "So you're really a doctor?"

"I'm a pediatric oncologist." Laney got ready for the onslaught of oohs and ahs. Most people tripped over themselves to celebrate her career choice making her into some humanitarian healer, all the while asking how she could handle such a depressing job.

His smile faded, the twinkle in his eyes cooled, and five nearly even lines cut across his brow. "I see."

She hadn't experienced this before. Was it her, or did he seem a little angry? Did he want to break their date because she was a pediatric oncologist? Men had broken dates with her for all sorts of reasons, but that had never been one of them.

"That's how I met Laney." Grace gently patted Luke's back. She was always touching her children—both her biological son and her three stepchildren. She made motherhood look easy. "I was working in the music lab with some of the kids, and Laney wheeled in the cutest five-year-old I've ever seen."

"Lara. She's adorable." And not doing well. Her leukemia wasn't responding to treatment. Every evening, Laney stopped by her room for a game of Uno. "Have you ever been to the Dell Children's Music lab? The patients love it, and it gives them a much needed distraction while they're in the hospital."

"No, sorry." He hung his head. All of the enthusiasm he's had for their date gone.

"Devon doesn't do hospitals." Grace touched his arm. "According to his mother, the only times he's stepped foot in one were his birth and his shoulder surgery."

"Do you have nosocomephobia—the fear of hospitals?" Laney's heart melted. He had a fear, and he was willing to overcome it because he wanted to go out with her. The caregiver side of her needed to make it all better. "Why don't we meet at the restaurant? What did you have in mind?"

"Dell Children's is fine. I don't have a fear of hospitals exactly, I just don't like them. Just like I don't like dentist's offices and the DMV." He smiled and his brown eyes twinkled in the sunlight.

How had he managed that? Did her eyes ever twinkle? She didn't ever remember twinkling.

"Six o'clock in the lobby." She smiled at him, and his eyes twinkled again. She tried to twinkle her eyes but blinked instead. When she got home, she was working on that twinkling thing.

"Ladies, come here." It was Charisma. "Coach Robbins wants us to talk about our last Ironman."

Since it had been on the local news, that's all everyone wanted to talk about. It wasn't that big of a deal. Teams worked together.

Laney kissed Luke's soft mass of blond curls, nodded at Devon, and gave Grace a little wave. She made it down the couple of steps and stood next to Nina.

"Guys, these women are incredible. Besides the fact that they can each swim almost two and a half miles, bike one-hundred and twelve miles, and run an entire marathon all in the same day without taking a break, they also care about their team." Coach Robbins looked at Charisma. "Ladies, please tell my team what you did for yours."

Charisma stepped forward. "We are one Tough Lady short today, but our teammate, Susie, is still recovering from surgery. Last month in Cozumel, ten miles from the finish line, she tripped and broke three bones in her foot. This was her first triathlon, and she'd trained so hard. We couldn't leave her."

Nina took a deep breath. "More than anything she wanted to cross the finish line. Susie couldn't walk on her own, so we took turns carrying her."

Charisma turned around so that the quote on the back of her Touch Ladies T-shirt could be seen.

January read it out loud. "*If you can't run, you crawl. If you can't crawl—you find someone to carry you.*"

"Joss Whedon wrote that. It was *Firefly* episode twelve." Devon called from the stands.

The fact that he knew that made him a thousand times more interesting. Laney's greatest passion outside of medicine was Sci-Fi. Especially, anything touched by Joss Whedon and Tim Minear.

Their eyes locked and a few small butterflies danced in her stomach. Well, not actual butterflies, she knew the sensation was caused by a rush of adrenaline and cortisol through her system due to arousal. As blood rushed to deep tissue, it shut down digestion and increased the heart rate resulting in the flutter in the stomach. For once, she wished that she didn't know the physiological reason and could just enjoy the fluttering.

Devon winked and blew her a kiss.

Laney felt all of the blood that should have been on the way to her brain rush to her face, breasts, and vag—she needed to stop the clinical analysis now and enjoy the arousal.

Nina elbowed her in the ribs and whispered, "Stop eye flirting with the hot offensive tackle. The chemistry between the two of you is starting to turn me on."

"Pervert." Laney whispered back.

Nina put her arm around Laney. "Everyone's got to have a hobby."

"Susie … well all of us, crossed the finish line together. While swimming, running, and biking aren't exactly team sports, we choose to be a team. If one of us stumbles," Charisma swept her arms wide meaning all of them, "we all catch her."

"What about your times? Weren't you a little pissed because you finished with longer times?" It was a large African American player with giant pecs and a gold front tooth.

"While it wasn't my best personal time, it was the best time I've ever had running ten miles." January smiled.

They'd taken turns telling ghost stories, making up poems, singing songs, and doing impressions to keep Susie's mind off of the pain.

"Wasn't she disqualified?" The guy hunched his shoulders. "Sure, she crossed the finish line, but it didn't mean anything."

Charisma arched an eyebrow and pulled herself up to her full height of four-foot-nine. "Her score might not have counted, but all of her hard work paid off. She didn't quit, didn't give up, and she didn't give in to the pain. She wanted to finish and she did. Winning isn't the only goal, sometimes finishing is more important."

The football player sat back in his chair. He'd backed down, just like everyone else who came up against Charisma.

"See guys, this is what's missing from our team." Coach Robbins pointed to the back of Charisma's T-shirt. "You need to be willing to carry your fellow teammate—"

"Coach, it's not that we don't want to carry our fellow players, it's more like we can't lift them. Keshaun, what do you weigh?" A lanky white man asked from the front row.

"Two ninety." He snarled. "If you can't lift two-ninety you need to find an easier sport like say, kickball or synchronized swimming." He pulled out his smartphone. "It says right here that the YMCA is putting together a belly dancing team. You'd be perfect."

"Kiss my ass." The first guy jumped up and onto the track. "I don't need belly dancing lessons." He ripped off his shirt and danced around.

Several of the players threw empty cups at him. She glanced up at Devon. He was watching her like a thirsty man drinking his fill—feature by feature—he was drinking her in. Her entire life, she'd only ever had one person look at her that way, and he'd been all of seventeen years old. Back then it had been worshipful and tender and a little overwhelming, and now, it was no different. She looked away.

Dinner tonight with him would be something completely out of her element.

Usually the unknown made her nervous, but this time she was excited. A new reckless experience. Maybe she'd even have a one-night stand.

Thirty minutes later, she and the other Tough Ladies made their way back out to the parking lot.

"Did you see how that Devon guy eye-flirted with Laney the whole time we were on the track?" January put her arm around Laney. "You should go for it. Have some fun and some raunchy gorilla sex."

Laney sucked on her bottom lip. "How is that different from regular sex? There are only so many places he can insert his—"

"Stop issuing a medical opinion. Just strip down and let him play with your girl parts. He looks like he'd be good in bed." Nina nudged her with her elbow.

"He had really big hands." January nodded. "You know what that means?"

"That's a myth." At least she thought it was a myth. Now that she thought about it, she remembered something about finger size. "Actually, I believe there is some research out of Korea that suggests that men with smaller index fingers in comparison to their ring fingers do have a larger than average penis."

"Crap, I didn't get a good look at his fingers." Nina's mouth pinched. "Did you?"

"No, he was too far away." January shrugged. "I guess Lanes here will need to fill us in."

Charisma opened her giant Louis Vuitton purse and dug through it. "You need to think about safety." She rooted around some more and came up with a handful of condoms. "Wait. Do you think he uses anabolic steroids? These may be too big."

She stuffed the condoms back in her purse.

"Research suggests that anabolic steroids don't shrink the penis but the scrotum—"

"Lanes, promise me that tonight you won't use the words, research suggests, penis, or vagina." Nina pointed at

26

Laney. "I need for you to have crazy, hot sex with this football player so that I can live vicariously through you. My current boyfriend is pink, vibrates, sounds like a lawn mower, and runs on D batteries."

"Please tell me you're practicing environmentally safe sex." January turned to Nina. Recycling was January's religion—some people worshipped Jesus and some people worshipped Buddha—January recycled.

"Duh, I use rechargeable batteries." Nina probably didn't, but if she admitted to using regular batteries, January would launch into a lecture that usually took at least two rounds of margaritas to finish.

Charisma pulled out the condoms again. "Here. I hope you use them all."

There must have been twenty condoms. "I don't think that's likely. According to the Kinsey Institute, couples between the ages of eighteen and twenty-nine only have sex one hundred and twelve times a year. That's a little over twice a week."

"Do you just spout this shit because you know we're not going to check it?" Nina smiled. "And if so, can you come up with some better statistics because I need to believe that if I'm ever part of a couple, I get to have sex more than twice a week."

"It's interesting. Research shows that on any given day over a hundred thousand couples have sex. So right now, sixty-thousand people are doing it." Laney loved to bore them with statistics. In fact sometimes she looked up completely useless info just to piss them off.

"Now you're just being mean. Sixty-thousand people are going at it right now while I'm left to dream about Leo the battery—oops sorry—the rechargeable battery operated love machine." Nina shook her head. "I feel so lonely."

"Don't worry, we're all lonely except Laney." Charisma slid her enormous bag back on her shoulder. "Tomorrow morning ... five-thirty. We're doing sprints, and we're expecting details. Since we all hate sprints, a good, long sexy story should take our minds off of them."

"Leave it to baby Hitler to come up with a way to combine sex and working out." January snapped her fingers. "I've got it. You should start a new workout routine that involves sex. You could do an entire line of DVDs and downloads."

Nina shook her head. "They already have that. It's called porn." Her phone beeped. She pulled it out. "Crap, I'm going to be late. I've got a laser hair removal appointment in ten minutes. Unfortunately it's on the other side of town."

She clicked her car alarm and jumped in her Corvette.

There was no doubt in Laney's mind that Nina would be there on time. It didn't matter that Austin didn't have a loop or that it would take a normal person in no traffic at least thirty minutes to get there. Nina was going to make it in ten minutes.

Laney took the condoms, stuffed them in her purse, and headed to her car. She had some shopping to do. Tonight, reckless was her middle name.

Chapter 3

Devon wasn't exactly nervous, he was excited and anxious, and well ... a little nervous. Tonight had to be perfect. All EJ needed was a little alone time with him, and she'd remember him. She was special and classy and so different than she'd been fourteen years ago. She probably loved art museums and the ballet and read War and Peace. It's not that he didn't like those things—he'd never read War and Peace—it's just that he, well ... didn't like those things. But he could learn to like them, even love them for Laney.

His plan was to spend as much time with her as she'd let him. Did they still have common interests? He let out a long, slow breath. Besides football, he liked cooking, Sci-Fi especially anything done by Joss Whedon. He was a simple guy. His idea of a perfect evening was a pizza and a *Farscape* Marathon.

He was a beer and barbecue guy, and she was probably a fancy champagne and French cuisine kind of girl. Years ago, her parents had been big on culture and society functions. They took her to art exhibits, the theater, and had forced her into years of cotillion where she'd claimed to have learned how to use all those little forks he'd only seen at fancy restaurants. He shrugged. He'd make it work.

It had taken almost fourteen years for him to find her again, and he wasn't about to screw it up.

His dad had screwed it up, and it had cost him six months that he could have spent with his mom. In light of the fact that his father had died when Devon was ten, he could have used that extra six months.

With his EJ—Laney, Devon didn't want to waste a minute. He knotted his tie. He was ready for his future, and Laney hopefully would play a huge part in it.

More than anything, he wanted her to remember him. It had stung this afternoon when she'd looked at him with only polite curiosity. He'd thought of her every day and today, she hadn't known him.

She'd become a doctor. The only thing she hadn't wanted to do with her life. He wasn't sure how he felt about that. It's not that he didn't like her being a doctor, it's more that he wanted to make sure that she'd been the one who picked it for herself. He could remember her overbearing father with great clarity. The man had grabbed Laney's arm and practically thrown her in the car. That day, her frightened Caribbean blue eyes had burned themselves into his memory. He'd run after the sleek gray Jaguar as it bounced down the dirt road that lead out of the camp until it had pulled out onto the highway and the receding taillights had faded into the expansive sunset.

Tears had streamed down her cheeks as she'd turned around in the backseat and watched him run after her.

His stomach muscles clinched. That had been the single worst day of his life. Over the years, he'd run through that day a thousand times in his mind trying to find a way that he could have changed things. But he'd been young and powerless and afraid he'd make things worse for her.

He shook his head. The past didn't matter; the future was where he should be looking.

Tonight he was taking her to an interpretative dance dinner theater thing that Seth Charming had arranged for him. Since Seth was the only person he knew from a rich, snooty family, he was the one to ask about cultural events. The rookie had hooked him up with some front row tickets, and Devon had agreed not to embarrass him for an entire week. It was going to be tough, but Laney was more than worth it.

"Do I get to meet her?" His mother walked into the master bedroom.

"Who?" He hadn't told her about Laney. Once he did, she'd hound him relentlessly to meet her, and then she'd spend hours telling Laney how he'd pined over her for months after he'd gotten back from camp. Or worse, what if his mother hated Laney for hurting her son. It had happened before. Call him crazy, but right now, he wanted Laney to think only nice thoughts about him. His mother, Sweet Louise, was a wonderful person, but she tended to go overboard with whatever she did. Whether it was gardening or loving her son, she went to extremes. That was fine with him, but Laney would get caught in the crossfire. He loved his mother, but she liked to walk in, take charge, and mess things up.

"The girl you just emptied your entire closet on the floor for. I've never seen you this nervous over a date. She must be something special." His mom picked up some trousers from the floor, walked to his closet, stopped, and turned around. "What am I doing? Your momma doesn't work here, pick up after yourself."

She dropped the trousers and walked to the door. "Don't do anything I wouldn't do."

She walked out into the hall.

Knowing his mother, there wasn't anything she wouldn't do.

Tonight was the first night of his life.

Three hours later, he wanted to cry. If he'd had less testosterone and no self-esteem, he might succumb to tears, but as he was a guy, that wasn't going to happen. Hands down, this was the worst date of his life. Not only was the night a total disaster, but she still hadn't recognized him.

"I'm pretty sure I got all of the Parmesan cheese out of your hair." He fisted and unfisted his hands. Tomorrow, Seth was a dead man. He gave Devon the tickets to the worst interpretative dance show in the history of the world. Naked people dancing around and throwing food at the audience wasn't art, it was weirdness.

Laney unlatched the gold clip holding her hair back and shook it out. It was graceful and sexy at the same time. He wanted to run his fingers through her hair, but instead stuffed his hands into his pockets. She was wearing a lacy blue clingy dress that showed off her toned body. And she'd done something to her eyes to make them appear larger and bluer. It had taken ten full minutes for words to come out of his mouth when he'd seen her walking toward him. And unfortunately, that had been the best part of the evening. It would be a miracle if she agreed to see him again after tonight.

He was trying so hard to impress her, but all he'd managed to do was coat her in parmesan cheese.

"It's okay. I don't think it would have been so bad if we weren't sitting on the front row." She opened her little gold purse-thing and tucked the clip inside.

"I can't apologize enough for this evening. The show was billed as provocative interpretative dance dinner theater. I was sure they meant provocative as in thought provoking and not as in naked." There was no way to salvage this evening. If only he could start again. He'd take her to the symphony or opera or to some foreign film festival where the subtitles had subtitles.

"And disturbing." She pulled another sliver of Parmesan cheese out of her hair. "I don't get why the guy rode a wheel of parmesan cheese out on stage, took off his clothes, danced with the cheese, and then shredded it all over the audience … and then there was the weird rant about the IRS."

"Don't forget the water balloons." Devon had buttoned his jacket to hide the huge wet blotch left by the balloon that had tagged him on the upper thigh. It looked like he'd peed his pants. Again, he just wanted to hit rewind and redo this entire evening. He'd tripped over the best foot he'd tried to put forward.

"Speaking of that, are you okay? A direct hit to the scrotum can be painful, but I don't think there was enough force behind it to cause any testicular damage." She tucked her purse under her arm. "I don't have my medical bag with me, but I can take a look if you're in pain."

If there was ever a time to die of embarrassment, this was it. He waited for a heart attack, or a lightning bolt, or for his head to explode, but nothing happened.

Laney didn't sound the least bit embarrassed. Then again, she was a doctor. The human body was nothing more than a machine that needed fixing.

They walked to his car—tonight he'd brought the Cadillac Escalade because she was a classy lady and needed to ride in a classy car for their uber classy date.

He opened the door for her and fought the urge to apologize again for the evening; he'd already said all there was to say. He offered his hand to help her in and her purse fell, bounced off the running board, and landed upside down in a puddle of mud. Could the night get any worse?

He knelt down and picked it up. Mud oozed through his fingers and the latch popped open. Six foiled condom packets, two pens, a credit card, and twenty bucks fell out. Out of nowhere a huge gust of wind blew the condoms across the parking lot. He grabbed the twenty dollars and the credit card before they flew away.

Did he go after the condoms or pretend that he hadn't seen them?

He glanced up at Laney whose cheeks were flushed as she watched them blow across the parking lot. One landed on the windshield of a gray Toyota Highlander and got stuck under the windshield wiper.

Given the last ten minutes, it was hard to pinpoint when the evening had actually hit rock bottom. Every situation had peaks and valley only this one had no peaks and a whole lot of flood-plain valley.

Devon closed her door and walked to the driver's side. It was safer pretending that he hadn't seen them. Six condoms. He smiled to himself. She had confidence in him that was for sure.

When he opened his door, he heard laughter. The sound soothed the part of his soul that was sure he'd never see her again. Laney was doubled over, tears running down her face, and laughing her ass off.

So the girl with the bizarre sense of humor was still in there. Good to know. Years ago, making her laugh had been his number one priority—the sound was still music to his ears.

He wanted to touch her... nothing too personal, but he needed a physical connection between them. Was running his fingers through her hair too much? He saw more cheese but picking it out reminded him of monkeys picking lice off of each other. What about stroking her back? He raised his hand, but couldn't quite figure out where to start. He settled for lightly patting her on the upper back. She didn't seem to mind. The lace of her blue dress—the same color as her eyes—was soft instead of itchy as he'd thought it would be. Finally, he settled a hand between her shoulder blades. His big hand covered a good portion of her back.

It took a five full minutes, but she finally sat up, wiped her eyes, and looked at him. Without a doubt, she was the most beautiful thing he'd ever seen—the laughter shining in her eyes and the moonlight in her hair. His mind took a snapshot so that fifty years from now he would remember this moment in great detail.

"Hands down, this is the worst date I have ever been on." Her smile made it funny instead of pathetic. "How about you?"

"This is definitely the worst date I've ever been on. Don't get me wrong, I've had some bad ones, but this is a new level." His bad mood was lifting. Just being near her made him happy. Would it always be like this?

"How do you think we could make it worse?" She smiled broadly, and he noticed a slight overbite. He didn't remember the overbite.

"You could turn out to be a vegetarian." He offered. She hadn't been all those years ago, but if she were now, it wouldn't be a deal breaker. He would know by now, but since they hadn't had dinner, he still didn't know what she liked to eat.

"Sorry to disappoint. I like meat. Cows taste good." She turned so that her back was against the door. "I could bring up how my biological clock is ticking and that I'm looking to get married soon and have lots of babies."

Strangely, he was okay with that, but that wasn't quite the response she was looking for.

"And I could bring up my liberal views on plural marriage. How would you like to get in on the ground floor by being wife number one?" He absolutely wanted only one wife, but she was right, it was fun talking about all the things he shouldn't say on a date. Since trying to impress her was out the door, the least he could do was make her laugh. "Did I mention that my parents met at a family reunion and that my eighteen brothers and sisters all live with me?"

"I have thirty-two cats, and they all sleep with me." She patted his arm. "In my free time, I knit their fur balls into scarfs for the homeless. According to the American

College of Allergy, Asthma, and Immunology, as many as one quarter of the population is allergic to cats, so at any given time twenty-five percent of the homeless in Austin are dodging a bullet every time their neck gets cold."

"The makers of Benadryl must love you." He said.

She had the most mischievous gleam in her eye that he almost forgot that he needed to keep her on the pedestal that he'd put her on. While the witty banter was fun, intelligent conversation was what she was used to. They should be discussing art or literature or global economics. He searched his brain, but he didn't know anything about art or literature or global economics.

"Besides tonight, my worst date was in college. This guy took me to Arby's and ordered for me. Don't get me wrong, I'm okay with a man ordering for me, I'm just used to him asking me what I want first. It turned out that he had a coupon for a free Beef and Cheddar. I appreciate that he was thrifty, but I wasn't in the mood for a beef and cheddar. He got so mad when I offered to pay. Then he took me to people watch at the mall. But the worst part was when he called me the next day to tell me that he'd had a dream that I was his soul mate and he asked me to marry him. Weird huh?"

Devon scratched the back of his neck and forced his facial muscles into a smile that matched hers. "Yes, pretty weird."

He'd been reluctant to bring up camp in the hopes that she'd remember him. Clearly that plan wasn't working.

"Until now, that was my gold standard for a bad date." Her voice was light, carefree.

"So tell me about yourself." The fact that he was hungry, she was covered in Parmesan cheese, and he didn't have a clue what he should do next, didn't stop him from diving right on in. "Did you go to any summer camps?"

He wasn't above begging.

"Sure. I think everyone has been to summer camp at one time or another." She sat back and thought about it. "I've been to water skiing camp, anatomy camp—not as fun as it sounds, drama camp when my mother was convinced I needed some culture, and robot camp where we actually didn't get to build any robots." She turned to him. "How about you?"

Drama camp rated above him?

"Just over-night camp." That he'd been forced to attend by court order on account of some less than stellar behavior that he wasn't about to bring up. It seemed that he was going to have to pry the info from her. "A place called Camp Huawni."

"Oh my God." She put her hand over her heart. "In Timpson, Texas? I went there. I met a boy there, DJ. He was so cute … taught me how to kiss … and a few other things." She fanned herself. "He carved DJ+EJ=4EVER into a tree trunk in the woods. We had a torrid high school love affair."

Devon's heart hammered in his chest. "What happened?"

"My father picked me up early from camp, and I never saw him again." She shrugged. "I gave him my address and my email, but he never wrote."

He sat up.

She most certainly had not given him her address or he'd have come to visit.

"Maybe he lost your address?" Devon scanned his memory for anything she'd given him with her address on it.

"I wrote it on the back of his favorite book. I don't remember the title but he always had it on him during meals." One corner of her mouth turned up in a wistful smile.

What book? He didn't remember a book. Wait a minute. He'd borrowed a book from his bunkmate so that he could pretend to read it while staring at her during lunch. At the end of the session, he'd given the book back to the boy who'd slept in the bottom bunk below him. Holy crap! Had some stupid book cost him years he could have had with Laney? He felt nauseated.

"How about you?" She waited for him to tell some camp stories.

Even talking about him, to him, hadn't sparked any recognition. Clearly she remembered their time together, but she hadn't put two and two together. Did he tell her that he was DJ? Was it too soon? A large part of him wanted so badly for her to come to that conclusion on her own. Whether it was pride or just the reassurance that they had a connection to one another, he wanted her to realize it in her own time. Plus, it was fun getting to know her all over again.

She checked her watch. "At the Lakeway Park, they show movies on Thursday nights. Tonight it's *Serenity*. If we leave now we can make it. Obviously, it's too late to get a good seat in the park, but we could roll down the windows and watch from the parking lot. Maybe order a pizza."

Her stomach rumbled, and she clamped a hand over it. "Sorry."

If he weren't half in love with her already, he would have fallen right then. She still wanted to spend time with him. She was giving him another chance. He wouldn't screw it up. Next time there would be flowers and dinner and a poetry reading.

Her smile was bright and lovely. "Just think, we don't need to order extra Parmesan cheese." She pointed to her head. "I've got it."

Spending time with her was such a gift.

"Sounds good to me." But he could do better than a pizza. What if he called Jeffrey's and had them deliver something wonderful or better yet, he could call The Emerald and have them set up a table in the parking lot.

They did personal catering that included a waiter. He glanced at Laney. Then again, a pizza, EJ, and his favorite movie sounded a whole lot better. He started the engine. Just this once, they'd go low-rent. After tonight, she was only getting the best money could buy. "Buckle up. The Lakeway Park it is."

They pulled into the parking lot just as opening credits started on the huge blow-up movie screen at the back of the park. Devon scanned the parking lot for the best vantage point, backed into the parking space, turned off the engine, and opened the back. Was it too forward to propose they snuggle in the back while watching the movie? It was early October in Austin. It might be too cold to sit with the back open. He was just about to turn the car back on when she opened her door. He threw open his door, jumped out, and was helping her out of the car before he realized what he was doing.

He pulled out his phone. "What kind of pizza do you like?"

"Meat lovers with extra cheese? Or whatever you like." She limped to the back of the Escalade and then eased back on the tailgate.

He called Dominos and explained that they were in the parking lot of the Lakeway Park. After some negotiating and Devon explaining who he was, they agreed to deliver the pizza to him.

He joined her on the tailgate. "Those are some shoes."

Laney leaned back so her feet dangled in front of her. "Cute, right? They're new … and painful."

Devon knelt down in front of her, slipped off one shoe and then the other. "Scoot back a little."

Laney inched back so only her feet hung out the back. Devon climbed onto the tailgate, gently picked up her right foot and massaged it. Touching her was wonderful.

Her whole body melted. "Mmmmmmm. That feels so good. Mmmmm."

He could stand to hear that sound a few billion more times.

"The best movie ever, meat lovers pizza, and a foot rub. You're fast becoming my most favorite person." Her eyes closed, and she leaned back on her elbows. "Mmmmm."

He felt the smile all the way to his soul. He was touching her and the simple pleasure in that was reward enough … but that purring sound was icing on the cake.

"Each foot has one hundred muscles and each one thanks you very much. And the twenty-six joints and thirty three bones are pretty happy also." She sat up and jerked her foot away. "Oops. I promised my teammates that I wouldn't bore you with trivia medical facts." She blew out a long breath. "Wait, I already talked about cat allergies and scrotum injuries."

"Can we agree to not use that word anymore?" He shrugged out of his jacket and winced as his right shoulder protested. He'd taken a hard hit in practice today and it ached.

"Sorry." Her gaze locked onto his shoulder. "Does it hurt? You've been favoring it all evening." She scooted over to him. "Take off your shirt."

The last four words replayed in his head over and over, but he didn't move. When he'd imagined getting her naked, it hadn't been in the back of his car, and it hadn't started with him.

"Take off your shirt." Lightly, she placed her hands on his shoulder. "I noticed the surgical scar today. Rotator cuff?"

"Yes. The surgery was a while ago, but I keep reinjuring it." Slowly, he unbuttoned his shirt. Normally, he liked showing off his body, he worked hard for it and was proud. But this was Laney. She was special. He wanted something real and permanent with her. This time, superficial wasn't enough. And while he wanted to sleep with her, he wanted to get to know her first. Not that taking his shirt off meant they were going to have sex, but well his mind had put two and two together. And being shirtless in practice was fine, but here and now it made him feel vulnerable.

Did she remember undressing him before? He looked nothing like that scrawny kid with a bad attitude she'd undressed years ago.

He unbuttoned the last button, and she peeled his shirt down his arms.

Gently, her fingers probed the wound. He closed his eyes and savored the feel of her hands on him. While there was nothing sexual on her part, the heat from her fingers ignited his body. He longed to run his hands along her skin and reacquaint himself with every square inch of her.

"You've dislocated it recently." She massaged around the shoulder joint to his upper arm.

"Last week." He could feel her breath on his neck and her touch instead of soothing was making him edgy. It seemed that she was all around him. Her perfume scented the air and the dark cocoon of the Escalade was intimate. She was trying to relieve his pain, and all he wanted to do was roll her beneath him and kiss her until she remembered him.

"I'm a licensed massage therapist. That's how I paid for medical school ... well some of medical school. Let me work on this for you." Her hands glided over his shoulder, and he bit his bottom lip hard trying to stay focused.

Massage therapist? That didn't make sense. When did she paint? She'd been a very talented artist back in the day.

She'd had to pay for her own medical school? But both her parents are doctors. Then again, he wouldn't put it past her ass of a father to never help her.

"You need to relax. Your muscles are so tight." Her hands kneaded, and his need for her grew.

It was too soon. Laney wasn't a one-night stand. The purse full of condoms notwithstanding. She was his future. Every girlfriend and every sexual partner faded into a nameless, faceless crowd. They had all been practice for her. Part of him wanted to skip over all the romance and get to their life together, but another part of him wanted to savor every new experience with her.

"Thanks." Devon covered her hand with his.

She batted his hand away. "I'm not finished. You need to relax. Lie face down, and let's see if I can get some of these knots out."

"No. I'm good." He turned around so they were face to face. "Thanks for laughing when you should have punched me. You're amazing."

He stared into her eyes and wanted nothing more than to crawl into them and stay forever. He willed her to remember him and to feel the connection they once had.

"You're not so bad yourself. Thanks for pretending not to notice the condoms. My teammates gave them to me. They think … I'm too uptight." She leaned ever so slightly and kissed him. Her lips were warm and soft. Fireworks didn't go off, and love songs didn't pound through his brain, instead, he felt like he'd come home. The restless part of him that was always wanting more, always searching for something was quiet and happy. It was exactly how he'd remembered it.

He cupped her face and deepened the kiss. His tongue darted into her mouth lightly exploring. He wanted more of her … all of her, but he'd have to settle for this perfect little taste. He pulled back and smiled into her dazed eyes.

"Wow. You sure can kiss." She sat back and her brow scrunched up. "Did I say that out loud?"

She was perfect for him … just a little awkward, but he loved that about her.

"You sure did." He nodded.

"Are you going to kiss me again?" She clamped a hand over her mouth and looked absolutely horrified. "I said that out loud too, didn't I?"

The fact that he'd gotten to her meant more to him than any Super Bowl win. She'd felt the connection too.

"Dominos." Someone knocked on the back window. "Pizza's here."

A Dominos deliveryman wearing the trademark blue shirt and red ball cap poked his head in the back. "Crap, you really are Devon Harding."

Devon worked his wallet out of his back pocket, extracted a hundred and handed it to the kid. "Keep the change."

His eyes turned the size of baseballs. "Thanks, man. Can I get a picture with you?"

The kid pulled out a smart phone and handed it to Laney. It didn't seem to bother her.

She took the phone, and snapped the picture. "Wait, let me take another one just to make sure."

She touched the button again and then handed it to the kid. "I hope they turn out."

"Do y'all need any red pepper or parmesan cheese?" He held up some little packets.

Laney's shoulders shook with laughter. "We're good on Parmesan, but we'll take some red pepper."

The kid gave her a handful of red pepper. He held up his phone. "Thanks man. You're so cool."

And then he turned back toward his car, his thumbs moving wildly across the keyboard, probably posting the pic to every social media site on earth.

Devon shrugged his shirt back on and buttoned it up halfway. Her gaze stayed on his chest. He'd caught her staring.

Pride had his cheeks flushing.

She shrugged. "You have nice pectoralis major ... and external and internal obliques and transverse abdominus

43

too." She waved to signal his entire chest. "That whole area is nice."

"You have fantastic legs. Well actually, all of you is pretty impressive." Devon allowed himself to look his fill. She was beautiful and lean with curves in all the right places. "You are the most beautiful woman I've ever seen."

Just because he meant it, didn't mean that it sounded any less hokey.

She flipped open the pizza box. "Thanks, but I'm average. It's okay, I'm good with it." She stretched her legs out. "I do have pretty good legs though. According to the body proportion calculator, they are a little too long for my body."

She tore open a packet of red pepper, sprinkled it on a piece of pizza, snagged a napkin, and picked up her slice. She gulped it down in three bites. It was impressive. He'd forgotten that she could eat more than he could back in the day.

She picked up another slice. "Grace said you were slick. She was right. How about we promise to only tell each other the truth from now on."

He wanted to tell her the truth, but more than anything he wanted her to find out on her own.

She bit into the pizza and sauce slopped down the front of her dress. With the corner of his shirt, he wiped it up.

After putting her slice on the cover of the box, she picked up his shirttail. "Why did you do that? Now your shirt is ruined."

"Your dress is ruined. I was hoping I could catch it before it stained." The red globs running down her dress meant he was too late. If only he had some Shout wipes. Should he take her to get some? Next time he'd have them in the glove compartment.

"It's okay." She hunched her shoulders. "I don't have anywhere else to wear this dress."

That didn't make sense. That dress was just the thing she'd wear to the ballet. He grimaced. She was trying to make him feel better. No more pizza. From now on they would only eat in places with cloth napkins.

"Don't you want some pizza?" She pointed to the open box. "Do you like red pepper?"

She waited for him to answer.

Eating? Christ he was so nervous that keeping food down seemed impossible. What if he told her that he wasn't hungry or ate earlier? His treacherous stomach growled.

Confusion crinkled in her eyes and then a dawning awareness took over. "Oh, why didn't you say something? You don't like meat lovers."

"No, I do. It's just that …" he swallowed the tidal wave of spit in his mouth, "I have a little bit of a nervous stomach."

That was the understatement of the century. He tended to vomit when he got super nervous. If he ate that pizza, he was sure to get sick. And wouldn't that be a fitting end to the evening? Him puking all over her.

"A nervous stomach, while it isn't a medical diagnosis, is usually caused by anxiety and stress." She moved the open pizza box to the side and faced him. "Do I make you nervous?"

"A little." It's not like he could deny it.

"Why?" Line creased her brow.

"You know … I like you …" he swallowed again. His mouth was making saliva by the gallon now. "A lot."

Always had … always would.

"I like you too." She inched closer. "You weren't nervous when you were kissing me."

"No." He hated that his voice shook, but there was nothing he could do about it.

"So you should probably kiss me again."

She didn't have to ask him twice. Softly, his lips took hers. She tasted like pepperoni and promise.

His hands slid into her hair, and his fingers lightly massaged the back of her head.

Every muscle in her body went slack, and she moaned, tilting her head forward. Her hand went to his shoulder sending a jolt of pain down his arm. He jerked back, cracking her forehead on his chin.

"I'm so sorry." Just when he'd thought the evening had taken a turn for the better, he knocks her on the forehead. Was God punishing him for something?

"Ouch." She rubbed her head and plopped down hard, cardboard creaked and then there was a wet-squishing sound. "Crap, I just sat in the pizza."

She rose to her knees and pepperoni, sausage, and cheese oozed down her backside.

Never in his life had a date gone so wrong. Besides accidentally running over her with the car or having her spontaneously combust, what else could happen?

His phone buzzed with a text from his mother. "Don't worry. Small kitchen fire. I'm fine, not much damage. Except the baby back ribs are ruined. Love you."

"Can you excuse me a second?" His heart hammered in his chest while he touched contact and waited forever for her to answer.

"I'm fine." His mother called over a den of male voices. "The Lake Travis Fire Department is taking very good care of me."

He sighed. "What happened?"

"A little grease fire. I was finishing the ribs off in the oven and they caught fire. I was busy and didn't notice. No big deal." She sounded so calm. He was a nervous wreck, but for her, it was business as usual.

"Whew … okay." His pulse was starting to head back to its normal level.

"It was quite a shock when the fire department pulled up and caught me and Reynaldo skinny dipping in your pool." His mother laughed.

"Better them than me. So long as you're safe." He let out a long slow, breath. "I'll call you later."

"Kitchen fire?" With a handful of paper napkins, Laney wiped furiously at the pizza sauce running down her legs.

"I'm so sorry, I forgot." He whipped off his shirt and wiped at her backside. This evening had so many lows that it was hard to pick just one.

Once they'd gotten most of the pizza off of her, she scooted down and out of the back of the SUV. He followed.

"I'm willing to admit defeat. You need to be with your mother right now, and I should be getting home." Laney smiled kindly. "I have sprints at five in the morning and still need to finish some charts from today's rounds. How about we call it an evening before something else happens."

She didn't sound mad, just resigned.

He really needed to check on his mother, but he didn't want to leave things like they were. "Can I see you again? How about breakfast tomorrow?"

Laney's shoulders shook with laughter. "Why not? This is more fun and humiliation than I've had in years."

They drove back to Dell Children's Medical Center in silence. She'd insisted on sitting on the pizza box instead of his jacket, which he'd gladly offered. It was on the tip of his tongue to apologize again, but she didn't seem mad only thoughtful.

After she directed him to the staff parking lot and to her car, he pulled up next to it and put the Escalade in park.

"If you're serious about going out again, hand me your phone."

He picked up his iPhone and handed it to her.

She thumb typed and then handed it back. "My numbers. Call me if you're serious about breakfast."

He wanted to touch her again … kiss her once more, but before he could make his move, she'd opened the passenger door. Lightning fast, he was out of his own door, taking her keys, and opening her car door.

"Manners." She nodded. "They're nice."

"That's what my mother is always saying."

She smiled and waited.

As crazy as it sounded, he was nervous to move in for the kiss. What with the pizza, the fire, and her cracked forehead which he'd noticed under the dome light in his car, was going to leave a bruise, he needed to work up a little courage to kiss her.

"You know, this would be a great time to kiss me." She winked. "Just FYI."

"I was working up the nerve." He smiled down at her. He liked that she was only a couple of inches shorter than him. Even fourteen years ago, she'd fit nicely against him and now, she fit perfectly.

He combed his hands through her soft hair. "Hair the color of peanut butter and eyes Caribbean blue."

He kissed her softly at first, and then his tongue darted inside her mouth. He loved her. It didn't make sense, but he had always loved her. All the years of wondering and longing both ended and began again. He pulled back and stroked her cheek. He wanted so badly to tell her how he felt, but even he knew it was too soon.

"Wow. Where did you learn to kiss like that?" Laney, dazed and breathing heavily, shook her head and rolled her eyes. "Duh, you're a professional football player. Are you that good in bed?"

Her eyes turned huge like she'd just realized what she'd said. She opened her mouth to say something else and then shut it again. She sucked on the inside of her cheek. "Could you pretend that I didn't just say that?"

"Not a chance." He kissed the tip of her nose. "I'll dream about you tonight."

He held her door open for her.

"Really? That's the best line you can come up with?" She grabbed a towel from her gym bag in the backseat, spread it out on the seat, and eased onto it. She pulled the door closed, put the key in the ignition, and rolled down the window. She hung her head out and looked up at him. "After all we've shared tonight, you're going to end it on that cheesy line?"

"What? It's true." He threw up his hands. "Nightmares are dreams."

He shot her a shit-eating grin.

"That's better." She waved and backed out of the parking space. She stopped and yelled out the window. "FYI—I'm going to sit by the phone and wait for your call. I'm kinda busy so can you give me an ETA on that?"

She laughed in a way that let him know that she really didn't think he would call.

"Give it about five minutes." He blew her a kiss and she drove off.

He ducked into the driver's seat and hit the phone button on the console. He found her number and hit call.

"Hello?" Laney answered the phone with the skeptical voice of someone who doesn't recognize the number.

"Just so you know, I'm terrific in bed." He kept his voice low and sexy.

Chapter 4

"Ricardo, is that you?" Laney laughed.

"This is Devon. Who's Ricardo?" His voice cracked so he cleared his throat. "Who's Ricardo?"

Of course she knew it was Devon, but messing with him was kind of fun. "He's my imaginary Latin lover. He's never actually called me before, but I'm hoping one day. Come to think of it, you don't have a Latin accent."

Nothing but silence from the other end of the phone.

"I'm messing with you." She laughed again.

"Whew. I thought I might have some imaginary competition." Devon sounded honestly relieved.

"You couldn't have mentioned the whole good in bed thing when we were face-to-face?" She smiled to herself.

"Safer this way." He said.

"I'm tired of safety. I want to do something outrageous." She took a deep breath. The evening already sucked, so she supposed added truth wouldn't make that much of a difference. "I don't suppose you're up for a one-night stand?"

"What?" He sputtered.

"I've never had one. Are they fun? Or is it awkward in the morning? For that matter, do you stay the whole night or is it customary to leave after sex?" She couldn't help the information gathering tone. She wanted to know.

"I guess it depends." He took a deep breath and let it out slowly. "Are we having this conversation?"

"I hope. How many one-night stands have you had?" Ten, twenty, two-hundred? What was the average amount of one-night stands for the American male? She'd have to Google that when she got home. Being a pro-athlete, she was willing to bet, he was way above average.

"I don't feel right talking about his with the woman I'm currently dating." His voice was higher than normal.

"Oh stop. You're a guy. Don't y'all brag about this to each other? It's a simple question. How many?" Laney found that she really wanted to know. Would she pale by comparison if indeed they actually did the deed?

"Usually I'm not one to easily embarrass, but this is making me nervous."

"Okay." For a football player he was certainly prudish. "Have you ever had crazy gorilla sex?"

Nothing but silence wafted in from the car speakers.

"Are you still there?" All she wanted was information. Devon was easy to talk to, most men didn't put up with her questions, but he didn't seem to mind until now.

"Yes, I'm here. You understand that I need to check on my mother…"

"Okay." What did questioning him about his sex life have to do with checking on his mother? He had hands free talking in his car. "So do you need to go?"

"No, it'll take me twenty or so more minutes to get home."

"About the gorilla sex? Is it different than regular sex?" Since she'd promised not to use the words penis and vagina, it was a little hard to ask for the mechanics.

He took a full minute. "You'll know after you have it."

"Well, if we ever do have sex, maybe you could point it out while we're doing it so I can see if I like it." She pulled onto IH-35 North and headed to her condo downtown. "My teammates seem to think that it's incredible."

"With you, it's going to be amazing."

"Again with the cheesy lines." She shook her head. "I really thought we were past that."

"You're never past a good cheesy line. They make the world go around." There was a smile in his voice.

"Goodnight, Devon." She needed to focus on driving and so did he.

"Goodnight, Laney." He didn't hang up.

Laney hit end and the call dropped.

It had been the strangest evening of her life, but not unpleasant. Devon was fun and hilarious and sweet in a way that a large muscular man shouldn't be. Still, there was something about him that was very familiar, and she still couldn't place it. It would come to her.

At five-thirty the next morning as she stood in a line with her teammates, she still couldn't figure out how she knew Devon. They didn't run in the same circles, by his own admission, he didn't come by the hospital, and she would have remembered meeting him before. He had a presence that was memorable. It was driving her crazy.

"You're awfully quiet this morning." January gathered her long hair into a ponytail and looped an elastic band around it to keep it out of her face.

"She's tired on account of the fact that she was up all night, with Mr. Football." Nina did some lunges to warm up her muscles.

"I wish. The evening was a disaster. It was just one awful thing after another." Laney told them everything.

"But he called you on the way home." Nina tried to see the good side to everything. "That means he's interested."

"If he were interested, she wouldn't have slept alone last night." January stretched out her calves.

"Not everyone's a slut." Nina tried hard not to laugh. "There have to be some people in the world with self-restraint."

Laney didn't make eye contact instead she balanced one foot on the guardrail of the bridge they were standing on and stretched her hamstrings. Sprints meant climbing Mt. Lakeway over and over again. The first two hundred foot climb over the super steep grade was fine, it was the thousandth one that sucked.

"Okay ladies, the first one to the top of the hill gets a donut." Charisma held out a box of Round Rock donuts.

"Oh goodie, I love sprinting for donuts." Nina looked around. "Where's the coffee?"

"That comes later. Donuts now." She opened the box and the smell of hot, sugary, fried dough wafted out. "Who wants a hot and gooey donut?"

"She does this every time and every time I want to kill her." January shrugged. "You'd think that after a while my rage would fade, but no, I still want to kill her, take all of the donuts, and run."

Charisma stuck out her tongue, closed the box, stowed it in her backpack, and shrugged on the pack. "Catch me if you can."

And she was off. Charisma might be little, but she was fast. No one ever caught her unless she wanted to be caught.

Two hours later, Laney's thighs and calves were aching, and her knees felt like they'd been replaced by concrete, but she'd eaten three donuts, and she'd caught Charisma. There was no small amount of pride in that.

"Way to go." Nina leaned over, catching her breath. "I'd punch you in the arm playfully, but I don't have the energy."

"What she said." January pointed to Nina.

"I don't know why y'all are so tired. We only ran up and down the hill twelve times." Charisma wasn't even breathing hard.

Nina looked up. "We can take her. We'll throw her body in the lake, no one will miss her."

"I can't move my legs so I'm thinking that overpowering her isn't an option." January turned to Charisma. "I don't suppose you'd tie yourself up and jump into the lake."

"Whine, whine, whine. I've raised a team of whiners." Charisma was extra cheerful and annoying.

"As soon as the lactic acid is flushed out of my muscles and I can move them again, I'm coming for you." Laney wagged her index finger at Charisma. "It may be tomorrow or the next day or possibly sometime next week, but you're going down."

Charisma laced her fingers together and cracked her knuckles. "Bring it."

"So cocky." January laughed. "I'd shake my head, but again, can't muster the energy."

Slowly, Nina straightened. "The hike back to the parking lot is going to be painful."

"Again with the whining." Charisma threw her hands up. "Would it help to know that I have another dozen donuts waiting in the car?"

January perked up. "You're a good person. I'm always saying that."

"I want some protein." Laney stretched her back. "Anyone up for breakfast?"

She checked her watch. "I have two hours before I need to be at the hospital."

"I could use some real food." Nina made her way to the parking lot.

"Not me." January followed her. "I'm in it for the donuts."

Laney caught up to Nina. "Magnolia Café, Kerbey Lane, or Maudies?"

Charisma jogged by showing off that she could go a hundred more miles before she dropped. "Magnolia."

"I could do with some gingerbread pancakes." January shrugged. "You know… after the donuts."

"A little protein once in a while won't kill you." Laney hooked an arm around January's shoulder. "You know, Fruit Loops and Pop Tarts aren't real food. Only children eat them. Adulthood is waiting, why don't you eat an omelet and try it out?"

"Never." January's mouth twisted in horror. "If you start eating grown up food then people start treating you like a grown up. First you give up the Pop Tarts, and then before you know it, you're working a dead-end job, driving a ten-year-old Ford Taurus, and clipping coupons so you can put more money away for retirement. No thank you. I plan on being young forever."

"Seriously, type two diabetes is a concern. I want you to live forever, that's why I'm harping." Laney smiled. "I need you around so that you can comment on how great my butt looks as I race past you."

"Bite me." January snorted. "I'm bloated. It makes me lethargic."

She glanced down at Laney's butt and then smacked it. "Nice ass."

Nina stopped short. "Lanes, I just realized that you haven't spouted one statistic today. Are you feeling okay?"

"Never better." Laney shrugged. It was odd that nothing statistical had come to mind, then again, she'd gotten home late and had fallen into bed without her normal medical research reading that she did to fall asleep.

"I, for one, am very …" Nina shaded her eyes with her left hand. "What the hell?"

Laney followed her line of sight. In the middle of the parking lot, there was a large round table set with white linen, china, and a huge bowl of fruit. There was a long rectangular table where a chef, complete with white coat and hat, stood behind a one-burner stove, making omelets. He tossed one up in the air and caught it in the pan.

"Maybe it's a wedding or something." Laney glanced around looking for the bride and groom, but didn't see anyone. "I'm pretty sure they won't want us in their wedding pictures."

"It's your football player." Charisma turned around to face Laney.

Devon, dressed in workout shorts and a T-shirt, waved from the driver's side of a black sports car. He opened the door and hopped out. "You said you'd have breakfast with me."

Laney's heart did a little flip-flop. It was just arterial flutter caused by the exercise and adrenaline, but damn it she wanted it to be because he'd done something nice for her. Now her wide smile ... that was all happiness. "I could do with a little breakfast."

Chapter 5

Devon smiled to himself. Last night, he'd told Laney that he wanted to buy her breakfast, and she'd thought it was a line.

"I thought you were kidding about breakfast." Laney shook her head. "Thanks."

"Why don't you introduce me to your friends?" He pointed to the three women currently staring at him. "I'm pretty sure coach introduced them to the team, but I was too busy staring at you to remember their names.

Laney waved them over. "This is Nina."

She pointed to a short dark-haired woman.

"This is January." It was the blonde surfer girl. "And last, but not least, this is Charisma."

Laney nodded to the tiny blonde with the purple highlights.

"My teammates." Laney shrugged. "And partners in crime."

His teammates were also his partners in crime. He'd wager that these women could get into some serious trouble.

"Nice to meet you ladies." He winked. "I'm trying to impress Laney so any tips would be helpful."

"That's so sweet." Nina cooed. "He couldn't make you breakfast in bed so he brought some guy to make it for you."

"Are those pancakes?" January was clearly all about the food.

Laney's hand went up to smooth down her sweat drenched hair, but she must have deduced that nothing short of a shower would fix it, so she dropped her hand. She was beautiful and he was dying to get his hands on her.

Devon walked right up to her and kissed her on the mouth. Sweat and muck be damned. He liked the way she looked … always. And she smelled fantastic.

"I know this is gross, but you smell fantastic." Devon whispered close to her ear. He took a deep breath, and his eyes practically rolled back in his head, "Crazy good."

Laney thought about it for a second. "*Psychology Today* did some interesting research proving that men like the way women smell when we sweat. It suggests that testosterone levels in men increase when they smell the sweat of an ov—"

"Excuse Lanes. She suffers from having a huge brain that leaks facts like a colander." Nina put her arm around Laney and stage whispered, "No random facts."

He loved the random facts. Trying to figure out how her brain worked kept him on his toes.

"It's okay. I like it." Devon nodded. Would he always be stupid happy just being around her, or would it fade after a while? "I read the same study. Men's testosterone levels rise anywhere from fifteen to thirty-seven percent. There is also a documentary done by *The Discovery Channel* called *The Science of Sex* that shows basically the same thing."

"Holy crap, he speaks Laney." Nina glanced at January. "There are two of them in the world."

"That's interesting. I'll have to look out for that documentary. It's on *The Discovery Channel*?" Laney nodded.

"I DVR'd it. We could watch it after dinner tonight?" Devon rocked back on his heels and grinned hopefully. Being a little nervous, he wasn't as smooth as normal.

"I suppose I could." Laney reached behind her to the zippered pocket and felt around. "I guess I left my phone in the car. I think I'm on call tonight so I might have to go into the hospital."

"As it happens, I'm also on call. If there's football emergency I'll have to head to the stadium." He may not be able to pull off smooth, but he could do witty. "I'm very important."

"I can see that and humble too." Laney nodded.

"Only thirty-seven percent of NFL football players consider themselves humble." Devon took her hand. "I like being in the minority."

"You made that up." Laney allowed herself to be lead to the large round table.

"Maybe, but it will give you something to look up later." He had made it up, but if she liked stats then he would give her stats.

"Did y'all just see that?" Nina called after them. "Someone just out stat-ed Lanes. I never thought that would happen."

January walked up to them. "So the trick is to make up some stuff, and then have her check it later." With her index finger, she patted her temple. "Got it."

"It could be true ... then again, it might not be." Devon hunched his shoulders. "Fun of the game."

"So, are we invited to this little breakfast soiree?" January grabbed a banana off the fruit basket in the center of the table. "Because I'm taking the banana."

Her tone suggested that if he crossed her, he'd end up buried in a shallow grave.

"Of course." He turned to the broad shouldered man in the chef's hat. "This is Mike from Kerby Lane. He's here to make whatever you want. The entertainment should be here soon."

Seth Charming had some serious humiliation coming. After last night, it was a miracle that Devon had let him live.

"Entertainment?" Laney stepped back weary.

He patted her arm. "No, it's okay. The rookie who convinced me that last night's provocative dinner theater was a good idea has graciously offered to do his own interpretive dance for us. He'll be wearing a grass skirt and a coconut bra." He leaned down and whispered. "He assured me that his clothes will be on the whole time and that no food will be thrown."

"Too bad." She smiled up at him. "I really like Parmesan cheese."

How could he not smile? She was so damn good for him.

He pulled the chair out for her and then seated her teammates. Manners were important. If his mother had taught him anything, it was that.

"So ladies, what will it be?" He glanced at Laney as he pulled a small notebook out of the waistband of his shorts and a pencil from behind his ear. He hadn't been able to find a server on this short notice, and the only reason he'd secured Mike was that he promised a huge tip and tickets on the fifty for the next three home games.

"I'll take some gingerbread pancakes, an omelet with ham, bacon, sausage, and whatever veggies you have, some biscuits and gravy, and a side of bacon." Laney grinned sheepishly. "You should know, I like to eat."

Thank God. He would have thrown his hands heavenward and genuflected, but he was all about convincing Laney that he was sane. Back at camp, she'd been able to put away seventeen waffles. It had been pretty amazing to watch.

"You're in for a treat." January peeled her pilfered banana. "Lanes can eat … a lot. Like more than two grown men. Don't get me wrong, I can put away some food, but she's a champion."

"And never gains an ounce." Nina helped herself to an apple from the bowl. "She's one of the few people who was able to finish the ten pound steak at the Lone Star Tavern—"

"Hey, if I finished it, I didn't have to pay for it." Laney crossed her legs at the ankle and relaxed back in her chair. "In medical school, money was tight so I'd eat anywhere they offered free food. If I had to eat ten pounds of meat to get it for free that was even better."

Hadn't her parents helped with college? He guessed not because she'd mentioned being a massage therapist last night to pay for college. He liked that about her. She earned her own way. Independence was sexy. And she smelled so damn good. Would it be too obvious if he leaned over and sucked in a deep drag?

"My momma's going to love you." Devon nodded as he wrote down her order. "Once she ate six barbecue chickens on a dare."

January smacked her lips. "Yum … that sounds good."

"My little gluttons, don't forget we're swimming tomorrow morning. I don't want you all to sink. Let's keep it under five billion calories today." Charisma, their coach if he remembered correctly used the same tone Grace used when talking to her children.

Devon took everyone's order, gave it to the chef, returned to the table, and sat next to Laney. "So what are you doing tomorrow night? I thought I'd go ahead and ask."

"She's going out with us." Charisma poured herself a glass of orange juice from the pitcher on the table. "It's her birthday."

Her birthday? Why hadn't she said something? That sucked. Now he felt left out. Maybe he'd get next year.

"Birthday, why didn't you tell me?" Devon tried not to sound pitiful.

"I've known you for all of forty-eight hours. It didn't come up." The look on her face suggested that it had never occurred to her to mention it.

It shouldn't have hurt, but it did. He should go ahead and tell her that he was DJ, but he still wanted her to remember on her own. It was important, he didn't fully understand why, but it was. At least, last night she'd talked about DJ as fondly as he'd remembered her.

"Then how about the night after tomorrow?" It was a consolation prize and there were no two ways about it.

"I really need to check my calendar. I feel like I have a function." She stood. "Let me get my phone."

Devon would have pulled the chair out for her, but she was already up. Slowly, she walked toward the parking lot.

"I don't envy her having to walk to her car and back." Nina blew out a long breath. "If her legs hurt half as badly as mine do, she'd be crying."

"We need to know your intentions toward Lanes." January's keen blue eyes were on him as she peeled her banana.

"If you break her heart, we'll kill you." Nina said in a super sweet voice as she picked up a butter knife and hacked off a good-sized pat of butter. The murderous intent was clear.

"I plan on spending as much time with her as she'll let me." Devon looked her straight in the eye so that she'd know he was serious without being creepy. He held her gaze and didn't blink first.

After a minute, Nina nodded. "Good enough for me."

"I think we should give him the inside scoop on Laney." Charisma sipped her juice.

"She's very intense on the outside, but is hilarious once you get to know her." Charisma yawned. "She's a fantastic doctor, but rarely talks about her patients."

"She is very careful to separate home and work." Nina shrugged. "I guess compartmentalizing is the only way she knows how to cope with her job. Sometimes, it's hard to watch the way she turns off her emotions."

"I don't think she turns them off, I think she bottles them up. I'm sure she gets it from her father." January rolled her eyes. "He makes robots look warm and fuzzy."

Charisma pegged him with her dark brown eyes. "We love her and don't want to see her hurt."

Everyone needed friends like these. He scratched the back of his neck. He hoped Laney would question his friends about him.

"Lanes likes to compartmentalize. Everything in its place … emotionally and physically. She's not OCD or anything, just particular … now her dad is OCD with a capital O-C-D. Last time I was at his house, I moved around all of knickknacks in his home office." January laughed to herself. "It took him forever to get them back in their places. Good times."

His gaze went to Laney who was walking toward them with her phone at her ear.

"That's her working face. She turns off emotion to deal with her patients. Something must be wrong at the hospital." Nina nodded. "Coping mechanism."

"Her father." January took a bite of her banana. "I'm pretty sure she learned it from him. Dr. Nixon, the elder, is an acquired taste."

"I'll just go and make sure everything is okay." He rose. Laney's face was blank, gone was the mischievous smile and all trace of her good humor.

She stopped about twenty feet away, turned away from them, and leaned against the tree talking quietly into her phone.

He put a hand on her shoulder and she flinched. She turned around, forced a smile, and held up one finger to give her a moment.

"Let's draw the labs again. Maybe yesterday's numbers were just a fluke." Her face may be blank, but her voice was hopeful. "I don't understand why her levels would fluctuate that much in a matter of days."

She nodded to whatever the other person on the phone had just said. "I agree. That's the best course of treatment at the moment. Thanks, Jake." She checked her wristwatch. "I'll be at the hospital in a couple of hours and I'll check in on her."

She nodded again to whatever was being said.

"Thanks again. I'll talk to you later." She hung up.

"Trouble at work?" Devon wanted to help in any way that he could.

Her fake smile got wider. "It's nothing."

He could tell by her tone, that she wasn't going to talk about it. Clearly, something was bothering her, but her friends were right. She compartmentalized and right now she wasn't at work so she wouldn't talk about it.

She tucked her phone in the little zippered pocket in the back of her running shorts. "No doubt in my absence, my friends have given you the run down on me and interrogated you about your personal life."

"They love you. I'm sure my friends will do the same when you meet them. God knows my mother is waiting to tell embarrassing stories about me. When she launches into the one about me driving across the border into Mexico—it's mostly a lie.

Laney's smile turned genuine, and then her shoulders relaxed against his hand. He could all but see her lock away the professional side of herself and pick up the off-duty version from a few minutes ago. "Mostly?"

"Okay—it may be more truth than lie, but I'd rather you not know the real me until I know you like me back." He replayed what he'd just said. "That sounded so much better in my mind." He should drop his hand, but he needed to touch her.

A bell dinged behind them and Devon turned around to find that the chef had placed four plates of food out to the side of the burner.

"If you're willing to forget about Mexico, I'll willing to serve your food." Devon grinned. "You look awfully hungry."

She laughed. "What happens in Mexico stays in Mexico."

He guessed that she'd successfully made the transition from doctor back to just plain old Laney. Why couldn't she mix the two?

"What's the most reckless thing you've ever done?" Her eyes were bright.

Had he missed something? "I don't understand."

"Reckless. What's the most reckless thing you've ever done?" She pegged him with her Caribbean blue eyes.

"Why?" He wasn't sure where she was going with this.

"I've never toilet papered a house, mooned anyone, or ding-dong ditched." She took a deep breath. "I've never done anything reckless."

At first he thought she was kidding. How had anyone gotten through high school without toilet papering someone's yard? Hell, his friend Clint and his schoolteacher wife Summer got hit at least once a semester. Well, until he and Clint had devised a little plan that involved motion-censored sprinklers on the roof. Anyone who tried to paint that yard white got a serious soaking.

Maybe all her questions last night really had been for informational purposes. More than anything he'd ever wanted, he'd wanted to spend the night with her. But sex was just sex and he wanted more from her and from himself.

"Reckless, let me see." He chewed on the inside of his cheek thinking. "You're going to have to be more specific—reckless physically, reckless emotionally, reckless stupid—I've done so many things I regret that it's hard to choose just one."

"See, that's what I'm talking about. I turn thirty tomorrow and I have no regrets." She shook her head. "It's pathetic."

"You could moon me right now, and I'll pretend to be shocked." He shaded his eyes with his hand as he scanned the area. "I see some condos over there. We could ding-dong ditch."

"That's a nice thought, but those aren't condos, that an Alzheimer's Care Unit. Ding-dong ditching people who won't remember seems kind of pointless."

"I see your point." He took her hand and slowly led her back to the table. "But I'm totally up for the mooning. I am here for you."

The bell dinged again. Devon glanced over. Mike waved with his spatula to come get the food.

"Let's put your recklessness on hold. Breakfast is ready, and Mike needs my help." He led her back to the table, pulled the chair out for her, and turned to the ladies. "Don't say anything else embarrassing about Laney ... until I come back. I'm your server today."

He walked to the table, placed the food on his arm diner-waiter style, and brought it to the table. He hesitated and then placed the food randomly in front of the women. After they all traded plates getting what they'd ordered, they settled in to eating.

Today, he'd learned some interesting things about Laney. First she didn't think of herself as reckless, but he remembered her being so daring at camp. Not cavalier, but willing to try anything and everything. Maybe that wasn't recklessness as much as curiosity, but still. This uptight version she saw herself as today wasn't the person he used to know or even how he saw her now.

Second, she used to wear her heart on her sleeve. This grown-up ability to turn off her emotions probably helped her in her professional life, but he hadn't remembered her doing that all those years ago. Back then, she'd been an open book and her face had shown whatever she was feeling. It's not that he didn't like the new Laney, he just wanted to understand her—get to know her all over again. And every once and a while, he caught a glimpse of that sweet, curious sixteen-year-old.

Chapter 6

At six o'clock that evening, Laney's doorbell rang. "Damn it."

She was still wearing her bathrobe, but at least her hair and makeup were finished. She unbelted the robe, slipped it off, and tossed it on her bed. She slid on some lacy black panties and a matching bra—an early birthday present from Nina—and grabbed her simple black cocktail dress. The doorbell bing-bonged again. Quickly, she pulled the dress over her head, smoothed it down, and yanked at the zipper.

The zipper tab broke off in her hand.

She shook her head. Could something go right, please? This was turning into the day from hell.

The doorbell bonged for a third time so she darted out of her room open dress flapping around her. She checked the peephole. Devon smiled in at her. She opened the door and was careful to use it to shield herself as much as possible.

Devon walked in holding a huge bouquet of flowers. He looked around taking in her condo. It was small and sparsely furnished. She didn't spend much time here and wasn't into decorating.

"These are for you." He handed her the bouquet.

Flowers for her? They were frivolous and cliché and perfect. She'd never gotten flowers before. She took them and did the girly thing and brought them to her nose and inhaling deeply. The orange roses smelled wonderful and would really add a splash of color to her beige condo. Why hadn't she thought to buy herself flowers before? They weren't particularly expensive and they made her stupidly happy. She hadn't bought them because they were frivolous and she'd been taught that frivolous was a waste of time.

Now she needed to put them in water, but she couldn't turn around and walk to the kitchen because her dress was hanging open. Could she back to the kitchen?

For that matter, what would she put them in? She'd never owned a vase in her life. Vases didn't have a function other than holding flowers and looking pretty…another frivolity. And Laney was all about the practical. Only now she was realizing that a little frivolity was a good thing. Well, tomorrow she was buying the stupidest, silliest, most un-practical vase she could find.

"Stop thinking so hard. They're just flowers. You look like you're working on some complex physics problem." Devon leaned down and kissed her lightly on the nose. "You look pretty when you're deep in thought, but you kind of look like your head's going to explode... you know, in a good way."

"Is there a good way for my head to explode?" The mental image was more than disturbing.

"Now, I can see that was a poor choice of words." He nodded. "Sometimes when I try to be witty it turns around and bites me in the butt." He grinned. "So what were you trying to puzzle out just now?"

"It's just that." She blew out a slow breath. "My zipper broke and so I was trying to figure out how to get to the kitchen to put these in water without flashing you."

"Earlier you did express a desire to moon someone. As a friend, I'm here for you. I'm willing to take one for the team." He put his hand over his heart. "That's just how I roll."

"Wow, Mother Teresa has some serious competition for Saintliest person. You're just one step below Jesus when it comes to helping humanity." Her mood was lifting. He had a way of breaking through her insecurities and making her laugh. She'd laughed more with him than she had in a long time. In fact, he always made her feel like she could be herself around him...insecurities, awkwardness, strange sense of humor, and all.

Better to get it over now. She turned around.

She hoped his quick intake of air was a good thing. "Can you help me out?"

After a minute or so, she glanced over her left shoulder. "Is the zipper completely broken? Can you zip it up?"

"Zipper?" Devon's breathing was rapid and shallow. "What zipper?"

His eyes were on her backside.

"The zipper that starts five inches below my bottom." If her hands weren't full of flowers, she'd reach around and show him.

"Sorry, my eyeballs won't move any lower than your underwear." His eyebrows bounced up and down. "That is the tiniest black lace thong I have ever seen."

"Come on. You're a professional football player. You have a PhD in tiny lace underwear."

"Yeah, but you weren't wearing it." He muttered under his breath.

"Can you hurry? I'm getting cold." Air-conditioned air swirled down from the AC vent above her. Always the practical one. Just once, couldn't she prance around in nothing but her underwear and the air conditioner be damned. That was recklessness, at least in some small measure.

He ran a finger down her back, grabbed the zipper tab, and yanked. It made it midway up her back.

"Crap." From behind her, Devon yanked hard enough for her to stumble backwards. "My cuff is stuck in the zipper."

Hysterical laughter bubbled up and she bit her bottom lip trying to keep it from blasting out. Her shoulders shook. This was ridiculous and so not typical of her life that it was funny as hell. She would have doubled over, but she was hauling around a huge football player.

He yanked some more and … nothing. "I can't get it out."

She couldn't contain it anymore. Laughter erupted out of her in a very unladylike snort. She'd never been a snort laugher before.

"Do I get to know what's so funny?" He didn't sound angry, just curious.

"It's us. Whenever I'm around you, my life is so much more fun—sure it's hell on my wardrobe, but I haven't laughed this much in years." Not since DJ. He'd always been able to make her laugh and they'd always gotten into the weirdest trouble. Like the night of the scavenger hunt. Neither one of them had any interest in scavenging for anything so they'd blown it off to go have some alone time by the lake. They'd taken the green paddleboat. Unfortunately it happened to have the final clue to the scavenger hunt written on the side, so when they'd paddled back to shore two hours later, there were lots of angry campers waiting for them.

"I am so sorry about last night's dress and this one too." There was way too much regret in his voice. He really thought this was his fault.

"Trust me, this is the most fun I've had all day." Late patients at her office had put her behind for rounds at the hospital and then there was Lara Brooks. She was dying of Leukemia, and no matter what she threw at the disease it was still winning. Laney didn't like to lose, especially when the stakes were so high. "Don't force it. I don't want you to rip your shirt."

Laughter had been in short supply until he'd stepped into her condo.

"Let's go into the kitchen. I have a pair of scissors." They'd have to cut the dress off, and she didn't have another to replace it. More than anything, she'd love to stay home tonight, order some take out, and watch a movie.

Like a couple of zipper-conjoined twins, they lumbered into the kitchen. She went to the drawer next to the sink, and pulled out the scissors.

"Did you just move in?" Devon looked around.

"No, I've lived here for almost four years." She followed his gaze. Now that she noticed, the kitchen was a little barren. No kitchen table, no homey curtains on the window overlooking downtown Austin, and the only appliance on the counter was her espresso machine. "I don't cook much or for that matter, spend much time here."

Her life was at the hospital and training with her team. Both of those things didn't leave much time for anything else. Why hadn't she noticed how barren her home was until now?

"I can see that. There's no 'you' in this condo." There wasn't any judgment in it, just a casual comment.

She'd never thought about it. She looked around. Everything was beige—it seemed to be her signature color. That added depression onto an already long day. Failure wasn't her favorite state of being, and clearly she'd failed as a decorator.

With the scissors, she started at the hem and cut.

"What are you doing?" Devon sounded honestly scandalized.

"Cutting my way out of this dress." She continued. She'd love to do something sexy right now, but she had scissors in her hand and she was pretty sure that running

72

with scissors was actually safer than sexy with scissors, at least in her hands.

"You're ruining it." It was sweet that he was more worried about her clothes than she was.

"It's the only way out. Unless you have another plan. And, it's not that great of a dress to begin with." She was waist high now and working her way up to the neckline. When she finally made it to the neckline, it was a huge relief. Now her dress hung open in front and back. Did she step out of it and parade around naked? It's not that she was prudish or self-conscious; it's just that she didn't do things like that. Would that be sexy or just awkward? She bit her lip puzzling through it.

"I promise to close my eyes like a gentleman if you want to change into something else." Devon's voice rumbled next to her ear.

It was better than standing here indefinitely. "I don't have anything else like this. I only own two dresses and the other one has pizza stains all over the butt."

Devon was hell on her wardrobe—not that her clothes were anything special. In fact, he was a very good excuse to go shopping for new ones. Except that she'd rather remove her own appendix with a dull knife than go shopping.

"Okay." She slid what had been a serviceable black dress down her arms and stepped out of it. She was halfway out of the kitchen when she turned back to find Devon's gaze glued to her body. "What happened to keeping your eyes closed?"

"I'm no gentleman." He was at her side in two strides. His hands went to her waist, he picked her up, wrapped her legs around his hips, and backed her to the wall. His lips were hot and demanding on hers. Not bruising, but not gentle either. His tongue thrust into her mouth and explored. His hands cupped her butt setting her firmly against him. She fisted his hair and pulled him to her.

Through the thin trousers of his suit, she could feel how much he really liked her lacy underwear.

His mouth left hers and trailed angel kisses down her throat.

"Are we about to have crazy gorilla sex?" She could have bitten her own tongue. Needless chatter wasn't exactly sexy unless it was something seductive. Dirty talk … that's what she should be doing right now. She scanned her brain and nothing came to mind. What exactly qualified as dirty talk? Surely penis was too clinical. Cock? That made her think of a rooster. Would he notice if she pulled out her smart phone and Googled dirty talk? She glanced down. She was only wearing her underwear so her phone was probably next to her purse on the front entry table. Did he have his phone? Maybe she could discreetly work it out of his pocket and find a couple of really dirty phrases.

"No." He traced her earlobe with his tongue. "No sex tonight … gorilla or otherwise."

"I disagree." She smiled sweetly. She would seduce him with the nastiest dirty talk he'd ever heard. God knew she could use some sex. The release would be nice after the day she'd had. "Let me borrow your phone."

"I can't imagine who you need to call right now." He pulled it out of his suit coat pocket and handed it to her.

"I'm not calling anyone. I'm about to seduce you with my filthy mouthed dirty talk." She took it, pulled up the web browser, and typed dirty talk. Several articles popped up. She pulled up the first one. "Okay, I'm supposed to make eye contact."

She looked him straight in the eye, but then had to look away to scan the phrases. They were all stupid, but she was willing to try it. "I want you to put your giant …"

The screen went black. She tapped on it. "I think the battery died."

"Well, I only had two percent left." Devon kissed the tender spot underneath her ear. "Dirty talk was never my thing. But if you want to turn me on, throw me some statistics."

"You like the random facts?" He seemed to this morning.

"I like everything about you." He kissed her hard on the mouth.

The doorbell bing-bonged.

Laney froze. It bing-bonged again. A chill ran down her spine. "Crap."

She'd meant to be gone by now because Daddy Dearest was coming over. Her latest tactic in daddy-daughter relations was to avoid him like the plague. She'd just pretend not to be home.

"I know you're in there. Your living room light is on." Her father's voice was brusque. It was always brusque because the man had that down to a science.

Devon unwrapped her legs from around his hips and gently slid her down his body. "What's wrong?"

"My father is here." She shook her head. "I'd planned on being gone before he got here."

If Santa Claus had a polar opposite, her father was it. He was tall, athletic, condescending, and hated all people in general.

His face blanched and then he turned angry. Did he know her father?

"Why don't we hide in the bedroom?" She didn't expect him to say yes, but it was worth a try.

"I don't hide from anyone. It's about time I met your father." Devon shrugged out of his coat, wrapped it around her, and smacked her on the bottom. "Go get dressed."

What did he mean it was about time he met her father? That was odd.

Her father started banging on the door. He'd never been much of a knocker.

Devon checked his watch. "We're going to miss our dinner reservation. How about take out?"

She kissed him lightly. "You read my mind. That sounds perfect."

The banging got louder.

Devon turned to the front door. "I'll answer the door. You get dressed."

She hesitated. "My father … let me apologize upfront."

"Go." He winked. "I can handle myself."

"My hero." She winked back.

Devon's face lit up.

Her pulse kicked up a notch, and she shoved the medical explanation aside and enjoyed the moment.

She escaped to her bedroom and threw on a T-shirt, a pair of jeans, and a fluffy pair of socks. Since her father always expected for her to look professional, even as a teenager, she'd dressed down. Rebellion came in all shapes and sizes.

The rumble of male voices carried into the bedroom. She zipped up her jeans, pulled on the socks, and took a deep breath. If was funny, she wasn't nervous to introduce Devon to her father, but to introduce her father to Devon. There shouldn't be a distinction between the two, but there was … a huge one.

Her father was cold, unyielding, and imperious, but Devon, well he made her happy. It was as simple as that.

Chapter 7

Having never actually met Laney's father until now, Devon didn't like him anymore than he had fourteen years ago. It was more than just coldness, there seemed to be an anger boiling in the depths of the man that didn't fully make sense. Was he angry at the world in general, his daughter for not waiting by the door for him to drop by, or because she had a man in her house?

Devon sat back, crossed his legs at the ankles, and continued the stare down he was currently having with Laney's father. Devon's eyeballs would dry up and fall out before he blinked or looked away first.

Silence crackled through the room, but he wasn't about to chat up a man who in his mind had taken Laney away from him.

Through his peripheral vision, he saw Laney walk into the living room and came up short. Because he couldn't analyze her face, he couldn't judge her emotions.

"Father." She called.

Her father turned to her, his eyes raked up and down her in disapproval.

Devon practically jumped up to go to her. Her father didn't have the right to disapprove of Laney in any way, and Devon wouldn't stand for it. She was lovely in jeans and a T-shirt.

He kissed her lightly on the mouth. "You look beautiful."

Laney blew out a slow, calming breath and laced her fingers through his. Nervousness radiated off her in waves.

"Want me to beat him up for you?" Devon whispered close to her ear. "I totally would."

Her father sighed loudly. "I came by to drop off your birthday present. I thought we might go to dinner." There wasn't the least bit of emotion in his bland tone.

Laney's whole body tensed like she was preparing for a fight and a forced smile contorted her lips. "Thanks, but I have plans."

Clearly, Dr. Giles Nixon wasn't in the habit of being rejected. "Your friend," he spat out the last word, "may come with us."

It was an order not a request.

"Sorry, we can't." Laney was firm. "Another time." Which sounded a lot like over her dead body.

Devon made a big deal of checking his watch. "So sorry, we have to go or we'll be late."

They'd already missed their dinner reservation, but he did have tickets to Ballet Austin, though it didn't start for another two hours.

Her father eyed Laney's clothes and shook his head. A muscle ticked in his jaw, but reluctantly he stood, pulled an envelope out of his breast pocket, and handed it to Laney. "Happy Birthday."

Her smile went from forced to fake. "Thanks."

"I'll see myself out." Her father headed toward the door and then turned around. He looked directly at Devon. "I know you from somewhere." His hawk-like gray eyes bore into Devon. "Ah yes, rotator cuff injury. You're a football player. The surgery took two and a half hours—

five or so years ago. One of my old partners did it and I assisted."

The man might be evil, but he had an impressive memory. He had no idea that Laney's father had assisted with his shoulder surgery. "That's right."

He nodded toward Laney and then he was gone.

Silence was heavy in the room. After a few moments, Devon put his arm around Laney. She stiffened slightly, but then relaxed into him.

"Let me get a sharp stick so you can poke it in your eye." She shook her head. "Or maybe I could run over you with my car." Tears rolled down her cheeks and she brushed them away angrily. "Both of those things sound like more fun than meeting my father."

More tears streamed down her cheeks. She didn't make a big production out of them or sob loudly; they were more of an annoyance and an embarrassment. She swiped at them and looked down. He'd never felt more helpless in his life. Laney who was smart, witty, and tough was crying. He would do anything to make it stop. He led her to the beige sofa, sat down, and settled her in his lap.

"Your dad wasn't that bad. Compared to Attila the Hun, Caligula, or the Rams defensive line, he's a pussy cat." Devon stroked her back.

"I like you so much and I was so worried to introduce you to my dad. I didn't want you to run away screaming." Her eyes squinted and sucked in her top lip. "I said that out loud didn't I?"

Devon felt the grin all the way to his soul. She liked him. It was a start. "I didn't hear a thing."

She returned his smile, and he noticed that the tears were gone.

He wanted to be there for her on good days and bad. More than anything, he wanted to share his life with her, and he wanted the same from her. "Tell me about your day."

"I don't want to talk about it." She tensed.

If she wouldn't share herself with him, how could they ever be together?

"I'd really like to know. You said that it was a long day, maybe talking about it would help take some of the burden off you." He wanted to know her ... everything about her.

She thought about it for a second or two. "I have a patient who is dying."

She didn't start off with the small and work up to the heavy. She jumped right in. He liked that about her.

She let out a long slow breath. "That's the first time I've admitted that." She shook her head. "Don't get me wrong, I've lost patients before and it always makes me feel like a huge failure. But this is different. Lara is so ... special. She was born addicted to crack cocaine, and her mother abandoned her at the hospital. After Lara kicked the drugs, she went into foster care, but was taken out of that home because of neglect. Before she could be placed in another home, she got sick. She beat Leukemia once, but this time it's back, which is bad." Laney closed her eyes for a moment and then opened them again. "She has no family. A social worker comes to see her every other week for about thirty minutes, but other than that, Lara is all alone." Laney shook her head. "She's so brave and funny and smart, and she won't see the age of six."

Devon rubbed Laney's back. She'd retreated into herself and her voice was the controlled physician. It was telling that she shed no tears.

"I deal with death every day and the only way I get through it is to compartmentalize, but with her, I can't turn off the emotion. Lara's never been part of a family, or lived in a loving home ..." Laney laid her head on his shoulder. "Today, I asked her if she could have anything in the world what would it be, and she told me that she wanted a family. I wish I could give her that—at least for the time she has left."

Devon's eyes strung with his own tears and he batted them away. If only he could make this better for her. Now he understood why she shed no tears. It's not that Laney didn't feel for her patients, she did, but she buried it under layers of professionalism. The only way to do her job was to focus on the disease and not the person.

Deep inside, Laney still had the tender heart he'd remembered. At camp, all those years ago, a baby bird had fallen out of its nest and Laney, careful not to touch it, had scooped it up with a piece of cloth, climbed the tree, scampered out on the limb, and returned the bird to its nest. It looked like she was still taking care of children. Maybe he'd misjudged her after all—she was following her passion of helping children.

He may not know anything about Leukemia, but he knew a lot about family. Lara wanted a family, he knew just the lady who could make that happen.

Gently, he set her off of his lap, stood, and held his hand out to help her up. "Grab your purse and whatever else you need, I'm about to introduce you to my mother."

Laney supposed that turnabout was fair play. Devon had met her father and now it was time for her to meet his mother. The gated community on Lake Travis where Devon lived was full of stately old-money mansions. It's not what she'd expected. He seemed more like a ritzy condo downtown, but they'd just turned into a—modest by mega-mansion standards—nineteen twenties Mission Revival. She was intrigued. He clicked a button in the visor of the Escalade, a wooden garage door rolled up, and they pulled in.

"I texted my mom that we were coming over, but I didn't hear back from her." He stepped out of the car, walked around to her side, and opened the door. "With my mother, it's best to call first."

"Okay. Do you want me to wait here?" She looked around. The four bay garage had one empty slot, a red Cadillac sedan in one bay, the black Dodge Viper he'd driven this morning in another, and now the Escalade. Were all of these cars his?

"Let's go into the kitchen." He settled his hand in the small of her back and led her to the door at the back of the garage. He opened the door and waited for her to enter.

Devon seemed nervous for her to meet his mother. That she understood. Maybe his mother was overbearing like her father?

"Give me a second. I'll go check the guest house." He led her into a huge kitchen. The entire back wall was windows overlooking a lush, green backyard. Off in the distance, an azure-blue pool winked in the waning sunlight.

Devon led her to a pair of overstuffed red leather chairs positioned in front of a massive indoor, outdoor fireplace in the middle of the wall of windows. He kissed her lightly on the cheek and then opened the door to the backyard and went to find his mother.

The kitchen was amazing. Two sets of commercial ovens, three stoves, and what looked like a wood burning pizza oven were surrounded by miles of marble countertops. Two huge islands made a large V in effect pointing to a large round kitchen table. There were groupings of sofas, end tables, and chairs. Without a doubt, it was the largest kitchen she'd ever seen. The colors and textures were done in warm browns, reds, and golds. Cheerful plants in colorful pots dotted surfaces and despite its size, it managed to be both homey and quaint.

If she ever took the time to cook, this is the kitchen she'd want to do it in. This room had life and love everywhere. It was used and cared for … and not beige.

Ten minutes later, Devon opened the back door and shaking his head, stepped into the kitchen. Disgust and horror mingled on his face.

Laney rose and went to him. "What happened? Is she hurt?"

She glanced outside looking for any sign of emergency. Off in the distance, a woman stepped out of the pool. Laney blinked to make sure her eyes were working. The woman didn't appear to be wearing a swimsuit or well … anything at all.

"What's the treatment for Post-Traumatic Stress Disorder? I'm pretty sure I have PTSD." Devon blew out a frustrated breath. "My mom was practicing her erotic, tantric swim routine. Apparently, she's making an instructional video."

"Wow." Was all Laney could come up with, "I don't know the protocol for PTSD, but I can find out."

"Mom is, well …" He looked around like the right words would appear from thin air. "She's a great mother, don't get me wrong, but she's um … different."

"How?" Since her own mother had died when she was thirteen, she was fascinated by mother-daughter relationships. From what she remembered of hers, it had been okay, if not a little formal. Her mother had been a world-renowned back surgeon who had pioneered many surgical procedures still in use today. But she hadn't been fun. While other kids' mothers took them to the park to picnic and play, her mother had taken her to the hospital to see patients.

"She's open … about everything. Don't get me wrong, she's a wonderful mother, but she … let's say… takes her sexual freedom very seriously. Ever since my father died, she claims to be exploring her sensual side."

"I'm sorry about your father. How long ago did he die?" With Laney, it wasn't just common courtesy that dictated the 'I'm sorry' but a true understanding of the finality of death.

"He died when I was ten."

"That's a lot of exploring." Laney couldn't wait to meet the woman who'd spent the last twenty years exploring her sensual side.

"You have no idea." Devon rolled his eyes. "You know that phrase about trying anything once, maybe twice … well, she's willing to try anything and she won't stop until she's conquered it. Ballroom dancing, bungee jumping, erotic ceramics, gardening. Unfortunately the erotic ceramics and the gardening were at the same time so I had a nipple fountain spurting water into a penis shaped koi pond."

His face turned an interesting shape of red. "I probably shouldn't have mentioned that."

"Your mom sounds like fun. My mom invented a new procedure to fuse vertebrae." Fun didn't exactly describe Dr. Marjorie Beaumont-Nixon. She was willing to bet that as a child Devon had birthday parties with silly party hats, cake, and ice cream. He probably got tons of presents. She got a check—not even a birthday card, just a check. As an adult that was fine, but as a ten-year-old, it left something to be desired. That was of course when they remembered it was her birthday. Her parents were important people whose careers left little time for family. Beginning in high school on her birthday, she bought herself some cupcakes, party hats, and birthday candles. If she were ever lucky enough to have a family, they would always come first.

"That's something. Your mom sounds very … um, smart." Devon shrugged out of his suit coat and tossed it on a chair. He rolled up his sleeves. "How about dinner?"

He went to the refrigerator and pulled out a bowl and a baking sheet covered with aluminum foil. "I've got macaroni and cheese my mom made yesterday and some beef ribs off the grill." He smiled sheepishly. "Leftovers are all I have. We could order something though."

"I love leftovers." She stood and stretched. "What can I do to help?"

"Nothing, Honey." A sultry female voice called from behind her.

Laney turned around and felt her mouth drop open.

A curvy blonde woman who had to be in her fifties sauntered up to Laney. In black silk slacks and a matching low-cut black silk top, she was sexy in a giggly nineteen fifties sexpot kind of way. Everything about this woman was sensual, but not trashy just plain *va-va-voom*. If this was Devon's mother, he must have to keep a big stick close to fight off all the men.

She held out her hand. "I'm Sweet Louise Harding." She nodded toward Devon. "Please excuse my son's manners for not introducing us properly. God knows I tried to teach him, but the boy's got a head twice as thick as his father's. And that man made a mule look like God's most biddable creature."

She took Devon's mother's hand, shook it firmly, and let it go. "It's so good to meet you. Devon talks about you all of the time."

Sweet Louise's cheeks flushed with pleasure. "All good I hope."

"Nope." Devon said under his breath.

"I apologize." She walked to her son and smacked him lightly on the back of the head. "No respect for his elders."

"What elders? You act like a horny teenager." Devon pulled the foil off the pan.

"You'd disrespect me in front of company?" The mock horror on her face made Laney smile.

"I think you took care of that by skinny dipping in my pool." Devon hip-bumped his mother.

She hip-bumped him right back. "It could have been worse ... a lot worse."

"I live in fear of that every day." Devon unwrapped plastic wrap from the bowl. "I already have several images that need to be burned from my memory."

He glanced at Laney. "Can that be done?"

She walked to the island they stood behind, pulled out a barstool tucked under the ledge, and sat. "Nope."

Devon grinned. "She's a doctor."

The pride in his voice shouldn't have made her heart beat faster but it did.

"A doctor." Sweet Louise sounded impressed. "That beats the … what was the last one you brought home? A bikini waxer?"

"That was like three years ago." He sighed heavily. "When are you going to let that go?"

"She was so dumb her tattoos were misspelled." Sweet Louise shot her a knowing look. "Hell's Angles. Can you believe that? I asked her if she was a mathematician. She told me she was a Baptist."

"Wow." Laney laughed. "Can I meet her?"

Maybe there was something medically that could improve her brain function.

"Sadly, Ms. Hell's Angle moved to… in her words, 'to one of those I states, you know, in the middle.' I hope she was good in bed, because I couldn't find any other qualities to recommend her." Sweet Louise spooned macaroni and cheese into a baking dish, covered it with foil, turned on the oven, and popped it in. "I'm pretty sure she got lost and is still looking for that I state in the middle. Too bad … she was a keeper. I'm sure she would have produced some high-quality babies for me to cuddle."

The eye roll was implied.

"Mom." Devon was mortified.

"What?" Sweet Louise hunched her shoulders. "I can't be having stupid grandbabies. And then they'd have babies and those babies would have babies. I'd be the matriarch of a dynasty of stupid people. I can't have that be my legacy. I need to be known for my love of humanity and my art."

She smiled at Laney. "You look like you'd give birth to really smart, beautiful babies."

Devon made a choking sound, turned on his heel, walked to a huge built-in cabinet on the left of the sink, opened it, and selected a bottle of what looked like Kentucky Bourbon. He unscrewed the cap, tipped the bottle to his lips, knocked back a good gulp, and screwed the cap back on. Without missing a beat, he replaced the bottle, closed the cabinet, and returned to the ribs. "Remember that offer of a sharp stick to poke in my eye. Same goes for you."

"At least he's not a closet drinker. That's got to count for something." Sweet Louise winked.

"Are you two always like this?" Laney grinned. Their house must be like living in a sitcom. Clearly, they loved each other. All the sparring back and forth was balanced with a deep affection for one another.

"Yes, pretty much. My son needs a lot of woman to keep him in line." Sweet Louise looked Laney up and down. "I think you may be just what he needs."

"Are you trying to drive me to the liquor cabinet again?" Devon's voice was higher than normal. He turned to Laney pleading. "Don't listen to her. The craziness in our family skips a generation."

Sweet Louise patted him playfully on the shoulder. "I'm so sorry it landed on you. At least my grandbabies won't be afflicted. That gives me comfort."

Devon went to the refrigerator and pulled out a small metal bowl, pulled up one corner of the plastic wrap, grabbed what looked like a fat paint brush from a red ceramic canister holding lots of paint brushes on the counter, dipped the brush into the bowl, and brushed a brownish liquid all over the ribs. "My secret barbecue sauce."

He brushed sauce on both sides of the ribs, opened a drawer in front of him, pulled out a box of aluminum foil, and ripped off a giant piece. He wrapped it around the ribs, opened a second oven, and popped in the ribs while punching in numbers to get the perfect degree of heat.

"Laney wants to do something reckless." Devon nodded in the direction of his mother. "Since you're the poster child for reckless, I thought you might have some ideas."

"Really?" Laney sat up. "Got any tips for the newly reckless?"

Sweet Louise brightened. "Well now, let me see …" She leaned against the counter. "Are we talking physically reckless, emotionally reckless, or stupid reckless?"

Devon nodded. "That's what I wanted to know."

Laney thought about it for a minute. "Physically reckless, I guess…to start."

Sweet Louise cocked her head to the right. "The first thing that comes to mind is the hobo hopping my best friend and I used to do in high school."

Devon stopped long enough to stare at her. "Do I want to know what hobo hopping is?"

"Train hopping. My friend Denise and I used to hop a cargo train at the railroad crossing in my home town and ride the train thirty or so miles to party in a college town. We'd hop a return train at three in the morning. So much fun." Sweet Louise nodded. "God, I miss Denise. After she married that Baptist preacher, she was no fun at all."

Devon's mouth was hanging open. "You hobo hopped trains? I don't even know what to say to that." He turned to Laney. "You're not allowed to ever do that." He turned back to his mother. "Neither are you."

"Like that was the most risqué thing I've ever done." Sweet Louise rolled her eyes. "I've skinny dipped in that big fountain outside of the LBJ Library. Luckily the cops were very nice. They told me to get out, put on my clothes, and go home."

Laney laughed at the horrified look on Devon's face. She propped her chin on her fist. "How old were you when you did that?"

"Fifty-five. It was last month." She grinned.

Devon's eyes got so big, Laney actually thought they might pop out of his head.

"If you want something sort of tame, try going through the McDonald's drive thru naked. They sometimes upsize your fries." Sweet Louise was enjoying her son's discomfort.

"Mom, stop talking. Forget I asked about your reckless adventures. I don't want to know." Devon looked horrified. "I thought you'd talk about driving the Jet Ski after dark, or riding your horse bareback, or maybe even how you 'borrowed' your father's car and accidentally broke the tail light sneaking back in."

"Please, I only told you the tame stuff. You asked for reckless and these are the things I could think of off the top of my head." She picked up a dishtowel and wiped down the counter. "Speaking of reckless, you've got your own stories. Have you told her about Mexico yet?"

His face turned an interesting shade of red.

Laney laughed. "We agreed to never mention Mexico, but I'd love to hear some other stories."

"He and his best friend used to race home. He had a '68 Mustang and his friend had a '72 Camaro." Sweet Louise was so blasé about the whole thing.

"How'd you know about that?" Devon put a dirty spoon in the sink.

"I'm a mother, we know everything." She folded the dishtowel and laid it on the counter. "I also know you drove to Austin almost every weekend in college looking for—"

"Would you like a glass of wine or something to drink?" Devon cut off his mother as he came around the bar, pulled out the stool next to hers, and sat down.

"I guess I'm supposed to be on my best behavior and not tell you all about the reckless stuff he's done." Sweet Louise glared at her son.

"I love you, mom." He shot her a super-sweet smile.

"Fine, I'll be good." She returned his smile.

"Water please." She pulled her phone out of her back pocket and set it on the bar. She needed to keep it close in case the hospital called. "I'm on call tonight so no alcohol for me."

"What kind of medicine do you practice?" Sweet Louise turned around, grabbed a large blue bowl full of peaches from the counter behind her, and set it down in front of her.

"I'm a pediatric oncologist." Laney watched as the older woman pulled out a small knife, and started peeling the peaches.

"Oh hon, bless your heart." Sweet Louise kept on peeling. One peach and then two and three.

"Tell her about your patient … Lara?" Devon covered Laney's hand with his big one. It was surprisingly gentle. In fact, for such a big man, he was always gentle.

"Why?" She didn't like to talk about her patients. Keeping work separate from home was how she dealt with things.

"Because if there was ever a mother who needed to coddle a child, there she is." Devon swept his free hand toward his mother. "Lara needs a family, and my mother could use a child."

"I have a child." Sweet Louise shot her son a look. "And he's a pain in the ass."

"Tell her." Devon nodded at Laney.

"I don't think it's a good idea." She bit her top lip thinking. Lara did need someone, but she needed someone to love her for as long as she lived. Not only was it a big commitment, more than likely, it wasn't going to turn out well. As much as she wanted a happy ending for Lara, she needed to face reality. Lara wasn't going to get any better and watching a child die wasn't something she would wish on even her worst enemy, much less a woman that she liked.

"Will someone please tell me about Lara?" Sweet Louise moved onto the next peach. "I'm making my famous peach cobbler, but I'm not giving either of you a bite until someone tells me about her."

"That's mean." Devon's tone was bland. "Her peach cobbler has won blue ribbons in five states. Just wanted you to understand the gravity of the threat."

Laney took a deep breath and told Sweet Louise all about Lara. The older woman listened as she peeled her peaches and when Laney was finished, the sheen of tears glistened in Sweet Louise's eyes.

"That baby just got herself a grandmother." Sweet Louise glanced at the clock on the microwave. "What time does she go to bed?"

"Nine or so, I think." Laney didn't know how she felt about this, but Lara needed someone … besides Laney.

"It's almost seven. We could pack up all this food and have dinner with Lara." Sweet Louise had already fallen in love with a child that she'd never met, it glowed in her eyes. A tiny bit of the fear at losing Lara eased—there was now someone else to watch over her.

Devon had done this, he'd seen how upset she'd been, and he'd done his best to take the burden. She'd never had anyone take her burden. It was nice for someone else to lighten her load, if just a bit.

Without thinking, she leaned over and kissed him lightly on the mouth. "Thank you."

"You're welcome." He looked overly pleased with himself.

In such a short amount of time, he'd come to matter to her. It had been a long time since someone had mattered in more than a professional way. She looked him over. This big man with gentle ways and kind eyes was special. Did he feel the same way about her?

Chapter 8

Dell Children's Hospital wasn't what Devon had expected. Yes, it was a hospital and had doctors and medical equipment, but it was focused completely on the children. The walls were brightly colored and several patients paddled down the hall on Big Wheels and tricycles. What medical paraphernalia he could make out was also brightly colored and more often than not tucked away in a cabinet or draped with stuffed animals. It still smelled like a hospital—antiseptic, Lysol, and apple juice.

His mother had insisted on stopping by the gift shop and buying the largest stuffed animal they had. Which explained why he was now walking down the hall carrying a giant stuffed pig wearing a purple tutu and rhinestone tiara. It didn't matter. Laney's face was no longer creased with worry, and his mother now had an outlet for all the love she needed to give. For that kind of payoff he'd gladly have worn a pink tutu and rhinestone tiara himself—thank God, he didn't have to.

He glanced back at his mother. She was nervous, wringing her hands in anticipation.

"Hey Dr. Nixon." A nurse called from a desk in an alcove by the double doors they'd just walked in from. "Did someone call you?"

"No, Joanna. I'm here to see Lara." Laney gestured to him and his mother. "I've brought some friends who can't wait to meet her."

"Lara's had a good afternoon. No nausea, but she didn't eat much dinner." Joanna smiled. She was short with huge front teeth and a ready smile. Her gaze locked onto Devon and her mouth fell open. "You're Devon Harding."

He shifted the pig and offered his hand. "Yes ma'am, I sure am."

"My husband is your biggest fan. He's always talking about your yards or downs or blocking or whatever it is that you do." She shifted from foot to foot. "We have your Fathead on our game room wall." She looked down embarrassed. "Can I have your autograph?"

"Absolutely." He balanced the pig on the bar top of the nurses' station and picked up a sharpie that was lying on top of a clipboard. "You know, we're going to be here for a while. Why don't you give him a call and see if he'd like to come by? I'd love to meet him in person."

Joanna's face brightened. "Really? Oh my gosh! This will make his day … no his year. He's been down since he lost his job at Barney's. After it burned down, they never rebuilt it. He was the pit master."

Devon glanced at his mother, and her eyes locked onto his. She was thinking the same thing he was. This was an amazing stroke of luck.

"He was the pit master at Barney's?" Devon would have gotten down on his knees and thanked God right here, but he was trying to keep an enormous pig from falling to its death. In his opinion, Barney's had the best brisket in the state of Texas. He'd mourned the day it had burned down. "I'm opening my own barbecue place and would love to talk to him about a job."

"I'll text him right now." Excitement radiated off Joanna. "Thank you."

If her husband really had been the pit master at Barney's, Devon was hiring him immediately.

Joanna pulled out her phone and stepped back in the alcove. He guessed she didn't need his autograph right now.

He picked up the pig. Laney leaned into him. "That was nice. Thank you. Joanna has four kids and has been working double shifts just to make ends meet."

There was a loud sniffle behind them. Devon turned around. His mother was wiping her eyes.

She shook her head. "I'm already a mess. I'm going to walk in to meet Lara and she's going to be scared because I'm balling like a baby. She won't like me, and then I won't get to be a grandmother."

Devon handed Laney the pig and put his arm around his mother. "She's going to love you. Just think, Halloween is just around the corner. You get to make her a costume."

His mother perked up. "I didn't think of that. And she'll need clothes—pajamas and such. I need to make those too. And probably she'll need a special quilt. When I get home, I'm getting my sewing machine out."

His mother loved to sew, but hadn't in years.

"You might need a new machine." Devon hugged her tightly and then let her go.

"I think you're right." Head held high, she fluffed her hair and walked straight ahead. "Which room?"

"At the end of the hall, last door on the left." Laney pointed. "What's a Fathead?"

"It's a life sized wall transfer of me." Devon took the pig from Laney and they followed his mother.

When they reached Lara's door, Laney stepped ahead of them, grabbed three-paper facemasks from the box by the door, and passed them out. "Lara's immune system is low because of all of the treatment, so anyone who comes in contact with her must wear a mask."

His mother took hers and looped it around her ears. "I can rock this mask like nobody's business."

Devon smiled to himself. By morning, his mother would have bedazzled her mask into something sparkly and bright. Laney slid her mask on and he followed. Lara must be sick if she couldn't breathe the same air as a healthy person. He knew Laney was a pediatric oncologist, but he hadn't fully understood what that meant until now.

She pushed the door open, and walked in. "How are you feeling?"

Devon girded himself for what would probably be a pitiful sight, but what he found was a cheerful little girl with curly red hair and freckles on her nose. She smiled and her two front teeth were missing.

His heart melted right there.

"I'm good today, Dr. Laney. I'm not very hungry though." She looked questioningly at the strangers. "Who are they?"

"This is my friend Devon and his mother Sweet Louise." Laney sat on the edge of the bed. "You're not hungry? How about a picnic?"

Lara sat up. "A picnic? I've never had one. You mean like outside and everything."

"I brought a blanket so we can sit on the ground." Sweet Louise grabbed the pig from Devon and set it in the chair next to Lara. "We found this pig roaming the halls looking for a kid to love it. Think you could help us out?"

Lara's whole face lit up. "You mean I can keep it … like forever?"

Her eyes turned world-weary. "No take backs."

Devon wanted to buy her every stuffed animal in Austin. Cute little girls with missing front teeth should never have to wonder if they get to keep their stuffed animals.

"No take backs." Sweet Louise crossed her heart. "Cross my heart."

"Wow." She reached over and picked up the stuffed animal that was twice her size and set it in front of her. "I get to keep it. Forever. My very own stuffed animal. I'm going to name her Princess."

She didn't have other stuffed animals? Devon looked around. Her room had no personal touches. It was brightly decorated, but nothing from home. His heart twisted in his chest. She didn't have a home from which to bring things. No special blanket or pillow or fuzzy bunny slippers. She was alone and had nothing to call her own. If she died, the only people who would mourn her were in this room. He glanced at his mother. From the look on her face, she too had just come to that conclusion.

He could do something about that.

He pulled out his phone and sent a broadcast text message to the team—tailgating at Dell Children's Hospital. Everyone bring something … either toys for the kids or food.

In less than thirty minutes the parking lot would be crawling with Lone Stars' players.

"I was thinking." His mother took the chair formerly occupied by Princess. "I need a granddaughter. Since my good-for-nothing son over there hasn't produced any grandbabies, I was hoping you'd agree to be my honorary granddaughter."

Lara rolled huge brown eyes up to meet his mother's green ones. "What does that mean, honorary granddaughter?"

"Well, it means that I visit you every single day, we hang out, play games, do silly stuff, and have a good time. Think you can handle that?" His mother smiled.

Lara thought about it for a second. "I guess."

"You need to give me a cool grandmother name like Nana or MeeMah or NeeNaw. The first grandchild gets to name the grandmother, it's a tradition." His mother took Lara's little hand in hers.

Lara's brow scrunched up as she looked his mother up and down. "I'm going to call you Honey."

His mother's smile turned up a notch. "That's what my husband used to call me."

"It's because your hair looks like honey." Lara reached out and touched his mother's hair. "Doesn't feel like honey." She yawned. "When's the picnic start?"

"Right now baby doll." Laney grabbed the wheelchair next to the door over to the bed. Laney attached the IV bag to the pole and then helped Lara climb into the chair. The little girl was wearing a tiny hospital gown with teddy bears on it. For a split second, it gapped open in the back and Devon caught sight of delicate vertebrae painfully close to the skin. The child was skin and bones, disease having ravaged her small body. She'd been through more in her five years than Devon had in thirty and yet Lara was upbeat and spunky. From now on, every time he hurt from a hit or his shoulder ached, he would cut out his own tongue before complaining. Lara was the bravest person he'd ever met, and he would move heaven and earth to make her life wonderful. She deserved the very best and he aimed to give it to her.

Laney fixed the gaping gown, made sure Lara was comfortable, looped a paper mask over the girl's small ears, and wheeled her to the door. It struck him that Laney was a warrior battling life-threatening diseases every single day. He nodded to himself. Now that he thought about it, he could see it. Her in armor with a sword, Joan of Arc style standing guard over sick children and fighting with all she had to keep them safe.

Laney had chosen to help those who could not help themselves. He saw her in a new light. He must have been staring at her because she turned to him.

"What?" One corner of her mouth quirked up in a half smile.

"You're amazing." He could hear the slightly shocked quality in his voice and hadn't meant it like that.

"Thanks. You're not so bad yourself." She blew him a kiss as she wheeled Lara into the hallway.

"Would y'all stop eye-flirting with each other in front of my granddaughter?" His mother rolled her eyes. "It's getting embarrassing."

In his mother's face, he saw heartbreak and love. He put an arm around each of his women. They were going to make his life interesting.

Forty-five minutes later the party was in full swing. Laney couldn't believe that Devon had pulled off something like this with one single text. Most of The Lone Stars football team was here and everyone had brought something. Someone had the presence of mind to bring tables, which now held food and mountains of toys.

"Dr. Nixon." Alan Busque's nasally voice called from behind her. Inwardly, she groaned. Alan was the hospital administrator and absolutely loathed all things fun. While she was sure he was excellent at something, though nothing came to mind, he was a huge, little—as he was all of five foot—pain in the ass. "Dr. Nixon, this is too much. Legally, we can't have all of these people milling around. Our insurance doesn't cover large gatherings, and how will the ambulances get through in case there's an emergency?"

Laney looked up. "The emergency bay is on the other side of the building, and there are less people in the parking lot right now than if it was filled to capacity with cars. I'm sure everything will be fine."

"I disagree …" His voice faded off as his eyes locked onto Sweet Louise.

Laney was noticing that the older woman had a huge effect on men. When she walked into a room, men climbed over each other to get to her. While she wasn't beautiful by conventional standards, she exuded a banked sensuality reminiscent of Bettie Page and Raquel Welch.

Sweet Louise sauntered up to Alan and let her eyes rake over him. "Is there a problem here?"

"N-n-n … no." He stammered and then licked his lips as he caught sight of Sweet Louise's more than ample bosom.

"Thank goodness, I'd hate to think that a big, strong man such as yourself wouldn't be up for a little fun." She ran a finger down his tie and then grabbed the end and pulled him closer to her. "We need more ice. Think you could help me out with that?"

"We have a commercial ice machine in the kitchen." He puffed out his chest importantly. "I can bring you all the ice you need."

"When I first laid eyes on you, I knew you were a powerful man who gets things done." Sweet Louise cooed. "And handsome too."

Alan swiped a hand over his comb-over making sure the three hairs he'd swirled over his bald spot were still camouflaging it. "I can get you whatever you need. Just say the word."

"Ice." She mouthed. "Now."

Alan swaggered off in the direction of the kitchen.

"How did you do that?" Laney had never met a woman with so much power over men. She wanted to see how Sweet Louise would handle her father. It would be interesting.

"It's all about attitude. Men have very fragile egos. Stroke it a bit. Works every time." She nodded in Devon's direction. "Except on him. He's wise to my ways."

"Devon is special." Laney watched him signing a football for a little boy in a wheelchair.

Sweet Louise nodded. "He's really into you. If you find that you don't feel the same way, I'd appreciate it if you'd let him down easily. It's been a long time since a girl has made him this nervous, and you rattle the hell out of him."

Wow, no pressure there. She knew Sweet Louise was only being a good protective mother, but the smallest bit of anxiety balled in Laney's stomach. Devon liked her and she liked him, well wanted to like him back, but it was too soon to tell.

"I make him nervous?" Laney never made anyone nervous. One of her gifts was putting people at ease, well at least, she hoped she put people at ease. Was nervous good?

"Child please. He's so nervous around you he can barely speak. And getting ready to see you, he went through twenty outfits trying to find one that would impress you. For him, women have rarely been more than a past time, but with you he cares … a lot." Sweet Louise patted her shoulder. "Be gentle with him."

The pressure increased.

Did she care about him? Of course she cared, but more than care? She liked him yes, but more than that? She didn't want to hurt Devon, but she wasn't ready to commit to anything. She'd known him for all of forty-eight hours. Although, it did seem like she'd known him for longer. She still couldn't remember where they'd met before.

Sweet Louise patted her shoulder. "You don't have to decide now. You only just met. I'm his mother so watching out for him is in my DNA."

"I promise. I won't hurt him." But that was an impossible promise. People hurt people every day—sometimes intentionally and sometimes by accident.

"I'm off to take Lara back. One of the player's wives commandeered her for a game of Uno, so now I need to steal Lara back before I'm usurped as Grandmother of the Year." Sweet Louise was fairly glowing. She and Lara had become fast friends.

"Thank you for …" Laney gestured in Lara's direction. "Everything."

"You never stop being a mother even when your child is grown. I didn't realize how much I'd missed being around a child. For them everything is possible. They believe in fairies and Santa Claus and monsters under the bed. I need that kind of hope and unwavering belief in my life. I need someone to nurture, and she's in need of nurturing. So thank you for giving her to me. You don't need to worry. I'll take good care of her—"

"But she's … she won't" Laney's voice cracked, "be around long."

Laney's heart broke at admitting it. She shouldered the burden of death every day, but she hadn't thought about the effect on other people. Now it was too late. Clearly Sweet Louise was attached, and she would take it hard when Lara died.

"I know. But it doesn't matter. I would rather have a few special weeks with her than never have met her at all. Love is funny that way. I would trade my life for hers, but it's a mother's curse at not being able to do that. So instead I'll fill the days she has left with love because that nourishes the soul—hers and mine. When the day comes that we must say goodbye, I'll hold her in my heart until I see her again in heaven. Everyone deserves to be remembered and loved after they are gone, and I will love Lara for the rest of my life." Sweet Louise's voice quavered but conviction shone in her eyes. She did love Lara—she'd known her for all of an hour and she loved her deeply and unconditionally.

Laney had never seen anything like it. Was this what love looked like? Her parents had loved her, but that love had limits—big glaring limits. As long as she did exactly what they wanted her to do, they showed her affection, but when she disappointed them, it was freezer city. With Sweet Louise there were no limits. When she loved, she loved completely and held nothing back. For Laney, that was both terrifying and hopeful. With her own children, would she love them wholeheartedly no matter what or would her love have conditions like her parents had for her?

"I've got to go find my Lara." The older woman sauntered off.

Laney had only known Devon for a few days, but in that short time he'd changed her life. Lara now had a family, and she had one less worry. She'd love to repay the favor, but she had no idea how to help him.

"Penny for your thoughts." Devon slipped an arm around her waist.

"I was just thinking that in such a short time, you've brought so much to my life. How can I ever repay you?" She owed him, and she didn't like owing anyone.

"My friendship doesn't come with strings. You owe me nothing. In fact, you've given my mother and me someone to care about. That's a true gift." He kissed her cheek. "But, if you'd let me buy you lunch tomorrow for your birthday, I wouldn't complain."

The bargain was still in her favor, but she wasn't going to argue. "Done. But we have to eat here, and I don't know what time exactly. I have a heavy patient load tomorrow."

Spending time with him was easy, and he made her laugh. That was enough for now. She refused to over think it. Feeling or no feelings, she was going to live in the moment if it killed her. Devon was handsome, smart, attentive, and thoughtful. She could love him, might love him … someday.

Stop with the over-thinking it.

"I'm flexible." He grinned. "I'm so flexible that I can put my legs behind my ears. Want to see?"

"Professional athletes are thirty-seven percent more flexible than the average person." Spouting facts was second nature, and it was a relief that he didn't mind.

"Wanted to let you know, the impromptu interview with Jason, Joanna's husband, went well. I hired him at double his old salary. He cried, my mom cried, and I damn near cried. He's a good man. I'm so lucky to have found him." Devon's hand slid down her back to rest on her butt.

"Your hand is on my butt." He wasn't handsy, precisely it was more about testing his boundaries.

He glanced down at his hand. "Well, what do you know … it is."

"Are you planning on moving it?" Laney grinned.

"Nope." Devon returned her grin. "I'm good."

"Okay then." She leaned closer into him. "I'm headed toward the food. Are there any ribs left?"

"A few. I've got more on the smoker." He pointed to the smoker he'd hooked up to his Escalade and pulled over here.

"Do y'all tailgate often?" He'd put this together so fast that they must do it quite a bit.

"Yes. Most of the team members are also my friends. And Sweet Louise is kind of the team Mom. She organizes the players and their wives for charity events and things. She's even got everyone organized now so that someone is with Lara twenty-four, seven. She will never be alone again." Devon scratched the back of his head. "I hope that's okay. She's already talked the administrator into moving a bed into Lara's room so she can stay there tonight."

"Lara's going to be so excited. She's comfortable in hospitals, but I know she's still scared of the dark." She still couldn't believe that Devon and his mother had done so much in such a short time.

"Does Lara need to stay at the hospital? Mom and I were thinking that we could bring her home … you know so she'd have some memories of home."

Laney didn't know what to say. It was one thing to talk about helping someone and another to bring them into his home—essentially give her a home.

"That's nice." Really nice. She'd have to look at Lara's latest blood work and think about it. Certainly she had patients who lived at home and received outpatient treatment, but Lara was a special case. "Let me get back to you on outpatient treatment for Lara. Her disease is pretty aggressive." She chewed on her upper lip. Lara had never had a good home and feeling like she belonged would go a long way in her treatment. There was something to be said for environment. Not that she believed giving Lara a home would cure her, but it might make her life better. "She'll still need to come to the hospital almost every day."

"Think about it. Mom's already talking about a pink princess room for Lara."

"Are you okay with this?" Laney knew that his mother was, but it didn't seem like she'd talked to Devon about his feelings toward her basically adopting a dying child.

"I think it's wonderful. Mom needs someone to love, and Lara's about the cutest thing I've ever seen. I'd love to bring her home right now. And buy her a puppy. She and a puppy could get into some serious trouble—it would be a blast to watch." He sounded so sure.

Devon moved fast it seemed, in everything.

"You do understand that there isn't a happy ending in Lara's future." It's not that she wanted to rain on his parade, but he needed to face the facts.

"Yes." Sadness crept into his eyes. "She won't see Christmas, but that doesn't matter. She's here now and for as long as we can, she'll know only happiness."

Laney didn't think that she'd ever met two such selfless people. "You're a good guy."

"No, I'm not. But I'm trying." He sounded embarrassed.

"Yes, you are." She was growing attached to Devon and she hoped that she could give him at least half of what he gave her in return. His mother's words about letting him down gently played over and over in her mind.

Chapter 9

The next day Laney leaned heavily on the door to exam room six. It was all of ten forty-five in the morning and she was thirty minutes behind seeing patients, she had a leg cramp from this morning's swim, and she was starving.

With all the strength she could muster, she stood upright, pulled up exam room six on her iPad, and scanned the patient information. It was a new patient with a referral from a hematologist. She checked his blood test results. Not good. He was all of ten years old. She closed her eyes, switched off her humanity, opened her eyes, and fixed on her polite doctor smile. She was a professional, and she would save his life.

Two hours later, she was ravenous, her leg cramp was worse, but she'd caught up with the patient load. Devon was meeting her for lunch in the hospital cafeteria across the street and she made record time down the stairs and across the street. She opened the double doors to the cafeteria and stopped dead.

Three of the four walls held giant banners proclaiming, "Happy Birthday Laney." They were draped like enormous ribbons decorating a wedding cake. There was a huge multi-tiered cake, and every single person in the cafeteria was wearing a pink party hat. Her smile was so bright that it hurt. This was her very first birthday party.

Devon stood next to the cake smiling like the cat that had eaten the canary. She looked around. Pediatric patients of all shapes and sizes were gathered in wheel chairs, standing, and seated. There was a clown making balloon animals, another doing magic tricks, and a third drawing caricatures. Where was the pony? That's all this party needed.

Devon walked toward her. "I tried to get a pony but the health department has some issues with barn animals inside a cafeteria."

It was like he'd read her mind. The man knew her better than she knew herself. That was both comforting and disturbing.

"This is wonderful." She hugged him. He was too much. Her heart went into overdrive … and this was too much. He gave more than she could ever give back. It's not that she didn't want to, it's just that she wasn't as free and easy with her emotions as he was. Trust was a problem for her. Part of her wondered what Devon's motives were. Clearly sex wasn't it or they would have had it by now.

It's not that she wasn't grateful for the birthday, it's just that this was a lot of pressure. She'd spent the better part of last night lying awake and thinking about Devon. His mother had asked her to let him down gently. This party was over the top. Anxiety made her palms sweat. She was seventy percent sure it was anxiety … okay fifty percent.

Things were moving too fast. She didn't move fast—never moved fast. For the love of God it had taken her two years to decide on a sofa, and she was barely ever home to sit on it. And here Devon was doing nice things for her and her friends. She'd wanted to spice up her boring life, but this was more…so much more. Sure, she'd wanted to be reckless, by skydiving or having an affair with a hot guy, but this was moving into emotional recklessness. That was so much scarier than physical recklessness. She liked Devon… a lot. She hadn't known him very long, but every time she saw him, her heart beat a little faster and her mood lightened. Smiling was easy around him. It hit her like a ton of bricks.

She could love him.

Little black dots danced in front of her eyes and she grabbed the nearest table for support. Her rational mind told her that either she was having a panic attack or her blood sugar had plummeted. She sat down hard in a plastic chair. When was the last time she'd eaten? Not this morning … last night? No breakfast and a three-mile swim—bad combination.

She could love him…was growing more attached to him every day. That scared the crap out of her. She hadn't loved anyone romantically since DJ. Love hurt too much. DJ had proven that to her. She tamped down her flight response—neither fight nor flight seemed like an appropriate response right about now.

"Are you okay?" Devon knelt in front of her. "Your face is kinda gray looking."

"Low blood sugar. I didn't have time for breakfast. Can you grab me a banana?" Here she was telling her patients to eat regularly and she didn't practice what she preached.

Devon was back with a banana and a bottle of water. He knelt down in front of her, peeled the banana, and handed it to her. "Here."

Her hands shook ever so slightly. Laney ate the banana without looking at him. This was embarrassing. Here he was doing something special for her and she nearly swooned like a heroine in a regency romance novel. Why did the realization that she was developing feelings for Devon make her nauseated? Did it make other people nauseated? She needed to research love and nausea. Maybe it was normal.

"Thanks."

"You need to take care of yourself." He tunneled his fingers through his hair. The look on his face clearly conveyed that he was frightened for her. He was certainly more emotionally invested in whatever it was that they had started. That was unnerving.

"I'm good now." Her head was no longer spinning from loss of blood flow and her stomach no longer growled. She stood and smiled at him. "Thanks for the birthday party. I wish I could stay longer, but I'll have to eat and run."

She had several more patients to see in the office and then hospital rounds.

"Okay, sit back down, I'll make you a plate and bring your present over." He held a hand out for her to sit. "Be right back."

He'd gotten her a present too? That made her uncomfortable. What if it was something expensive? Hopefully, it was something small.

Her gaze followed Devon. He walked over to where a small group of pajama clad kids were huddled around something. He snaked in between the kids, said something that made everyone laugh, and bent down. When he stood and turned around, Laney's breath caught in her throat.

Devon was holding a squirming puppy with a big red bow around its neck. Her heart melted … well not really, it was just dopamine flooding her brain and increasing her heart rate, but it didn't matter. For as long as she could remember, she'd wanted a puppy. How had he known?

She shouldn't accept it. She didn't have time for a puppy. She bit her lip. She wanted to hold the squirming bundle so badly. Holding out her hands like a child waiting for her next Christmas present, her legs vibrated with anticipation.

No one had ever given her such a wonderful gift. Devon seemed to know her…understand her better than she did herself.

Devon placed the dog in her lap and the little thing, took one look at her, licked the side of her face, curled in a ball, and fell asleep.

Devon patted the sleeping bundle. "She's an English bulldog. Very good with kids and hypoallergenic. I was thinking you could take her to work with you. Bulldogs are good with children, and they're real sturdy so they can handle playing even with rough kids." He cocked his head to the left. "I know dogs are a lot of work, but she's smart."

She snored lightly.

"I can see that." Laney picked up the sleeping dog, tucked her into her shoulder like a baby, and gave in to the love she already felt for the dog. So she could feel love. That was good. "What's her name?"

"She doesn't have one. Lara wants to call her Kisses. I already introduced her, and they hit it off. Lara says that she's available to babysit any time you'd like."

Laney held the dog out in front of her. "Are you a Kisses?"

One eye opened regarded her sleepily, and then shut again.

"I'll take that as a yes." What on earth was she going to do with a dog today? Maybe tomorrow she could arrange to bring her to work, but she had nowhere to keep her today.

"Let me get you a plate." He made his way to a long row of tables that held aluminum foil covered pans of food. Did he make all this food? If so, when had he done it? He'd made the food for last night too. He must have been up all night cooking. Wow, when he threw a party, he went all out. A weariness over his abundant generosity picked at her. Kisses stirred, licked Laney's neck, and then wiggled back into a comfy spot and went back to sleep.

"Can I hold your dog?" A little boy in fire truck pajamas shyly walked over. She didn't recognize him, and he didn't have an IV. He must be here for some sort of treatment.

"You bet." She handed the puppy to him.

"I gotta dog named Scout at home. He sleeps with me." He was maybe seven.

"Where are your parents?" Laney looked around.

"My mom died and my dad's at work." He petted Kisses. "He comes to stay with me at night."

Another lonely kid.

"Josh, it's time for your medicine." A scrub clad female walked over. Laney recognized her as the nurse on the transplant team. Doris or Dorothy.

So Josh had recently gotten a transplant. His color was good, and he was up and around. Children were little miracles, they could be sick one minute, but give them a new liver or kidney and they were up and about the next day.

"What room are you in?" Laney took the puppy from him.

"Four seventeen." His blue eyes glanced up.

"How about if I bring Kisses by later. Think you could babysit her for me?"

His face lit up. "Sure."

He patted Kisses one more time, turned toward the door and the waiting Doris, and went with her.

In giving her Kisses, Devon had given her the means to brighten many a child's day. That was an even bigger gift. She should do something for him ... but what? Without a doubt, she was the world's worst gift giver. Her teammates understood that for Christmas and their birthdays, they were going to get something they'd have to return. In fact, it had turned into a little game where she went out of her way to buy something so awful that most of the time they couldn't figure out what it was. Laney was the best white elephant gift giver in the world.

Devon returned with a plate with half a smoked chicken and three kinds of potato salad. "Mom and I are trying out different potato salad recipes for the restaurant. Tell me which one you like best."

She smiled. He was a good businessman. He'd turned her birthday lunch into marketing and market research—cunning and practical. Devon had game.

"Thanks." She was so ravenous, she could have picked the chicken up by the leg and gone all caveman on it, but instead she used a knife and fork. She handed Kisses to Devon who tucked the puppy in his arm football style.

"I have a confession to make." Devon petted the squirming puppy. "Originally, I bought the puppy for Lara." He threw a hand up. "I didn't re-gift her... but well I thought you could share her. I was going to buy two puppies but my mom wouldn't let me. Kisses could stay with her during the day or something like that. A kid needs a puppy. Households with pets have been proven to be healthier and happier. And sixty-three percent of all American households have a pet."

He'd done his research and was proving his case. As if she needed proof.

Laney looked around. "Where is Lara?"

"She's upstairs. Her treatment took a lot out of her." Devon glanced at his watch. "When I left her fifteen minutes ago, she was sleeping. She wanted to sleep with Kisses, but well ..."

"Let me guess, your mom sweet-talked Alan into letting her keep a puppy in the hospital." Laney was amazed by just what Sweet Louise could get away with.

"Sweet-Talk is my mother's middle name." He smiled to himself. "She's sewing matching blankets and dog beds as we speak. She sends her love, but she won't leave Lara's side."

"Your mother is a special lady." And he was special too.

"That's putting it nicely. We both know "special" is code for crazy." Devon watched every move she made. It was both unnerving and comforting. He was into her…got her. "I have something else for you … that I got before the puppy."

"Another present? Really, we don't know each other that well. I hope it's something small." She didn't want to sound too negative, but she needed to set some boundaries. He needed limits. They both did. She didn't do whirlwind romances; in fact, she didn't fully understand the concept. Wasn't a whirlwind like a mini tornado? What did emotional attachment have to do with tornadoes?

He thought about it for a minute. "Well, it's smaller than some things and larger than others."

"That's not comforting." Now was not the time or place to get into the limits talk. "Am I going to be shocked?"

He smiled. "Probably."

After finishing the chicken, she tasted each of the potato salads. All were wonderful, but one was extra special. "I like this one." With her fork, she pointed to the slightly yellow-i-er one with chopped up bits of boiled egg.

"That's my favorite too, but mom says that it's not fancy enough." Devon rolled his eyes. "We differ on what we want in a restaurant."

"I'm sure you'll work it out."

"Have you met my mother?" Devon shook his head. "She's not big on compromise. She's more of a her way or the highway kind of person."

"That explains where you get it." She took a small bite of potato salad. It didn't matter what the obstacle, he'd mow it down to get what he wanted.

"So you see me as uncompromising? That's funny. I don't see myself like that." He didn't seem angry, merely thoughtful.

"Neither does your mother." Laney grinned and patted his hand. "Okay, now show me the present that's probably going to shock me. Just so you know, I have a high shock tolerance. It better be impressive."

More than likely she would make him return the gift, but it would be interesting to see exactly what he'd come up with. Kisses was the best gift she'd ever gotten. Let's see if he could top that.

"Let's take Kisses for a walk outside. That's where your present is." He set the dog on the floor, pulled a pink leash out of his coat pocket, and clipped it to her collar. "She's not real good on the leash yet."

Kisses bit at the leash, growled, and then ran around in a circle chasing it.

"She's just seven weeks old. She'll get better." Devon gently pulled her on the leash. "I hope."

"I'll take her to puppy school." She glanced down at Kisses whose tongue was lolling out the left side of her mouth as she played the leash game. Laney stood.

Devon settled his hand at the small of her back and guided her out the door, down the hallway, and into the lobby. Kisses tried to keep up, but ended up lying down at the entrance to the hospital and shot them a look that said "I'm not going any farther and you can't make me." The puppy was breathing hard.

"Poor thing." Laney scooped her up. "Her little legs have to work four times as hard as ours."

Kisses licked her face, and Laney could swear she smiled. Not well versed in canine anatomy, she couldn't say if it was possible or not, but she was choosing to believe that it was.

Laney stepped outside and shaded her eyes with her hand. Right in front of the hospital, double-parked, was a brand new, dark blue Mustang convertible with a huge red ribbon on the hood.

It was the car that she'd always secretly wanted.

She almost dropped Kisses and then looked around incase this wasn't her present and it was for someone else.

Devon smiled from ear to ear as he took on the role of car salesman. He walked around the car. "It's called deep impact blue and is almost the color of your eyes. It has four hundred and thirty-five horse power and four hundred pounds of torque."

Laney couldn't claim to have been speechless ever before this moment. She had no words. Just like the puppy, she'd always wanted a Mustang convertible, but she couldn't keep it. It was too expensive of a gift to take from someone she hardly knew. How had he reached into her mind and pulled out two of the things she'd always wanted, but wouldn't allow herself to have?

"It has Bluetooth everything, SYNC, and a kickass sound system. This car practically drives itself." He waved a hand grandly game show hostess style to indicate the interior. "The leather is so soft you feel like you're sitting on a cloud."

The longer she stared at it, the more confused she became. She was starting to have feelings for him, but he clearly had stronger ones for her. She chewed on her bottom lip, trying to think of something to say.

Why couldn't they have a normal relationship beginning? He wanted to jump into things like they had been a couple for years. It was a lot of pressure. True, her parents hadn't been the best role models when it came to relationships, but Devon's buying her expensive presents didn't feel right.

"I can't accept it." She was quiet but firm. "It's too much too soon."

It felt like way too much too soon. What were his motives for giving her this gift? In her mind, it came with strings—nothing was without strings. She didn't understand the rules. When had their relationship or whatever they had moved to grand gestures?

The boyish grin in his face crumbled. "I want you to have it."

"That's very sweet of you, but I can't take it." She took a deep breath. "This is a large and expensive gift. It feels like you're trying to impress me. I don't need a car to like you. I already like you. So, I'm going to say thank you, but no thank you."

He walked up to her and held his hands out. "That's not it. I'm not trying to impress you. I just think that this car is more you than the Volvo. You're a top-down, radio blaring kind of woman. I'm just trying to help you achieve the real you."

"Did you just say that you're trying to help me achieve the real me?" Was there something wrong with who she was? True, she probably wasn't as splashy or exciting as the other women he'd dated, but she'd never thought of herself as defective. It was starting to piss her off that he wanted to change her into someone she wasn't. The urge to yell at him was almost overwhelming. "I'm sorry, I'm late. I've got more patients to see."

She never lashed out … ever. It was unproductive and uncivilized. Yelling only made things worse.

"Wait, I'll walk you back to your office." He sounded desperate and not a little mad himself.

"No thanks. I need a few minutes to gather myself before I head into the office." All she wanted was five minutes alone to puzzle out the fact that she was possibly falling for a man who wanted to make her into someone else. Just once she'd love an uncomplicated relationship. Did those even exist?

"Okay, but hang on. Let me get Kisses' things out of the trunk." He called after her.

She turned around to find him pushing some buttons on a key fob. The trunk popped open. He rushed around to the back of the car. A few seconds later, he brought her an armful of puppy things. A bed, a bag of food, several toys, and a rawhide bone that was approximately four times larger than Kisses. She held her free hand out to take the load, but he stepped back.

"I'll carry this up for you." Every word was clipped. He was angry. That was fine, because so was she.

In stony silence, they walked through the lobby of the professional building, got into the elevator, and rode to her office on the fourth floor.

When the elevator door opened, Devon turned to her and said, "It's just a car. Nothing more."

"It's more than that and you know it. What did you say? You're trying to help me achieve the real me." She matched his chilly tone. "What's wrong with this version of me?"

He studied her face letting the words sink in. "That's not what I meant. I don't want you to change, I just thought that you were more of a fast-driving convertible girl." His voice faded away as understanding dawned on his face. "Crap, I just screwed up big time, didn't I?"

How did anyone stay mad at this man? She bit her bottom lip to keep from smiling and nodded.

"Are we still on for tomorrow night?" He wasn't pleading, but it was close. "I can fix this…you know, once I figure out exactly where I went wrong. I can fix it."

How was she supposed to say no to that?

"Yes, we're still on for tomorrow night." She shook her head. "You're just so damn cute, sometimes I want to smack you."

"If I promise to stop being cute and apologize for…" his tone implied it was a fill in the blank question like the sum of two plus two is…

He opened the front door to her office, waited for her to walk in, and set the dog things on the closest chair. He turned to go. "That sounded a little desperate, didn't it?"

She squeezed her thumb and index finger about an inch apart. "Just a little."

"I'll work on it." He shook his head. "That was even more desperate."

"Thanks for my birthday party. It's the first real party that I've ever had." She snuggled Kisses.

Devon sucked in a deep breath and let it out slowly. "You're welcome. Can I call you tonight?"

"Tomorrow would be better. I'm going out with my teammates tonight."

His face fell as he turned on his heel and walked to the elevator.

She needed some time to think. Devon wanted more from her than she wanted from him. He'd bought her a car and a puppy. She couldn't help but feel pressure even if he didn't mean for there to be. Things with Devon had just become complicated.

Chapter 10

Devon wanted to beat someone up ... preferably himself. He sat in the new Mustang in the hospital parking lot trying to figure out his next move. The car had been too much too soon, but he'd been driving by the dealership and he'd remembered that she'd wanted one all those years ago. He thought it might trigger her memory of him, but all it had done was make her mad. Now that he thought about it, he was a little angry himself. He'd done everything he could think of to get her to remember him, but nothing worked.

Did that mean that she hadn't felt the same way about him? His mind was willing to go there, but his heart wouldn't let him. She had loved him and he would stick with that story until she told him otherwise.

At least he'd gotten her to keep the puppy. That was something.

What should he do next? Did he hang onto the car in case she wanted it later?

His phone rang. He worked it out of his front trouser pocket. It was his mother. He slid his finger across the bottom of the phone to answer the call.

"Hello."

"Since I can see you sitting alone in the Mustang, I take it Laney wasn't excited about the car." Her tone was soothing.

"You can say I told you so." Devon nodded and then looked around. "Where are you that you can see me?"

"I'm in Lara's room. Look at the last window on the far left of the fourth floor."

He glanced up and saw a figure waving in the last window on the left.

"Please, I would never say I told you so because it's always implied. And I never state the obvious." She laughed quietly.

"I know I shouldn't have bought it for her, but I couldn't resist. I want her to have nice things, and I want to be the one who gives them to her." He sounded sad and pathetic even to his own ears. And he wanted her to remember him. He couldn't get it out of his mind—if she remembered him, they were meant to be together.

"I know. You want to be her hero … just like your father. He didn't buy me a car, but a washing machine. On our second date, I came home to find that my washing machine was dead. The next day a brand new one was sitting in my driveway with a red bow on top. Based on the bow I see from all the way up here, you had the same idea." The smile in his mother's voice lightened the heaviness around his heart.

He loved hearing stories about his father. For five years after he died, she couldn't talk about him because it was too painful. "What did you do?"

"I made him return it. It was too big of a gesture too soon. He gave it expecting nothing in return, but it still made me uncomfortable. Even though he gave it with no strings attached, I wanted to attach some. Think about it this way, if she'd accepted such an expensive gift this early in the relationship, would she really be someone you could see yourself with long-term?"

He'd dated more than his fair share of gold diggers. One woman had come straight out and stated she expected expensive presents regularly and then helpfully gave him a list of acceptable gifts. That hadn't worked out.

But Laney was different. What they had together started a long time ago. The Mustang had been one of her dreams back then and now he was able to make that dream come true. It was more than just buying her things, it was taking her back to the past so hopefully she could see what was right in front of her.

"What did Dad do with the washing machine?" Devon rubbed the tense muscles at the back of his neck.

"He did what you're going to do. Park it in the garage until she's ready to accept it. Just because she won't take it now, doesn't mean that she doesn't want it." His mother always knew the right thing to say.

"You are wise Master Yoda." He felt like he'd lost any ground that he'd gained with Laney. Had he actually said that he wanted to help her find the real Laney? Now that he thought about it, that sounded terrible. She was perfect just the way she is, but he'd made her feel imperfect. It tore at him…like little cat scratches to the soul. He'd hurt her, he hadn't meant to, but he had.

"Give her some time. Let her finish her workday and then text her. Go with a simple 'I'm sorry' and for goodness sakes, don't send her flowers or some other gesture. Just a simple 'I'm sorry'."

He had to admit, sending flowers had crossed his mind … more than once.

"A grand gesture followed by another grand gesture only works when you've done something to piss her off that's not related to a grand gesture." His mother rattled something that sounded like a candy wrapper. "You're coming on too strong. You should dial it back a little."

He couldn't dial it back. He'd waited so long to see her again, he didn't want to waste a minute of time with her.

His father had lost six precious months with his mother after he'd met her. Devon wasn't about to lose any time with Laney.

It was time to come clean with his mother. "Remember EJ? That's short for Elaine Janece."

He let that grenade fall between them.

There was nothing but silence from the other end of the phone.

"And Laney is short for Elaine and Laney's middle name is Janece." He rolled his eyes. Clearly a lost night of sleep was costing his mother some brain cells.

"Oh." He heard the phone shift like she was sitting up. "OH. I'm going to need a notebook to keep all of her nicknames straight."

"I recognized her, but she hasn't recognized me." That was downright depressing. It scared him that she hadn't remembered him. Was that a sign that he'd been in love with the wrong woman for almost half his life?

"I'm sorry baby. That sucks." He heard the sewing machine she'd brought to the hospital whirl in the background.

"How's Lara?" He should consider putting the top up, he was getting sunburned. He hit the button on the visor and the roof unfolded from the back.

"She's sleeping. That kid could sleep through an F5 tornado."

"That's good I guess. What does she think about coming home with us?" The more he thought about it, the more he wanted to make whatever kind of home Lara wanted. It had been just him and his mother for so long that it would be nice to have someone else around.

"She's excited I think but also a little scared. The hospital is all she knows … or all she can remember. It's safe here and she knows what to expect." His mother continued to sew.

He understood the need for safety. "Whenever she's ready, I think we should move her in."

There he went again with the grand gestures. Was there something in his DNA that made him go big or go home? But he'd never been this way before. He liked to do things for his friends and family, but not on this scale. Did Laney bring out this need for him to take care of people?

He kind of liked that about himself. It was comforting to know that she brought out the best in him. Did he do the same for her?

"Why haven't you told her that you're DJ?" He could hear the reproach in her voice.

"Because I want her to figure it out." Something inside him wouldn't let go of the dream that Laney would come to her senses and realize he was DJ. At first, it might have been pride, but now it was more than that. When she did put two and two together, it would be validation that they were meant to be together.

"Have you ever thought that she might be mad that you didn't tell her?"

He sat back. Why would that make her mad? If anything she should be embarrassed that she hadn't remembered him...that is if she actually had feelings for him back at camp.

"No." He traced the stitching on the steering wheel. Laney might be embarrassed, but not mad. "What do you mean?"

"There is the possibility that she might feel duped. She's a pretty headstrong and upfront kind of person. Don't you think she might not be too pleased that you've failed to mention something of this importance to her?"

Women. They were so complicated. Laney mad because she hadn't remembered. It wasn't his fault she didn't remember him. Was there seriously a possibility of her blaming him for not remembering? That was the dumbest thing he'd ever heard ... but so like a woman. God knew they didn't make sense. Had they ever made sense—had Eve been a perfectly rational being not capable of yelling at Adam for forgetting to take out the trash until that whole apple thing had messed her up? Or had God's companion creation for man evolved into something that He hadn't quite foreseen?

"I'm just saying that she might not be too happy that you've kept this from her." The sewing machine stopped.

"I haven't kept anything from her. I just didn't point out that she should remember me. That's all." He was in the right on this. It may be the only thing he was in the right on, but by God he was right.

"Whatever." His mother sounded frustrated.

He glanced at the clock on the dash. "Sorry mom, I've got to go."

He was going to be late for practice, and that would cost him a few miles around the track. What a sucky, fitting end to a terrible day. He'd woken up in such a good mood and then everything had gone downhill from there. The only thing that could turn his day around was a smile from Laney.

Good God, he was pathetic.

"He bought you a car?" Nina's eyes turned the size of Oreos. "And you're not sleeping together?" She shook her head. "What is the world coming too? My view of life in general has just taken a serious hit. It's like learning that Santa Claus is actually your parents. I just can't go back from that."

Laney had been on edge all afternoon, and now her friends were taking her out for her birthday. They wouldn't tell her where, and she was starting to worry. Lara was babysitting Kisses. Her little puppy had followed her around all day like a mini medical assistant listening intently while she talked to patient's parents and then playing her heart out with the kids. At the hospital, she'd gotten smiles wherever she'd gone. And Lara was happy to watch her. They had played and wrestled a good portion of the afternoon.

Now, Laney and her teammates were all crammed into her Volvo roaring up Research Boulevard. The only reason they were roaring instead of creeping was that Nina was behind the wheel.

"So he likes you enough to buy you a car, but not to sleep with you?" January glanced in the rearview mirror and made eye contact with Laney in the backseat. "That's a little strange don't you think?"

"It's nice." Susie with her foot still in a cast sat next to Laney. "Maybe he's saving himself for marriage?"

Susie always saw the glass as one hundred percent full, thought everyone in the world was good and kind, and believed implicitly in true love. Basically, she was Snow White with a broken foot. Even her coloring—black hair and green eyes—lent her the appearance of Dopey and Sleepy's mistress.

"You think everything is nice." January rolled her eyes.

"That's because it is." Susie leaned over and thumped January on the back of the head. She didn't always act like Snow White.

"Ouch." January rubbed the back of her head.

"Laney, what do you think?" Charisma leaned forward, looking past Susie so she could make eye contact with Laney.

These were her closest friends—her sisters—she could tell them anything. Right?

She took a deep calming breath and dove into her feelings. "He makes me nervous. I get the impression that Devon wants more from me than I can give him. Now that I've had some time to process it, I think he actually bought me the car because he wanted me to have it. It wasn't some flashy move to impress me, I think he truly wants me to have it." She took another deep, calming breath and let it out slowly. Emotions were hard for her—logic she had in spades, but emotion—not so much. "That's what scares me. He isn't out to impress me, because he feels like I'm already his. Not in a creepy stalker kind of way, just in a really likes me kind of way."

That's what made her nervous. Not that she couldn't see herself with Devon, but that she wouldn't be able to give him back emotionally what he gave her. She wasn't even sure that she was capable of love. Her mind went to Kisses. No, that wasn't right. She was capable of love, but possibly not the deep intimacy that Devon deserved.

"Wow. That's a lot of pressure for a new relationship." Charisma leaned back. "How does that make you feel?"

"Nervous, scared and I don't want to hurt him." Which was ridiculous since she'd already hurt him. "His mom wants me to let him down easy if I don't return his feelings."

"Jesus, the lead weight on your chest just got heavier." Charisma shook her head. "I don't know what to tell you."

"Yeah, there's more at stake than a car." Nina smiled at her through the rearview mirror.

"Want my advice?" January turned around so she could look in the backseat.

"Does she have a choice?" Susie grinned.

January stuck out her tongue.

"Of course I want your advice." Laney ever the peacemaker jumped in before the yelling started.

"Get out of your head and live in the moment. Stop analyzing everything and just enjoy it. If something happens with Devon then great and if not, it will end and you'll find someone else. Personally, I think the fact that you're so worried about it means something. How about Dr. Dick last year? He was in love with you, but you didn't care. You broke his heart—if he had one—and didn't think twice about it."

"He wasn't in love with me, just my feet." Laney shivered in disgust. "He used to sniff the inside of my shoes." It was weird … so weird. "I could never figure out why he went into gynecology instead of podiatry. Clearly, feet were his thing."

"How come we didn't know about the feet?" Nina eyed Laney through the rearview. At least she didn't take her gaze off the road too long.

"Yeah, it's our responsibility to hear all facts— especially the weird ones—pertaining to your relationships." January nodded. "It's part of the whole friendship thing."

"I thought I'd told you." Laney nodded to herself. Why hadn't she told them? Because he hadn't mattered enough. When she'd broken it off, all she'd felt was relief and not the least bit of sadness. What did that say about her?

Devon mattered. It was foolish to pretend that he didn't. It still didn't make sense to her that she could come to care for him in such a short time. But it didn't feel short…it felt like she'd known him forever.

"Oh no, now you're off in your head again." January grabbed her heavy golden hair, pulled it into a ponytail, and wrapped an elastic band around it several times. "Stop analyzing things. Dr. Dick was a freak. There is no hidden meaning in his freakiness."

January was right, Laney needed to stop analyzing things to death.

Susie touched her arm. "Feel free to analyze things, but you do need to give equal time to living in the moment. Devon sounds like a good guy. It's okay to like him back. And for now, that's enough. Don't worry about what the future holds."

Changing Lanes

"When did y'all get so wise?" Laney knew they were right, but sometimes she couldn't help the over-thinking. It's what made her a good doctor. "So where are we going?"

She glanced at all the ladies in turn, and every single one of them had an I'm-not-going-to-tell grin.

"Do I get any hints?" Laney liked surprises … and if she told herself that a thousand times a day, maybe it would be true.

January thought about it for a minute. "It's reckless and involves changing clothes … sort of."

"Well that narrows it down to about half a billion things." Laney rolled her eyes. "Can you give me a little more?"

"We're going to iFly." January turned back around.

Laney waited for someone to tell her what iFly was. "What's iFly?"

"Indoor vertical wind tunnel. It's skydiving minus the parachute and plane." January smiled. "It's controlled recklessness. You should start small."

Controlled recklessness sounded like a good idea. Just jumping into skydiving or racecar driving might be a bit too much. Although part of her didn't want to start off slowly, she wanted to do something drastic like base jumping or cliff diving. When she did something she was all in.

"And then after, we're going to Chez Zee for an all dessert dinner party. There will be only dessert—all carbs, no protein." Nina added.

"Now that's living on the edge." A slow devious smile crept across Charisma's face. "And we'll have to do twice the workout tomorrow to compensate."

"Spoken like a true sadist. I'm sure there's a psychological diagnosis that explains you." January looked at Laney. "Help me out here."

"You called it … sadist. That's someone who likes to inflict pain and clearly we are all masochists because we like the pain she inflicts or we'd leave." Laney thought

128

about it for a second. "Although the definition of a sadist is that he or she inflicts pain on unwilling victims, so I guess that doesn't apply."

"See, I'm not the one with the problem. I'm perfectly normal." Charisma nodded.

"Normal in the way Hitler was normal … scary normal." Susie smiled. "Yeah, scary normal works for you."

One thing was for sure, this was going to be a birthday to remember. She'd gotten a puppy, semi-skydived, and had almost gotten a car. She's won the birthday lottery—too bad she didn't feel like a winner.

Chapter 11

Devon was sure that coffee and a scone wasn't a grand gesture. Laney loved to eat and he was merely providing the food. It was harmless...he was harmless. The next morning should be long enough for her to forgive him. He'd have come last night but both CoCo and his mother had talked him out of it. He'd made her feel like she wasn't enough...like he wanted her to change. He hadn't meant it that way. She'd told him that it didn't matter, but it mattered to him. Laney was perfect and he wanted her to know it.

He juggled the two beverage carriers full of coffee and the three large bakery bags that he'd gotten at Starbucks. Since he hadn't known what Laney liked, he'd bought a little of everything. It wasn't a grand gesture, it was indecision. Besides, he could pass it off as he was bringing something for his mother to eat.

Using his butt, he pushed open the double glass doors to the professional building at Dell Children's, walked to the elevator, and used his left elbow to press the up button. Once inside, he used his elbow again to press floor number five.

His nervous stomach reared its ugly head, and he nearly vomited up the water he'd had in lieu of breakfast. Anticipating the nausea he always felt when stressed, he'd purposefully skipped his normal eggs and ham for room temperature tap water.

He would have put a hand over his stomach to calm it, but his hands were full. The elevator dinged heralding the arrival of floor number four and Devon leaned heavily against the back wall.

He was a badass football player who regularly intimidated other badass football players. He could handle a hundred pound doctor with commitment issues. Last night as he'd babysat Grace and Chord's kids, HW, Cart, Coco, and Luke, he'd devised a plan. Or rather ... Coco had. Since she was the only female around, he'd listened to her. The fact that she was sixteen and thought she knew everything had made the groveling apology she'd helped him write sound plausible. Now, he was rethinking the advice from a sixteen-year old.

The elevator doors swished opened and there was the front door to her office. The hall to her office seemed to elongate like something from The Twilight Zone. He stepped onto the tile floor and made his way to the door. Since he didn't actually have an appointment, he was counting on sweet-talking the receptionist into sneaking him back. That shouldn't be too hard because he'd been sweet-talking women since he'd learned to form words. The only person he couldn't sweet-talk was Laney. He totally loved that about her.

With his forearm, he wiped the sweat running down his brow and opened the door. The waiting room was unlike anything he'd ever seen. There was a huge round aquarium in the middle of the room surrounded by cubicle like enclosed rooms. Every single room was brightly colored, had a TV on the wall, and was filled with toys and books. Because some of her patients were susceptible to common diseases, she'd sectioned off the waiting room to keep everyone safe. It was ingenious and fun.

A small round woman who bore a striking resemblance to Danny DeVito sat behind a half wall. As he got closer, he could make out a full-on mustache. Maybe this was Danny DeVito in drag? No wait, the hair wasn't right. He was balding while this woman had a full head of dyed black hair. She had on black scrubs with pink bunnies all over them. Her name tag read, "Helen Reichs-Chief Smile Officer."

True to her station, she smiled as he reached her desk. "May I help you?"

"I'm here to see Dr. Nixon." He held up the bags. "We have a breakfast date."

She tapped some keys on the computer and squinted at the screen. "That's funny, I don't have you on the schedule."

"It's okay, I'm her boyfriend." He propped the coffees and bags of food on her desk, and leaned closer. "I screwed up yesterday—you know on her birthday—and I'm trying to make it up to her. Say, you wouldn't happen to know if she's a mocha latte, Frappuccino, espresso, or plain black coffee kind of girl? I have them all."

"Laney's plain black and so dark you could tar a roof with it." She continued to smile.

"Thanks, you wouldn't be a mocha latte, Frappuccino, or an espresso kind of girl?" Sweet-talking was one of his finest features.

Her smile turned kind. "You could talk me into a Frappuccino."

He pulled one out of the holder and handed it to her. "How about some breakfast too?" He opened one of the bags. "I have a little of everything."

"Just the coffee for me. You can feed the rest to Laney. She's an eater." Helen looked over her right shoulder and then leaned in conspiratorially. "Go on back. She should be in any minute. You can wait in her office. Spread out a little picnic on her desk. She'll love it." She winked.

"Helen, you're a good woman." He opened the door that separated her from the rest of the world.

"Are you the guy who gave her Kisses?" Helen sipped her Frappuccino.

"Yes, ma'am." He nodded.

"Thank you." She reached out and touched his hand. "You made so many children smile yesterday that Laney is going to bring Kisses to work every day now. It takes someone special to make a kid smile, especially when they don't have a lot to smile about."

Devon's queasiness eased. He'd known the puppy was a good idea and now that he had proof, he felt better about this morning.

A door opened somewhere in the back of the office.

"Oh, that will be her. Quick, her office is around the corner and all the way at the end." Helen pointed to the corridor on his left. "I'll stall her as long as I can."

Helen was fast becoming one of Devon's favorite people.

"Thanks." Devon called over his shoulder as he dashed down the hall and into her office. He had just enough time to set down the coffees and the bags of food and sit down across from her desk when she walked in. Kisses ran to him, hunched down on her two front paws like she wanted to play, and barked. Her tail wagged so fast that it looked the blades of a helicopter. He half expected her to take flight.

Devon scooped up the puppy. He needed something to calm and run interference for him. Kisses seemed like the perfect tool.

Laney just stared at him for a full minute and then shook her head. "Good morning."

"I'm here to apologize." He held up his hands. "Now hold on. I've brought breakfast as a peace offering." He picked up the coffee. "Plain black just like Helen said you liked it."

"Thanks." She looked a little confused.

"I have my apology all worked out." He set Kisses on the desk while he patted his pockets for the piece of notebook paper he and Coco had written it on. "Just give me a minute, I have it somewhere."

Devon finally found it in his right trouser pocket. As he pulled it out, Kisses noticed the bags of food, walked right up to the first bag, and pounced on it like a cat stalking a mouse. She lay on top of the bag in case it was going to slither away. He picked her up, flipped the piece of paper open, and skimmed it.

Laney watched with one eyebrow curled up.

"Okay, I'm very sorry—wait …" he sat down, "I'm supposed to be seated when I say all of this."

"You brought a speech?" She folded her arms. "Does this apology come with a multimedia display?"

"No, just some heartfelt paragraphs of humble groveling. Last night was my night to babysit Grace and Chord's kids. Their oldest, Coco—she's sixteen—helped me work it out. I'm supposed to compliment your shoes and promise to never buy you a car again. FYI-I was adamant that you wouldn't want an apology video on YouTube or a mix CD of apology songs. Trust me, those were steps in the wrong direction." He leaned over the desk. "So let me see your shoes so we can get the ball rolling."

She held out a foot. He glanced down and grimaced. She wore the single ugliest pair of shoes he'd ever seen. They were black plastic clogs.

"Can I borrow a pen?" He nodded to the cup full of pens on her desk.

"Sure, do I want to know why?"

He grabbed a pen and marked out the first two sentences on the notebook paper. "Needed to make a small adjustment because those shoes um … no longer apply."

She bit back a smile. "They're my surgery shoes. Good for standing, but not particularly aesthetically pleasing."

"Okay, so here goes." He took a deep breath and let it out slowly. "I am deeply sorry for buying you such an expensive gift. It was too …" He squinted at the paper. The writing had smeared. He held it up to the light thinking he could see the original pen strokes and make out the word, but that didn't work.

"Give me a hand here." He held the paper out to her and pointed to the word. "I can't make out this word."

Dutifully, Laney took the paper and analyzed it. "Soon."

She handed it back to him.

"It was too soon. I like you just the way you are. Any implication that I wanted you to change in any way was a mistake. Where you are concerned, I'm over eager—"

"Let me stop you right here. I thought we'd resolved things yesterday." Laney shook her head, but there was a smile on her face. "Does anyone stay mad at you?"

The nausea that had been plaguing him all morning vanished and his stomach rumbled. "Well now, let me see."

She sat at her desk and opened the bag closest to her. She pulled out a chocolate muffin, broke it in half, and handed him a chunk. She licked the caramel oozing out of the center. "My favorite, chocolate caramel muffins."

He forced his eyes to glance away from her flicking tongue as he filled chocolate caramel muffins under her favorites list in his head. "In the third grade, I accidentally knocked out Ted Garcia's two front teeth with a baseball bat. I'm pretty sure he still hates me. And then in high school, I broke up with Jena Menkins the day before prom, and I know she still hates me. Then there's my mother who I seem to piss off on a daily basis. After last week's game, the Denver Broncos aren't too happy with me right now."

He bit into his muffin and it was pretty good.

"You're forgiven," Laney rolled her eyes, "am I?"

She bit into her muffin half.

"For what?" He said around his bite. She'd done nothing wrong. Well, except for not remembering him.

"I was unforgivably rude. You threw me a party and gave me some wonderful presents, and I was rude. I'm sorry." She wouldn't make eye contact.

He smiled. Her sense of fair play was still going strong.

"Does this mean that you're taking the car?" This was great, better than he'd expected.

"No, I can't accept it. It's just too much." There was real sorrow in her voice. Did she want to take the car?

"How about we agree on visitation? You could babysit it once a week and come over anytime you want to see it. I named her Blue Lightning. She's really fast. I'm thinking of having some silver lightning bolts painted on the sides." He picked up the mocha latte and took a sip. While he would have gladly given it to her, he was happy she hadn't wanted it.

"Let's hold off on the silver lightning bolts for a while." She took a sip of her coffee. "Just until we get a feel for whether her name is really Blue Lightning. What if she's more of a Blueberry or Beth? Let's not jump into anything."

Here they were discussing the name of the car she wouldn't take yesterday. It was progress. "How was your birthday?"

"The best I've ever had. This super cute guy threw me my very first birthday party. My teammates took me to iFly, and we pretended to skydive. They called it controlled recklessness." She grinned. "I would have preferred some actual recklessness, but I guess you have to start somewhere."

"Baby steps." He managed to keep most of the needy out of his voice. If she wanted reckless, he'd give it to her. "Can I take you out tonight?"

"That depends, are you planning on buying my anything that costs more than this pen?" She held up a cheap plastic gimme pen.

"Dinner only and I hope it costs more than that pen. I think even the value menu at McDonald's is over that budget." Instead of a fancy restaurant, he'd take her for a picnic and some adventure. He was beginning to see that Laney wasn't into the finer things in life, which was fine because he wasn't either.

"Okay." She slumped back in her chair. "Wait … what kind of date is it? I don't have any more dresses. Please say its casual dress because I have a couple of biopsies this afternoon, and I don't have time to go shopping."

"How about if I go shopping for you?" It was his day off, he could manage it.

One eyebrow shot up. "You're not going to buy me a fur coat or diamonds? And sexy underwear at this point would be creepy." She sighed heavily. "I'll agree to one condition, I pay for the clothes."

He opened his mouth to argue, but she shot up an index finger. "I pay or no deal."

He tunneled his fingers through his hair. She was a tough one, but he could play hardball. "Fine, but the money you reimburse me, I'll donate to charity."

She shrugged. "Fine by me. As long as I pay my own way, what you do with your money is completely up to you."

She peeked into the open bag in front of her, stuck her hand in, and came out with a piece of coffee cake. She unwrapped part of it, took a taste test, nodded, and took a bigger bite.

"What size do you wear?" He'd judged her for a six, but he needed to be sure.

"I wear a six, and my shoe size is a nine and a half." She said around the cake.

"Shoes too?" He grinned. It was stupid to be this happy about going shopping for her, but he was.

"Unless you want to see these unfortunate things all evening." She held a blue scrub clad leg up for his inspection.

"Good point." He chewed on his bottom lip. How long would it take to find the perfect outfit for tonight? Based on the amount of time it took him to dress himself, he'd need about a week to find her something to wear.

Laney pursed her lips and then sucked on the bottom one. It was sexy as hell. "Can I ask you something that may or may not piss you off?"

"Sure." What else was he supposed to say?

"What's your end game with me? I can't figure it out. I feel like we should have a talk about boundaries, but honestly, I don't know you that well." She tapped her fingernails on the desktop. "And the thing is, I do want to get to know you better, but I feel like there's a lot of pressure that comes with that."

The queasiness was returning with a vengeance. He put a hand over his stomach. It didn't seem like a good time to mention that he was in love with her.

"I don't mean to put pressure on you. I didn't know that I was." He could feel the muffin and mocha latte turning on him. "I like you a lot. I feel like you could be someone special, and I want to know everything about you. It's not often that I find someone I'm interested in." He hoped that was vague enough. It was definitely too soon for talking about spending the rest of his life with her. This whole love thing was complicated.

Her sigh of relief was a kick to the heart. "Thank God. I want to get to know you too, but I'm not sure I'm relationship material." She shook her head. "I know myself, and I'm not certain that love is in the cards for me."

"You must have been in love at some point." At the age of sixteen, she'd professed her love for him. Had that been a lie? It hadn't felt like it at the time.

"Of course I've thought I was in love, but I was very young. Puppy love." She pointed to Kisses who had curled up in a ball and fallen asleep right on top of her bag of now-squished goodies.

"Tell me about it." Devon's nervous stomach turned anxious. Please let it be him.

She shook her head. "It was nothing."

That was a blow to the soul.

"You really want to know?" She bit her top lip.

He nodded because his voice would have given away the hurt he felt.

"His name was DJ, and I thought I loved him. We met at camp—it sounds silly now—but I thought it was the real thing. For two weeks we were inseparable." Her voice faded away like she was lost in memory. She picked up Kisses and settled her on her lap. Absently, she stroked the back of the sleeping dog.

After a minute or two, he asked, "What happened?"

Laney started like she'd forgotten he was there. "Camp ended … well my dad picked me up early, and I never heard from DJ again."

He slid his hand into his trouser pocket and clasped the leather bracelet she'd made for him all those years ago praying to God that she would see him as DJ, but it wasn't time yet. She needed to work it out for herself.

"Did you ever try to find him?" God knew he'd tried to find her.

"Yes." She clamped a hand over her mouth. "I've never admitted that to anyone including myself. I don't know his last name. His first name is DJ, and I don't know if that's short for something or his real first name. At the time, he lived in Dallas." Her shoulders shook with embarrassed laughter. "I actually chose to do my residency in Dallas because some part of me thought that if it was meant to be, we'd bump into each other. How corny is that?"

And he'd moved to Austin in the hope that he'd bump into her. He'd turned down much more lucrative offers to join a new NFL franchise, The Lone Stars, because it was in her hometown.

"Tell me about him." The fact that she'd truly loved him and had been in some way looking for him like he'd been looking for her was heartbreaking and beautiful. The part of his soul that had died the day she'd left began to heal and give him hope for the future.

"He was big and strong and tough, but the kindest person I have ever known. He had a tattoo on his left shoulder of a Chinese symbol that he told me meant courage, only I looked it up and it actually meant chicken eyeball. One day I hope to find him and tell him that it needs to be removed."

A fact he'd learned in a Chinese restaurant in college when his waitress had wanted to know why he had chicken eyeball tattooed on his shoulder. After ten painful laser treatments and a scar from a shoulder surgery, the tattoo was nothing but a memory.

More than anything, he wanted to pull out the leather bracelet and tell her the truth, but he'd made a promise to himself, and he kept every promise he made.

"He was into sports and we'd go jogging every morning. I think he played football too. Back then he'd been at camp under court order. I don't think that he knew that I knew that. He'd been arrested for stealing cars and it was either summer camp or jail." She was beautiful lost in thought … softer somehow.

He loved seeing himself through her eyes. "So you're into bad boys?"

"No, not really … just him. He was big like you, but a little on the pudgy side … not fat, but big. You could tell that he was destined to have a beer belly someday. It was wonderful. I was just me around him and that was all he wanted."

Devon patted his flat stomach. He did not have a beer belly, but that's because football had conditioned all that extra fat into lean muscle. Back then, he'd drank enough beer to create ten beer bellies because it had made him feel like an adult, but a tough coach with a heart of gold had given him a choice, football or the highway. Only his love of the game had gotten him through those terrible months after EJ.

"Not that I'm an expert, but it sounds like you loved him." He sat back and crossed his ankles. "I don't think age matters. When you find the right person, you just know."

"How about you? Ever been in love?" She moved from the coffee cake to a scone. It still amazed him how much she could eat.

He thought very carefully about what he should say. "Yes and I too fell in love in high school. Also, a summer thing. She was smart and funny and beautiful. She seemed to calm the restless part of me. I liked who I was when I was with her. She made me want to be a better man." He was careful to use the past tense, but in his head everything was present tense. His mind screamed for her to remember him. "I loved the little zing I got every time I saw her … you know the rapid heartbeat and throat thickening. Sometimes I'd just sit and stare at her trying to convince myself she was real."

"I didn't know men ever got sappy." She smiled. "It's nice."

"Excuse me, sappy?" He took off his jacket and flexed his biceps, which were very noticeable in his short sleeves. "I'm a manly football player. We're never sappy."

She put her hand over her mouth. "I beg your pardon. I wasn't referring to you."

"Thank God." He grinned.

"What happened to her?" Laney propped her chin on her hand.

"Same as you. We lost touch." And he'd been looking for her ever since.

"That's too bad—well not for me—because if you'd kept in touch I wouldn't have known you." She thought about what she'd just said. "That was very self-centered. Sorry."

"No worries." He nodded.

She had loved him, it was a start. He was willing to slow down as long as he knew that they were going in the same direction. She had loved him. It was a balm to his soul.

Chapter 12

When Laney had agreed to let Devon shop for her, she'd thought he'd come up with a sexy dress or something short and silky, but the reality was more flame retardant and resembled a jumpsuit. A white Formula One jumpsuit with a red stripe down both sides and driver booties to be precise. To give him credit, he'd wrapped them all in a huge box complete with big red bow and left it on her desk. The card on top said that he'd pick her up out front at six.

She checked her wristwatch. It was five minutes to six now. She slammed the door to her office shut, and quickly changed clothes. She pulled on the booties and finally figured out how to tie them. For clothing that was completely fire proof, it was surprisingly light and comfortable. She hit the stairs running and made it out the front door and into the parking lot at five after six.

Devon leaned against the Mustang, arms crossed, and grinning. He was wearing a matching red jumpsuit with a white stripe down the sides.

"Sorry, I'm late." She pulled at the elastic at her waist. "Not what I was expecting."

"But cool right?" He tossed her the keys. "You drive. It will get you warmed up for our date."

"I take it we're not going to the symphony." She smiled. "Thank God."

"We're picnicking at Circuit of the Americas and then we're racing Formula One cars." Devon opened the driver's side door for her.

She couldn't say no, it would have been rude. She slid behind the wheel, used the buttons on the side of the seat to change it to her liking, and shoved the key in the ignition. "You found a way to get me behind the wheel."

"I'm good." He nodded. "Really good."

"And modesty absolutely pours out of you." She watched as he lowered himself into the passenger's seat. For such a big man, he was so graceful—it still shouldn't amaze her but it did.

"Just wait and see what I can get you to do later—I'm very talented." He winked.

"Good God, I hope its sex." She shook her head. "Crap, I said that out loud didn't I?"

She wanted to slap herself on the forehead, but that was never a good idea in public.

"I didn't hear a thing." His shoulders shook with laughter, and he leaned over and kissed her gently.

His lips were soft and undemanding. Trouble was, she kind of wanted demanding. She may not know exactly what her feelings were toward him, but she knew exactly what her body wanted from him. It occurred to her that was very shallow and she'd never been shallow in her whole life. So he brought out the shallow in her, what did she bring out in him?

"Stop picturing me naked, it makes it hard to concentrate." He shot her a look.

"Are you picturing me naked?" It was out before she had time to sensor it.

"I am now." He shook his head. "Drive before I yank that zipper down just to see what you have on underneath."

The temptress that she'd always wanted to be finally came out, and she pulled the zipper down past her chest almost to her navel. The fabric slipped open about three inches.

Devon's gaze fastened on the lacy blue demi bra and stayed there. After a good minute, he licked his lips, and closed his eyes. He turned away. "Do you realize that we're in the parking lot of your workplace and my mother is watching us from Lara's window?"

Laney froze and then looked up. Sure enough two figures, one small and the other adult-sized, waved from Lara's hospital room window. Kisses sat at Lara's foot. In no time flat, she whipped the zipper up, threw the car in reverse, checked the backup camera, and zoomed out of the parking space. "Oh my God. The one time I decide to do something risqué, is in the parking lot at work. Maybe in a few years I'll be able to look back on this and laugh, but right now, it's not that funny."

"I think it's hilarious as hell." He was laughing so hard his eyes were watering.

She punched him on the arm. "Shut up."

"Ouch." Devon gingerly patted his arm. He wasn't faking, something was wrong.

She pulled out onto the feeder road to Interstate Thirty-Five, went under the bridge, and onto the on-ramp for Highway Thirty-Five South.

"What's wrong with your arm?" Laney shot short glances his way.

"Just took a pretty bad hit yesterday in practice." He raised his arm and winced.

"Let me see." For the most part, she kept her gaze on the road, but glanced over at him.

He unzipped his jumpsuit to the waist and gently wriggled his arm out. "Wait a minute, this isn't some ploy to get me to take off my clothes, is it?"

"We're in the middle of the highway, if I wanted you to take off your clothes, it would be a little more private." She glanced over and winced too. A bruise the size of a softball mottled his arm black and blue. But his back was worse. The bruising there covered him from shoulder to shoulder and all the way down to the small of his back. "What happened?"

"I took a hit. Every single game is like being in a car wreck. That's why this is my last season." Slowly, he pulled the jumpsuit back up his arm and zipped it up.

"I'm glad. You must be in some serious pain. Why didn't you say something? We could have stayed home tonight and watched a movie." She glanced in the rearview and then the side mirror before changing lanes.

"I'm fine. It looks worse than it is." He put his hand on her thigh. It was more of an unconscious gesture—like he needed to touch her not something sexual.

"You should be in bed icing that back down. It's a wonder you can move much less spend the day shopping for me." She took the exit for Circuit of the Americas and followed the signs. There were exactly two cars in the parking lot so she pulled up to the space closest to the front entrance. "I've never been here before. It's really big."

"It's huge and since it's across the street from The Lone Stars' Stadium, traffic's a nightmare when we have a home game and they have an event. We're trying to coordinate with each other's schedule, but it doesn't always work out." Devon was out of his seat and coming around to open the door for her before she had time to open it for herself. "I like that you open doors for me. I know it's old fashioned, but I still like it."

"Mom insists. Once when I was ten, she sat in the car a whole ten minutes before I realized why. I was already in the house and ran out to open the door for her. I never forgot after that."

"In case I forget to tell you later, I had a wonderful time tonight." Laney leaned up and kissed him lightly.

He deepened the kiss and pulled her gently to him. She put a hand on his arm, and he jerked back reflexively.

"I'm so sorry. I forgot about your arm." She wanted to get a closer look at it and see if there was anything she could do, but he was adamant that he was okay.

"It's nothing." He said through pain-gritted teeth.

"Really, why don't we just go home? You need to rest." She turned back to the car, but he caught her hand and gently pulled her toward the front doors.

"I want to see you drive a Formula One racecar. I can't wait." There was a smile in his voice. Come to think of it, she wanted to drive one too.

Her stomach rumbled so loudly that he glanced at it.

"Sorry, no lunch—too busy." She patted her flat stomach. "Food please."

He just shook his head. "Do I have to bring you food three times a day in order to make sure you eat?"

"That would be helpful." She lowered her gaze and looked up through her lashes. "I'm not going to lie. I don't cook. It's not my thing."

Devon jumped back in fake astonishment. "No, I don't believe it. You definitely had me fooled."

"What gave it away? The fact that I'm always hungry."

"Nope, it was your kitchen. Do you know that you still have the original tape holding your oven door closed from when they installed it?" One corner of his mouth turned up. "And your espresso maker has the original Styrofoam it was packed in."

"Wow, you're very observant." She eyed him skeptically. "Creepy observant."

"I notice kitchens because I like to cook. You notice body ailments because you like what you do." He looked down at her. "So if you don't like espresso, why do you have an espresso maker?"

"Ex-boyfriend gave it to me for Christmas last year. It's funny. I dated him for almost a year, and he didn't know me half as well as you do." She waited for him to open the door for her, and then she stepped inside. The lobby or front gate or whatever was different than she'd expected. It was all glass and a fancy mural that spanned one entire wall. It looked more like an upscale restaurant than a racetrack.

"So what did he do wrong?" Devon whispered close to her ear as he led her down a hallway and then outside.

"Dr. Dick—his real name is Richard Helms, but my teammates call him Dr. Dick—was into feet ... really into feet." She shivered and Devon thinking she was cold put his arm around her.

"Huh?"

"He always wanted to do strange things with my feet." She could feel her gag reflex coming on but swallowed it down.

"Like what?"

"Well, one of the more tame things he liked to do was have me put on different shoes and then take pictures of my feet. And sometimes, he liked to paint my toenails." She should have listened to her inner voice and never gone out with him.

"I don't mean to be rude, but your feet aren't exactly your best feature. Don't get me wrong, they're nice feet, but I've seen better."

"Hey, see if I ever let you suck my toes." She would have punched him again in the arm, but she remembered the bruising.

"Sorry Babe, toes aren't my thing. There will be no toe sucking ... ever." His tone was final.

"I'm inclined to agree. Toes aren't my thing either. The first time he did it I almost vomited. We'd been to the rodeo, and I was wearing flip-flops. We'd spent the afternoon walking through all of the show barns and I'd stepped in all sorts of nasty stuff. Later when he kissed his way down my leg to my feet, all I could think of were the germs teaming on my feet. It was disgusting." She shivered again.

"That is really gross." He opened the door that lead out to the track for her. "As long as we're grossing out, I dated this woman once who was into food—not eating it, but wearing it. She liked for me to spread food all over her. Now, I'm okay with chocolate syrup and whipped cream, but baked beans? That's just nasty."

"Yuck." Laney laughed. It was good to know that Devon had dating horror stories too. Thank God it wasn't just her.

Something white caught her eye and music started up. She shaded her eyes. In the grassy area in the middle of the track, there was a romantic table set for two, a string quartet was set up behind the table, and a large white folding screen was behind them. A waiter in a black tuxedo waited to pull out a chair for her.

"This is the fanciest picnic, I've ever had." Especially in the middle of a Formula One track. This was the second time he'd surprised her with an upscale picnic. How did he get those tables right where he wanted them on such short notice? "Do you have a table rental company on retainer?"

"No, I'm very persuasive." He led her to the table, the waiter pulled out her chair, and scooted her in. He flipped open her napkin and placed it delicately in her lap.

Devon seated himself and opened his own napkin.

The waiter disappeared behind the screen and came out with a pitcher full of water. First he poured her a glass and then one for Devon.

"Sorry, we can't have champagne because the track has a strict policy on alcohol before getting behind the wheel, but I've arranged for other drinks for us." Devon covered her hand with his.

"Ma'am we have fresh squeezed lemonade, water, sparkling water, or iced tea." The waiter said nonchalantly like he always served people sitting in the grassy knoll in the middle of a Formula One racetrack.

"I'll have an Arnold Palmer—half iced tea and half lemonade." Laney sat back in her chair. The sun was starting to go down, and it was surprisingly peaceful. The music was subtle and calming.

"That sounds good, I'll have the same." Devon said. "And you can bring out the first course when you're ready."

There were multi-courses? "When you picnic, you go all out."

"I like food, and I like feeding you. Let's see if you are up to the challenge of The Emerald's four-course chateaubriand dinner. I know linebackers who can't finish it." Devon toasted her with his water glass. "I have faith in you."

"Please, chateaubriand—I can do that in my sleep." She clinked glasses with him. "I won't let you down."

"I'm counting on it." He set his glass down.

The waiter, hefting a huge tray, made his way to the table. Without missing a beat, he set her Arnold Palmer in front of her and then Devon's in front of him. Then he set a huge bowl of French onion soup in front of Laney. It smelled delicious. She noticed that the bowl holding the soup was actually an enormous hollowed out onion. With a flourish, the waiter poured something on the top of the soup, struck a match, and the soup erupted in a blue flame.

"Feel free to blow it out." The waiter's bored tone almost made her laugh. She blew out the flames. The waiter set Devon's soup in front of him, lit it on fire, and then disappeared behind the screen.

Devon blew his flaming soup out and picked up the large soupspoon next to his plate. Laney followed suit. She broke through the crusty-melty cheese and scooped up a spoonful. As soon as the soup hit her tongue, she sighed. It was delicious—truly the best French onion soup she'd ever tasted.

"This is fantastic." She scooped up another bite and pretty soon all of her soup was gone. It was funny. Having the soup only made her hungrier. She drank her Arnold Palmer, and as soon as the empty glass hit the table, the waiter set a fresh one down. He was good.

Devon ate more slowly. He seemed to be savoring every single bite. True, the soup was savor-worthy, but the next course wasn't likely to come out until he was done. Since she didn't want to delay him any further with small talk, she glanced around the track.

Devon watched her every move. "Is something wrong?"

"No, no finish your soup. It's really good." Maybe if she imagined him eating faster he'd subconsciously get the point and shovel it in. She concentrated really hard, but he kept on with the dainty little bites.

She downed her second Arnold Palmer and a third was brought out. At this rate she'd be joining AARP before Devon finished his soup. Would it be rude to pull out her phone and play a game of solitaire?

Devon grinned. "Are you ready to kill me yet?"

"What?"

"My mom hates eating with me because I'm so slow. Why don't you help me out?" He picked up her plate and set his down in front of her. "I'm not as hungry as you are."

"Are you sure?" Laney didn't wait for an answer but picked up her soupspoon. She finished that off in a matter of minutes.

After the waiter cleared the soup dishes, he brought out the salads and a basket of bread. She plowed through her salad and the entire basket of rolls before Devon had eaten half of his salad. The waiter brought out another basket of bread, and she ate that. Devon finally gave up on the salad and called for the waiter.

"Please bring the main course." He wiped his mouth.

The waiter cleared the salad plates and returned with a huge tray with three plates. He set two in front of Laney and one in front of Devon.

"I took the liberty of ordering you two servings. I hope you don't mind." Devon grinned. "I bet you still eat them both before I finish."

Laney dug in. The chateaubriand was so tender she used her fork to cut it. The carrots and potatoes surrounding the meat were glazed in a butter wine sauce and melted in her mouth. The potatoes were stuffed with breadcrumbs and butter. Hands down, it was the best food she'd ever had.

"You have a real gift. Ever think about competitive eating? I think you could dominate the sport." Devon sipped his first Arnold Palmer.

"Eating is a sport? Wow, I feel like I just wasted the last few years of my life training for all of those triathlons when I could have been eating." She wiped her mouth.

"Speaking of triathlons, after this football season is over, I'd like to train for one. Nothing like the Ironman, but maybe a mini." He cut another dainty little bite of meat. "Maybe we could train together?"

"I'll have to ask my team. We're an all-girls team, but they like you so we may be able to work something out." She grinned. "How do you feel about drag? We could dress you up like a girl, and then we'd still be all girl-ish."

"Not going to happen. It's too complicated being female. All that makeup and all those face creams and stuff. Not to mention the dozens of bottles of shampoo—why do y'all need all that stuff?" With his fork, he placed the little meat bite in his mouth and chewed.

Sight impaired quadriplegics didn't take this long to eat. Devon was maybe a quarter of the way through his steak and she was starting on her second meal. She should feel bad, but … she didn't. Devon liked that she was an eater, and he didn't make her feel self-conscious about it at all, in fact, he encouraged it.

It dawned on her, he liked her for exactly who she was. He'd never suggested that she wear something different or that maybe she shouldn't eat so much or that she talked too much about her work. With the exception of DJ, Devon was the only other man who liked everything about her—no qualifiers or limits. They could talk about anything and he never made her feel inadequate or uncomfortable.

She was happy. It shouldn't have surprised her, but there it was. Devon made her happy. She looked forward to seeing him.

Chapter 13

Devon wiped his mouth with his napkin. It was crazy, but he enjoyed watching her eat. Laney could put the away food. Where it went, he couldn't tell, but man, she could eat.

"You're making me nervous." She forked in a huge bite of meat.

"Sorry, it's just so much fun to watch you eat. I keep wondering how you don't weigh three hundred pounds." He finished his chateaubriand and carrots but left the potatoes. He had to watch the carbs or he'd weigh three hundred pounds.

She finished the second chateaubriand and all the vegetables. After she mopped up all of the sauce with the last piece of bread, she popped it in her mouth, chewed, and swallowed. "That was delicious. And I don't know how I eat so much. I do exercise a lot, but still. Maybe it's because I don't eat regularly like I should."

She shrugged. "Food tastes good."

"Is there anything you won't eat?" Devon was taking more mental notes.

"I don't like beets or sweets and meats together—like the new idea that all of the hamburger buns in Austin should be sweet." She grimaced. "It's like eating a couple of donuts with a hamburger patty in between. Or waffles with fried chicken all covered in maple syrup—yuck. Sweet and meat don't go together."

"So beets and sweet plus meat. That's it. You'll eat anything else." He bet she got more than her money's worth at a buffet.

"Well, I'm not that into sushi. It's not that I don't like the flavors, it's more of a mouth-feel issue. Sushi is a little bit slimy and sometimes mushy, so I don't like the way it feels in my mouth. But don't get me wrong, I'll still eat it if it's the only thing around." She sat back and crossed her legs.

"What's your favorite food?" So he was interrogating her… he needed to know these things.

"I like meat—all kinds of meat."

If he didn't already have a thousand reasons to love her that would be one. The meat reminded him. "You said something about when you were in college and eating at places that didn't make you pay if you could finish a huge plate of food because money was tight. Didn't your father help you with college?"

And she'd said something about being a massage therapist to pay for medical school.

She refolded her napkin in her lap. "Since you've met my father, I don't need to explain that he can be difficult. When I applied to colleges, I didn't apply to his beloved Stanford, but instead to U.T. For him, that was bad enough, but then I went and majored in art."

"So you're an artist." She had pursued her art … at least in the beginning. He wanted to high-five her, but then he'd have a lot to explain so he controlled the urge.

"At one time I'd thought of myself as an artist, but unfortunately, I'm not that great. I struggled and struggled and barely produced terrible art. I had the mechanics down, and my technique was flawless, but I didn't have the heart of an artist. It took me a while to admit that I loved the idea of being an artist instead of actually being one. I didn't have the natural ability and passion that goes into the work. So one day I went to my advisor and changed my major to biology. In that, I found the passion I was missing."

"So your father wouldn't pay for art school?" He still couldn't understand how her father wouldn't let her major in whatever she wanted.

"Something like that. And after I changed my major to biology and he was thrilled, I already had my massage therapy license and didn't want his money. When you take money from someone, there are always strings—the kind that choke you like a noose." She sounded so matter-of-fact that it made him angry at the man who'd given her this jaded view of the world.

"Not everything comes with strings." He didn't want to argue with her, but it needed saying.

"With my father, they do." One corner of her mouth turned up in a rueful smile. "When I declared my specialty to be pediatric oncology instead of orthopedics, he didn't talk to me for six months."

The fact that some part of her thought that was her fault made his hands fist. He wanted to punch her asshole of a father more than he wanted to take his next breath. Instead, he asked, "What made you choose pediatric oncology?"

"Residency. I did a rotation at Children's Medical Center in Dallas. There was a real need for pediatric oncologists, and I love the challenge of fighting against nature." She smiled to herself. "I've never thought about it until now, but I do. Saving a life is a powerful thing."

Her smile faded. "And losing one is a defeat that you never get used to or get over." She took a deep breath and let it out slowly. "Can we talk about something else, please?"

Her teammates thought that she turned off her emotion to work with the sick, but they were wrong. She felt deeply and that's what drove her to do better. He wondered if she knew that about herself.

"How about your mother?" Dutifully, Devon changed the subject. Where Laney was concerned, he had an insatiable appetite for knowledge. While he knew her mother was dead, he couldn't remember the particulars.

"She was very important." Laney said.

He waited for more, but that was it. "Back surgeon right?"

"Yes, according to the medical community, she was the best. I don't remember much about her other than she worked all of the time. She died in a car accident when I was thirteen. Drunk driver." There was no sadness in her voice, because this was simply the way life was.

"And your father never remarried?"

"Honestly, I don't think the thought ever entered his mind. He likes his life, and someone new would disturb that. He's a creature of habit and trust me, no one would enjoy living with him." Again with the matter-of-fact. Based on her words, there should be venom and hatred, but instead indifference.

"If you could do one thing differently, what would it be?" Devon was like a sponge soaking everything up.

"I'd have recognized my need to be an artist as a form of rebellion instead of a calling. And, I would have never waited around by the phone and computer for DJ to contact me. It sounds silly now, but when I look back, it seems like a pivotal point in my life. Innocence lost or something. It taught me to be guarded and more pragmatic about relationships. I didn't have the normal high school experience in regards to boyfriends. I wasn't allowed to date, and my father saw anything extracurricular as a waste of time. I studied a lot and I had friends, but they were also overachievers with demanding parents. Meeting DJ at camp—in a place not controlled by my father—was a luxury."

"If DJ was sitting directly across from you right now, would you recognize him?" Holy giant hint Batman. Devon sat on the edge of his chair willing her to recognize him.

"I think so." She cocked her head to the left. "Although people rarely look the same fourteen years later, especially adolescents who are now adults. The impractical part of me knows I will recognize him, but the practical side says that's impossible."

"What if he remembers you?" Devon's heart was pounding.

"Then I would hope that he comes up to me, kisses me, and calls me EJ—that's what he called me." She grinned. "Not likely."

"What if he does recognize you and you don't recognize him, but he doesn't tell you because he wants you to come to it on your own?" He might as well pull out the bracelet now and show it to her.

She shook her head. "That's the dumbest thing I've ever heard. If he felt or feels the same way about me that I do about him, he wouldn't want to waste a minute not together."

Oh crap … he hadn't thought of that. This was bad. Should he tell her now and risk her anger? It didn't seem like the best idea.

He'd been avoiding the subject long enough. It was time to get to it. "I leave for Seattle in the morning. I'll be there for a few days, and then we come home after the game on Sunday."

"Oh." Laney let out a long breath. "I'm going to miss you."

She sounded surprised by that.

"I'm going to miss you too." It made him smile that she was surprised by her own admission.

"I've never been to a professional football game … or watched one on TV. Perhaps I'll watch your game with Lara." She wiped the corners of her mouth with a napkin.

"I'll blow you a kiss." He'd find a way to do it on national TV or die trying.

"Okay, it's a date." She winked. "Maybe you'll invite me to a home game sometime?"

"How about Sunday after next? We're playing the Saints at home." He would be so proud to have her in the stands rooting for him. Maybe she could sit with his mother, Summer, and Grace. They all sat in the stands instead of the skybox because they wanted to be closer to the field.

"I can't wait." She sat forward. "Do they have hot dog vendors who roam the stadium like at baseball games? Not to brag, but I am the U.T. Baseball Disch-Falk Field hot dog eating champion. I'm looking to expand my territory into professional sports."

"Sadly, no roaming hot dog vendors, but for you, I'll hire one." This woman was perfect for him. Knowing that she would be watching him gave him an ego boost that just about made him invincible.

Over Laney's right shoulder, a man in a black jumpsuit waved as he walked toward them. That must be the man Devon sweet-talked into giving them a Formula One driving lesson.

The dark-haired lanky man held out his hand for Devon to shake. "I'm Ricky Sussmann, and I'll be your instructor. If you're finished with dinner, let's walk over to the garage and take a look at the cars. We need to go over the cars and some safety issues before we get behind the wheel."

Devon rose, walked around the table to Laney, and pulled out her chair. "Y'all go ahead. I need to settle a few things here, and I'll be right behind you."

Not only did he need to pay the musicians and the waiter, he needed a moment to wrap his head around things.

Laney and Ricky made their way toward a large outbuilding with several sets of garage doors. Devon pulled two envelopes out of his breast pocket and handed one to the waiter, "The food and service were incredible as always."

The waiter nodded and then walked behind the screen. He was a man of few words, Devon could appreciate that.

He turned to the short male violinist whose name was Bob and handed him the other envelope. "Thank you so much for coming out on such short notice. The music was perfect."

"You're welcome. It was our pleasure. Feel free to call Three Girls and a Guy Strings anytime." He shook Devon's hand.

"Absolutely." Devon nodded. "Now, if you'll excuse me, I've got to learn a few things about racecars."

He waved and walked toward the garages.

Laney had said that the impractical side of her brain would know him. How did he bring that out in her? Should he just come clean? This was turning into somewhat of a mess. He'd done everything except come right out and tell her that he was DJ. He massaged the tense muscles at the back of his neck. He had a sneaking suspicion that his mother was once again, right.

If he told Laney now that he was DJ, she would be angry. And he wasn't confident that her feelings were strong enough that she would let him make it up to her. He sighed heavily with resignation that he had indeed screwed this up big time. He should have thought this out ... had a plan, but when she'd walked into the football stadium, and he'd lost his mind. He doubted that temporary insanity would be an excuse Laney would accept. It was slightly better than "the dog ate my homework."

The time had passed for him to reintroduce himself so now all that was left was for her to remember him.

Chapter 14

"How's my favorite patient this morning?" Laney walked into Lara's now thoroughly homey room. Sweet Louise had created a tent-like canopy made out of pink and purple silks over Lara's bed. Pink sheets, fluffy purple pillows, and two matching quilts had turned the hospital bed into a chic and comfortable princess fairyland. There were toys everywhere, a purple area rug, and a miniature white wrought iron table with two matching chairs set for a tea party.

"I'm feeling pretty good today." Lara smiled and her missing two front teeth twisted Laney's heart. Lara's color was bad, her kidneys were failing, and there was nothing Laney could do about it. This was the beginning of the end. Laney had seen it too many times to count.

The little girl's sallow skin was quite a contrast to the bright pink pajamas that swallowed her tiny body. Laney looked around. It appeared that Sweet Louise and Kisses the dog had on matching PJs. Kisses had spent the night with them as Lara had claimed that only Kisses could scare away the monsters under the bed.

"My girl's doing well this morning." Sweet Louise picked up Kisses and headed for the door. "I'm going to take this little rascal out for a walk and give you two ladies some privacy."

Lara's gaze followed Sweet Louise out, and when the door had closed behind her, Lara turned to Laney. "Do you believe in Heaven?"

Laney fitted her stethoscope in her ears and listened to Lara's breathing. "Yes."

She needed to believe that her patients went to a better place after they died. It didn't quite make sense, but it didn't not make sense either.

Her lungs were clear that was good.

"I'm going to die soon. I know." Lara placed her hand over Laney's and patted. "It's okay, I'm ready."

Laney wasn't ready. That was a mule-kick to the chest. She knew it was only a psychosomatic response to anxiety, but it felt like a mule-kick.

She swallowed down the lump of grief that threatened to choke her. It was too early to be mourning this sweet little girl, but her heart already felt the loss. "Yes, your body is failing."

She couldn't lie to this wonderful little girl no matter how much she wanted to.

"Honey and Devon still believe that I'm going to get better. Why is that?" Lara looked so grown up ... too grown up. Little girls shouldn't be having this conversation ... ever.

"Because they love you, and they have hope. Their belief that you'll get better comforts them because when you love someone you want to be with them ... see them. It's easier to believe that you'll get better than facing the fact that someday you'll be gone." Laney knew she was talking about herself. Only she didn't have the luxury of hope, it's not that she didn't have hope, but she wouldn't use it as a crutch.

She'd lost patients before, but it had never felt like this. When Lara died, part of Laney's soul would go with her—

she could actually feel her heart breaking right this second. She searched her mind for a medical reason that would explain the pain in her chest, but there wasn't one. It was love … love that was twisting her inside out.

"You know, there are tiny little babies who get sick and die. I'm lucky. I got to have a family. That's more than those tiny little babies." Lara reached up and touched Laney's cheek. "Don't be sad for me. I'm going to Heaven."

Laney nodded because she didn't trust her voice.

"Sweet Louise says that everyone's Heaven is different. There's pearly gates and that stuff, but everyone's Heaven is different. Mine's going to be made of strawberry ice cream and stuffed animals. I'm going to look down from Heaven on the people I love and that love me. That's the nice part, now I have people to look down on." She shrugged her thin shoulders. "Well, besides you. You've always been my family."

The knife in her heart twisted, and she couldn't seem to fill her lungs with air.

"In my Heaven, I'm going to have hot chocolate for breakfast every day and cheeseburgers for lunch. My dinner will be all red Skittles. I can't wait." Her brow screwed up. "They have food in Heaven, right?"

Laney nodded again. She took a deep breath, wrapped her stethoscope around her neck, and gave up the pretense of doctoring. If it gave Lara comfort that she would get to eat her weight in red Skittles, then by all means she should believe it. "You bet, kiddo. Eat some Skittles for me."

"What's a will?" Lara relaxed back against the raised bed. "I saw some people reading one on TV last night after their mother died."

Laney thought of the best way to explain it. "It's sort of a letter you leave for the people in your life telling them what to do with your things after you die." She pulled the closest chair up to Lara's bedside and sat.

"Now that I have some stuff, I guess that I need to make one." Lara scratched her head. "Can you write it out for me?"

"Of course." Laney pulled out her prescription pad from her white physician's coat pocket. Her heart ached that this little girl was so chipper about writing a will. "Go for it."

"I'd like for you to have Princess. I was thinking you could put her in your office with a sign that said, "Free hugs" so the kids would have something to hug and not be so scared. I'd like my tiara collection to go to Honey. She's going to be sad when I die and those will cheer her up. I'd like Devon to have Cuddles," she pointed to a purple stuffed hippo wearing pink ballet shoes, "besides Princess, she's my second favorite—don't tell Devon that, I want him to feel special."

It was like Lara was making out her Christmas list— so excited. The heartache was turning into a hollow sadness. Laney concentrated on taking notes instead of the fact that she was writing the last will and testament of a five-year-old.

"I'd like all of my other stuffed animals and toys to be given away to the other kids in the hospital." Lara looked around. "And I'd like for my room to stay just like this ... it could be called the Princess Room; maybe it would make some other sick girl smile." She shifted and played with a loose thread on the quilt. "Don't tell Honey, but I'm a little bit scared. Is it going to hurt when I die?"

Tears strung Laney's eyes, and she bit her top lip willing them away. She was a doctor and this was her patient, emotion never played into the doctor-patient relationship. Only, this time, Lara was more than just a body that needed fixing. She was a perfect little girl who'd been through so much and had so much to give. The barriers that Laney had erected so that she could do her job crumbled. The only defense she had against the dark side of her chosen profession was gone. She was vulnerable and the grief seeping in threatened to strangle her. Yet, she sat there taking notes because it was the only way she could help this wonderful little girl.

"I don't know if it will hurt or not. I guess it depends on how you die." She didn't want to say on which organ fails first causing cardiac arrest. Laney hung her head. For the first time in her life, she wished that she didn't know the facts. She wanted to un-learn the human body and tell Lara that she would fall asleep and go peacefully, but death was harsh and painful and the result of trauma to the body or in her case, a disease that greedily sapped the body of life. "I'll do my best to make sure that it doesn't hurt."

The best thing for Lara would be to slip into a coma, but Leukemia wasn't kind. Right now, she would give anything not to know what the future held.

"What happens right when I die?" Lara's serious eyes had seen so much in her short life.

Laney was fairly certain she didn't want to know the physiological explanation, but the spiritual one. "Honestly, I don't know. There have been people who've died and come back saying that you simply float out of your body and go into a bright light. And others say that your mind takes you through your happiest memories before you enter the white light."

"I hope I get to go through my good memories, that way I'll get to relive this last week." Her eyes were bright at the prospect. "I wish I could die and then come back and tell you what it's like."

Laney wished the little girl didn't have to die at all. It was so unfair. There were murderers and rapists who lived, but this precious child was dying.

"Me too. I wish you could come back and stay forever." Laney said it before she'd thought about it. More than anything, she wanted to hug Lara forever and keep her safe, but that was out of her control.

"Dr. Laney," she looked Laney right in the eye, "thanks for all that you've done for me. You did your best to make me better, and you gave me a family. Thank you."

This time there was no stopping the tears. She concentrated very hard on ripping the paper off her prescription pad, folding it, and putting it in her pocket.

"I'll hold onto this until its time." Her voice was shaky.

"Thanks." Lara's eyes were getting heavy.

"Why don't you take a nap, and I'll check on you this afternoon." Laney lightly patted the thin arm, tucked her quilt around the little girl, turned out the light, and left the room.

It was useless pretending that she didn't love Lara. And it was useless pretending that she'd ever been able to separate her job from her heart. She'd mourned the loss of every single child she'd failed. It had always been more than a defeat, it had been devastation. All these years, she'd been lying to herself. She'd kept every child she'd lost close to her heart. But Lara was special. Laney would love her for the rest of her life and the hole left in her heart would never go away. She couldn't turn off her emotions around Lara and she was tired of telling herself that she could.

The tears were coming faster now and the hospital was no place for them. She hurried down the hall and nearly knocked Sweet Louise over.

"I'm so sorry." Laney righted the older woman and would have continued on her way if Sweet Louise hadn't touched her arm.

"Child, what's wrong?" Sweet Louise's voice was so light that for a split second, Laney thought it was her imagination.

"Nothing." She swiped at the tears. "I need to get to the office."

It was a lie she only wanted to be out of here.

Sweet Louise clamped a hand down on Laney's upper arm and held tight. "We're going for a walk. True, I've just taken Kisses out for one, but we're going on another one. Let me just tell Lara."

"She's napping." Laney gasped out. She was losing the battle against sobbing. Tears were one thing, but sobbing was a whole different ball game.

"Good, let's go." She pulled Laney to the elevator and hit the down button.

"I can't. I have patients." Laney wanted to escape to her office where she could shut the door and cry in peace.

"They'll keep. Doctors are never on time." Sweet Louise wasn't taking no for an answer. Now she saw where Devon got it.

The elevator door dinged open and Sweet Louise dragged her in.

Her colleague, Dr. Rosenberg a hematologist, followed by a small crowd of medical students began to step into the elevator but Sweet Louise glared at him.

"We'll take the next one." Dr. Rosenberg stepped back.

The doors closed and the elevator descended.

"Really, I'm fine." Laney almost choked on the words.

Sweet Louise held Kisses out in front of her. "I don't believe she's fine, do you?"

Kisses looked bored.

"Where's Kisses?" Sweet Louise tucked Kisses under her arm.

Laney managed a smile through her tears. She loved that damn puppy so much. Hell, it looked like she loved everyone and was turning into a blubbering fool.

The elevator dinged the arrival of the first floor and the doors rolled open. Sweet Louise pulled her through a side door into the three-acre healing garden. Sunshine blasted them and they stepped under the covered walkway.

"You need to allow yourself a good cry." Sweet Louise pulled her to the nearest picnic table.

Laney looked around. They were all alone. "I can't."

"Stop looking around trying to see if anyone is watching us. It doesn't matter if they are. You need to cry. Emotion isn't a weakness, but a strength." Sweet Louise set Kisses down.

"But …" The tears came faster and the choking, halting sobs started up.

Sweet Louise put her arms around Laney. "Child, let it all out. You keep yourself so tightly buttoned up, it must be killing you."

Laney put her head on Sweet Louise's shoulder and let go. The older woman stroked Laney's back as the grief and desolation and utter helplessness Laney felt bubbled to the surface.

"That's right. Let it all out." She continued to gently pat. "You battle disease every single day, you deserve a good cry. You can't relieve your soul until you've cried out all the sadness."

"She's dying, and I can't fix her. She's dying." Laney's control was gone—broken by the need to be comforted. For once, she was going to let someone else shoulder the burden, if only for a little while.

"I know, but Lara's ready." Sweet Louise just patted and let Laney cry. "It's not fair, and I hate it. Trust me, when I meet God face-to-face we're going to have words. He's got some 'splaining to do."

Laney managed to laugh between sobs. "I'd pay money to see that conversation."

"Trust me, the angels will be weeping by the time I'm done with him." Sweet Louise pulled out a wad of tissues from her pocket. "Here."

Laney mopped her face but kept her head on Sweet Louise's shoulder.

"You know in some religions they believe that when a soul has learned all of its earthly lessons, it may choose to come back to teach others. I see that in Down's Syndrome kids whose love of life makes me smile. And I see that in

Lara. She teaches me love and humility every single moment that I spend with her." Sweet Louise's voice shook. "Maybe it isn't true, and I just tell myself that because it gives me comfort, but I don't think so. When I look into her eyes, I see a generosity of spirit and a selflessness that's missing from most of the population. She's had a huge impact on my life in the short time that she's been in it. Because of her, I've decided to redo all the rooms on her floor with different themes."

"Think Alan will let you get away with it?" Laney shouldn't have even asked. The administrator would have given Sweet Louise the shirt off his back and his car if she'd only asked.

"Child, please. The day I can't handle the Alans of the world, is the day they lower me into the ground." She stroked Laney's hair. "Don't beat yourself up about things you can't control. Torturing yourself because you couldn't heal Lara is a fruitless waste of time. Instead rejoice in the fact that because of you, she's lived a longer and happier life than she would have without you. You gave her love and a family when she was alone. Whether you're ready to admit it or not, you love each and every child that you treat. It's what makes you a good healer because you see more than a broken body, you see the lovely human being in front of you. Don't hate the part of you that cares. Rejoice in it."

"But it hurts to lose them." Laney sat back. She missed the comfort of having her head on Sweet Louise's shoulder. "And I need to separate my emotions from the patients. I can't give them the best treatment, if I don't see them as just broken bodies."

Could she? That was contrary to everything she'd ever told herself.

Sweet Louise shook her head. "I don't know. I'm new at this sick kid thing. I don't have the same view of it as you do, but from what I've seen, you can't help but fall in love with each and every kid. Maybe caring is what makes you such a good doctor. Ever think of that?"

"No." She really hadn't.

Sweet Louise regarded her with shrewd eyes. "How many patients have you lost in your career?"

"Thirty-two. Want me to name them?" Every single name was tattooed on her brain and the picture of their bright hopeful eyes were tattooed on her soul. Her failures—the ones she couldn't save.

"The fact that you know exactly how many and their names says more about you than your curriculum vitae. Life isn't about counting your losses, but reveling in your victories. Do you know how many you've saved and their names?" Sweet Louise smiled.

Laney searched her brain for a number. "No."

"I think you need to take a moment and remember the faces of those you've saved." She pointed to the trail meandering through the healing garden. "Take a fifteen minute walk and see how many you can call to mind. Any halfway decent coach will tell you that counting the wins if far more important than the losses. Just think about how many families you've saved because you cared enough to go to battle for their child. How many lives have you touched because you refused to give up? That's love right there. You can't fight that hard, if you don't care." Sweet Louise put her arm around Laney. "Along the way, someone told you that caring was wrong, whoever that was is a big, fat idiot."

That would be her father who showed her that emotions were messy and just got in the way. Every other bit of advice he'd given her had been wrong, why was this any different.

"Will you walk with me?" Laney felt a kinship with this woman that went far beyond friendship.

"Kisses and I would be happy to join you." She stood and tugged gently on Kisses' leash. "Now tell me about the first patient you can remembering saving."

Laney thought about it. "Harrison Schiller. He was twelve when he was first diagnosed. Last year he graduated from high school."

She stopped and took a moment for it to sink in. He'd graduated from high school because she fought like hell to heal him. That was a miracle. She'd helped to produce a miracle. The heaviness in her heart eased slightly. It was clear to her now that the professionalism she'd thought she'd donned when facing a patient was an illusion and served only to pacify the analytical part of her brain that wanted to control the situation. The truth was that she couldn't control it, had never been able to control it.

With each step and each remembered name, Laney finally understood that caring for her patients was part of what gave her the courage to face down terminal illness and to never give up.

Chapter 15

"You might want to give Laney a call, she's had a rough day." Devon's mother said on the other end of the phone.

"What happened?" He sat up. In his empty hotel room in rainy Seattle, he felt cut off from the ones he loved. "Is she okay?"

"She's fine. I think she finally accepted that Lara's dying and that she can't hide from her grief. Do you know she can name all of the patients she's lost? Every single one. But this afternoon, I asked her about the ones that she saved, and she had a hard time remembering a handful of them." His mother sighed. "It breaks my heart. She feels things deeply but crams it down because it hurts."

He felt so powerless to help her. He stood and paced the length of the tiny room. Laney was hurting. She needed him, and he was stuck in a dreary hotel room on the other side of the country. Why hadn't he quit football last season? Then again, he wouldn't have re-met Laney if he had. Should he fly home just to see her? He'd miss practice tomorrow and get in all kinds of trouble. That didn't bother him as much as his teammates counting on him. "But she's okay now, right?"

"She's fine. Summer and Grace and all the kids are coming over to the hospital, and we're having a block party of sorts in Lara's wing. We were going to do it outside, but it's raining cats and dogs over here." He heard his mother's eye roll. "It never rains in Austin except when I want to throw a party."

"You throw lots of parties." Devon would give anything to be there.

"That's beside the point."

"So is the hospital okay with you throwing a block party on Lara's floor?" He doubted that his mother had asked. She did what she wanted and sweet-talked those who stood in her way. He totally loved that about her.

"Please, if I wanted a surgery suite and a scalpel, Alan the administrator would gladly hand over both." She yawned. She hadn't been getting enough sleep at the hospital.

"Why don't you go home for some sleep tonight? It would do you good." Devon shook his head. She wouldn't do it and he shouldn't have wasted his breath, but he worried.

"I'm good. Lara's sleeping now so she can be at her best for her block party hostess duties." The concern in her voice made his heart ache. He gave up the pacing and sat on the bed.

"How is she?" But he already knew she wasn't good.

"Today wasn't a good day." She took a deep breath and let it out slowly. "She's slipping away. It's like watching a blooming rose wither on the vine. I know the end is coming, but I didn't expect it this soon. I want to hold on tight to her and beat back Mother Nature, but there's nothing I can do."

"Are you kidding? You're doing more than anyone. We both knew the outcome wasn't good, but we want Lara's last days to be the brightest of her short life. That's a gift that you've given her … the most important gift. You didn't take the easy way out and dismiss her—you dove in headfirst. Not many people would have done that."

"And not many sons would have intervened on a little girl's behalf and given her a family." His mother's voice caught.

"Listen to us. We're our own fan club. Who needs The Lone Stars' Cheerleaders?" His sweet Lara wasn't going to make it much longer. The hole in his heart threatened to swallow him.

"You sure don't. You stay away from that little brunette with the huge fake ta-tas. She wants to shake her pom-poms for you." The playfulness was back in his mother's voice. "You can't be messing around with her. What if she gets pregnant? I don't want any grandbabies with fake ta-tas."

"The only woman I'll be impregnating is Laney." He grimaced. "That came out wrong."

"Either marry her or I'll start dating your friends." His mother didn't make idle threats. "Don't screw it up."

"I'm working on the marrying part, but unfortunately she's cagey. I'm doing my best not to screw it up. She's the one for me. All the other women in the world are faces in a crowd." He smiled to himself.

"Thank God. I need me some smart grandbabies. Not that I don't think you're smart, but let's face it, Laney's got you beat."

Just to keep her on her toes, he said, "What if we decide not to have children."

"I-am-hanging-up-now. I can't be wasting my time talking to crazy people. I love you. Talk to you tomorrow." She hung up.

Devon scrolled for Laney's number and pressed the telephone icon.

It rang once.

"Laney's house of pain. Our whips give a lickin' and keep on tickin'."

He pulled the phone away from his ear and checked the number. It was Laney's phone number, but it wasn't Laney's voice.

"Crap. Give me that." It was Laney. "Hello."

"Sounds like you're having way more fun than I am." Devon settled himself against the headboard.

"Nina dropped by my office to make my life a living hell, and now she won't leave." The smile in Laney's voice made him grin.

"Some people always outstay their welcome."

"Hey, I brought ice cream." He heard Nina call from the background.

There was some shuffling.

"Are you Amish?" Nina asked.

"Give me the phone back." Laney yelled.

"No, I need to know if he's Amish because this no sex thing between the two of you is starting to affect me. I can't live vicariously through you if you're not having sex." She huffed out a sigh. "You and Laney need to do the deed, and it better be epic because we both know that Laney is a terrible liar so embellishing the story isn't an option. You better be at the top of your game. I won't tolerate any slouching."

Devon laughed. He couldn't help it. He could all but see Laney's face turning tomato red.

"Oh my God. I don't even know where to start apologizing for her." Laney was back.

"Adios people, I've got a plane to drive. I have the Maui route for the next week so I won't see you at practice." He heard kissing in the background. "Take care."

A door slammed in the background.

"Again, I don't know what to say about Nina." Laney's voice was higher than normal.

"Have you met my mother? She makes Nina look harmless." He stuffed some pillows between his back and the headboard, and then crossed his legs at the ankle.

"Yeah, but your mother isn't trying to force us to have sex." Laney sounded honestly embarrassed.

"Oh yeah, I just got off the phone with her, and she's talking about the smart babies she wants us to make. Talk about pressure." What if they didn't have genius IQs?

"She's just worried about you." Laney laughed. "I hope she gets some smart grandbabies or you'll never hear the end of it."

He could read between the lines. She hadn't said 'we'd' never hear the end of it. That hurt. He understood that she was guarded, but that hurt.

"I've decided to take you up on your offer to babysit The Bluebird." Laughter lingered in her voice.

Huh?

"Is that code for something? If we're going to start talking in code you need to give me a heads up." He rubbed the spot right above his heart. She didn't see them as a long-term couple. Would he be able to change that?

"The Bluebird. That's what I decided to call the Mustang. Bluebird because she flies. Anyway, if you don't mind, I'm going to trade her out for Viola my Volvo this afternoon." She sounded eager—younger.

It was a step in the right direction. Every time she took two steps back, she took a baby step forward. It was progress … slow … but progress all the same.

"That sounds fun. I wish I was there." He really did. Away games had never hit him this hard before. He'd made fun of his buddy Clint for moping during away games, and here he was doing it too. It would be seventy-two long, grueling hours before he'd see Laney again. It loomed like a wasteland of devastation. And the worst part was, that this was just the beginning of the season. There were several more away games on the roster.

He kicked off his loafers and wiggled his toes.

"Can I ask you something?" Laney walked somewhere and then a door closed.

"Where are you?"

"In my office." It sounded like she sat down. "You didn't answer my question."

"Sorry, yes, ask me anything?" He wanted to touch her … to see her just to remind himself that she was back in his life.

She sounded different. Thoughtful or playful maybe?

"Do you love me?"

Devon sat up and actually stopped breathing for a moment. Had he heard her correctly? Seconds ticked by.

"Um …" He wasn't sure what answer she was looking for. He swallowed a mouthful of saliva. His heart hammered in his chest. He may be a lot of things but he wasn't a coward. "Yes."

"I thought so. I don't love you yet, but I'm working on it. I had an emotional meltdown or breakthrough depending on how you look at it, and I realized that I'm falling in love with you. It scares me … a lot." She made it sound like a clinical observation. It might not be romantic, but it was romantic for Laney.

"Why?" Loving didn't scare him, it probably should, but it had always been with him just like she'd always been with him. His life had always had a purpose because in some way she'd always been in it.

"What if I'm not the person you think I am? What if I can't give you what you need?"

"You're more than I ever expected or hoped to find. Stop second-guessing yourself. You're perfect just the way you are. From your peanut butter colored hair to the toes on your not-so-attractive feet, there is nothing I would change." Devon's heart was approaching stroke status. She was falling in love with him. His sweet, wonderful, smart, and funny Laney was falling in love with him again. This was more than he'd ever hoped to have.

His world was just about perfect.

"What if this doesn't work out?"

And then she had to go and dump cold water on his perfectly good mood.

"What if it does?" He smiled to himself. That would give her something to think about.

"Oh crap, I have to go. I'm late for the block party." Laney said. "I almost love you."

"I love you. Okay if I call you after the block party?" What the hell else did he have to do but count the minutes until he could talk to her again?

"Sure. Just so you know, I'm counting on some phone sex. I'm going to research it, so be ready." She hung up.

He laughed until his eyes watered.

He could see their future so clearly. There would be a house full of loud, rowdy children—his house that's where he saw them making a home. Toys and books would litter the floor—not messy just lived in—and they'd have big dinners full of family and friends. On the days when she was busy at the hospital, he'd pile the kids in the car and take them all to have lunch with her. They'd have a sweet little girl with peanut butter colored hair and huge blue eyes named Lara. Not to replace the original but to honor the beautiful child. When his Lara smiled with her two front teeth missing, he knew she'd melt his heart.

Chapter 16

Laney couldn't help but be impressed with the block party. Sweet Louise had outdone herself. There was a luau theme complete with tiki torches—unlit of course—and limbo, grass skirts, flower leis, and a roasted pig. There was even a green screen where patients could have their picture made pretending to surf. It appeared that no one in the Harding family did anything halfway.

This evening she'd limbo-ed, learned the hula from real Polynesian dancers that she was pretty sure Sweet Louise had flown in from Hawaii, and eaten poi which tasted and looked like wall paper paste, but she'd had a wonderful time. Now as she sat at the nurse's station drinking a glass of what else—Hawaiian Punch—she watched as a line of laughing kids led by Sweet Louise attempted a conga line of wheel chairs.

"She's pretty amazing." Summer Grayson said as she patted the back of her two-year-old daughter asleep in her stroller.

Laney was usually uncomfortable around new people, but Summer was the kind of person who made others feel good. She was warm and charming and genuine. Laney couldn't help but like her.

"Tell me about it. I want to be her when I grow up." Grace Robbins sat beside Laney. "Are you sure you don't want me to take him?"

She was referring to her baby son Luke who was asleep in Laney's arms.

"No, you get to hold him all of the time." Laney smiled down at the sweet little bundle of joy making small sucking sounds in his sleep. "I don't get to hold babies very often."

"So you and Devon." Summer raised her eyebrows. "I'm glad. He talks about you all of the time. He's very proud of you."

Devon talked about her? Adrenaline made her heart beat faster—no, she was choosing to ignore the adrenaline and think of it as love.

"You're the first one he's fallen for since high school." Grace nodded. "He thinks we don't know about his torrid high school love affair, but Sweet Louise told us the story. It's so sweet—"

"And tragic at the same time." Summer touched Grace's arm. "He loved her so much."

"Oh my God, did she die?" Laney sat forward careful not to jostle Luke.

"No, no." Grace shook her head. "They met the summer after his senior year. According to Sweet Louise it was love at first sight. To hear her tell the story, it's another love-on-the-wrong-side-of-the-tracks type thing. She was from a wealthy family, and he was from a poor one."

Devon's family had been poor? He rarely talked about himself, in fact, he never talked about himself. All they talked about was her. Why hadn't she seen that before?

"What happened?" Laney realized that she was sitting literally on the edge of her seat waiting for more.

"It was a summer thing. They had two weeks together and then lost touch." Grace put her hand over her heart. "Sweet Louise told me that years later he accepted a job with The Lone Stars because Austin is her hometown. He hoped they'd run into each other. Isn't that the sweetest thing?"

"And have they?" Laney's voice was harsher than she'd wanted. Was she keeping Devon from the love of his life? Did she believe in that sort of thing? Her heart screamed, "yes" while her mind had other opinions. Well, at least she'd believed in life-long loves thirteen years ago.

"Not that I know of. I guess he gave up when he met you." Summer smiled at her. "He's so happy."

"I don't understand. If he moved here because this is her hometown, where did they meet? Didn't they go to the same school?" This story didn't make sense. The more she thought about it, the more there seemed to be something missing.

"No, they met in the summer." Grace chewed on her bottom lip. "It was camp … summer camp. He was there by court order. "

The hair on the back of Laney's neck stood up. The fact that she didn't immediately pull up the medical explanation spoke volumes. This story was familiar. It sounded a lot like her story.

"They met at camp." Laney's palms were damp and lead weights played bumper cars in her stomach. "Do you know the name of the camp?"

Could Devon be DJ? But his last name was Harding— that didn't start with a J. Then again, her last name was Nixon and that didn't start with a J. The sinking feeling got worse.

"I don't know." Grace shrugged and then yelled, "Hey, Sweet Louise, what's the name of the camp where Devon went his senior year."

Sweet Louise paled and stopped the conga line. Wheel chairs holding smiling kids crashed into each other like a trail of falling dominoes. Sweet Louise's eyes found Laney's. The apology she saw in them cut her to the core.

"Camp Huawni." Sweet Louise mouthed more than said.

No. Laney shook her head. No. It couldn't be. But her heart knew it was true. Devon was DJ, and he hadn't told her. Maybe he hadn't known, either? But it seemed that Sweet Louise knew.

Laney searched her memory for clues as to whether Devon had recognized her. He'd said something about her peanut butter colored hair. Hadn't that been what he'd called it all those years ago? And the Mustang … she'd told him that she wanted one back then.

She slumped back against the chair.

He'd recognized her. That was certain.

Why hadn't he told her the truth?

It didn't make sense.

Mental eye roll. She'd poured out her heart to Devon about DJ, and he'd said nothing. What possible reason could he have for not telling her?

Luke stirred in her arms and looked up at her with wise baby-blue eyes. If only he were older and could interpret the male mind for her.

"Let me take him. He's probably hungry." Grace scooped him up before Laney could protest.

Sweet Louise leaned on the nurse's station right in front of Laney. "Child, before you go off on him, try to remember that he's a guy. That predisposes him to stupidity. Don't get me wrong, I love my son, but sometimes his male genetic disorder makes it hard." She pointed in Laney's direction. "Ladies, meet EJ—Devon's mystery teenaged fling."

"What?" Summer looked from Laney to Sweet Louise and back again.

"Laney is the girl Devon met that summer at camp. He had faith that they'd meet again, and here she is." Sweet Louise watched her like a hawk.

"Wait … you're the girl?" Grace stared at Laney. "Why didn't you say something?"

"I didn't know." Thoughts tumbled through Laney's mind. Devon was DJ. The slightly pudgy guy she'd fallen for was the super fit football player she was now seeing. She just couldn't wrap her head around it.

Did it change things?

Absolutely.

"That's so sweet." Summer was all smiles. "You were meant to be together, and you found each other again."

It didn't feel sweet. Laney wasn't sure what to do. Should she yell at Devon for not telling her or be embarrassed because she hadn't recognized him? And back then, why hadn't he called after camp?

Oh crap and just this afternoon she'd told him that she was falling in love with him. This was a mess, a big f-ing mess.

She needed to get out of here, go for a jog, and clear her head. She glanced at the window across the hall. It was pitch black and must be past nine. It looked like the treadmill would have to do, which sucked because head clearing worked so much better outside.

She stood. "I'm about luau-ed out. I think I'll head home."

She glanced at Lara who was holding a sleeping Kisses. She'd leave them to be together for the night.

"Summer and Grace can y'all watch Lara, I'm going to walk Laney out." Sweet Louise stretched and yawned. She waited for Laney to step out from behind the nurse's station.

It looked like there was no escaping Sweet Louise. As they walked down the hall toward the elevator, the older lady kept silent. She pushed the down button and just stood there.

Laney didn't know what to say. Clearly his mother had known all along.

The elevator dinged and the door opened. Laney followed behind Sweet Louise onto the elevator. Both women turned around to face the closing door.

"He pined after you something fierce." Sweet Louise's voice was little more than a whisper.

"Then why didn't he call or email me? I gave him all of my information." Laney's thoughts were a tangled mess.

Sweet Louise touched her arm. "Child, if he'd known how to get in touch with you, he'd have moved in with you. He's looked for you in the face of every woman he met."

"I wrote all my information on the back of the book he always had with him." She remembered doing it so clearly. He'd left it on the lunch table while he went to get something from his cabin. She'd borrowed a Sharpie from the activities table and written everything on the back cover.

"Book? What book? Devon doesn't read for pleasure, never has. He's more of a movie person." Sweet Louise looked like she was plowing through memories trying to find the right one. "I can tell you for sure that he didn't come home with a book from camp. I know because I unpacked his trunk. There was only a lot of dirty laundry."

"But I wrote it in the back of the book he always had with him." Laney knew that for sure. Right now she may not be sure of anything else, but by God she knew that.

"Did you tell him about the book?"

"No." Laney shook her head. "I wanted it to be a surprise."

Looking back on it, she was willing to admit that might have been a mistake. Anything could have happened to the book. It was possible that he hadn't known she'd written in it and had left it at camp in the book exchange. Now it seemed impossible that one simple mistake could have caused so much heartache.

"Talk to him about it. Let him explain himself. For the record, I told him it was a bad idea not to tell you." Sweet

Louise shrugged. "But he's a guy so that bit of advice went in one ear and out the other."

"How long have you known?" Laney couldn't help the feeling of betrayal. The logical part of her mind understood that this wasn't all Devon's fault, but her heart didn't care.

"Since your birthday. He was upset about the car and thought you would never speak to him again. By the way he's not about to let you walk out of his life again. Once my son latches onto something he's there forever. Even if you break up with him, he won't move on. He believes in love at first sight and soul mates. He will never give up on you. I know that puts a lot on your shoulders, but I thought you should know. He loves you, and that makes you the most important person in his life. Whatever he has to do to win you, he's going to do it because he knows in his heart that there is no one else for him but you." Sweet Louise didn't say this grudgingly, but thoughtfully. Just a mother giving insight to her son's girlfriend.

Devon loved her unconditionally. She knew it down to her soul. Just like DJ. There was comfort and fear and more than a little piece of mind in that. He would always be there for her no matter what.

Laney needed some time to think this through. Yes, she was falling in love with Devon, but this felt like a setback instead of a confirmation of her feelings.

The door bonged once for floor number one and the doors opened.

"He never got over you. He never had a serious relationship after you and dated only to pass the time. My boy has a romantic streak three miles wide, and he truly believed that one day he'd see you again. That has to count for something. Don't let your embarrassment and confusion over this one detail ruin something special. Devon should have handled this differently, but it's done now, and it can't be changed." Sweet Louise pulled Laney into a tight hug as the doors closed.

She released Laney and hit the door open button. "Go take a little time for yourself, and then talk it out with Devon. You two belong together, and you get a second chance. That's more than most people ever get."

Laney stepped out into the hallway and the door closed again. She needed time to think, but she also needed to see Devon. She glanced at her watch. It was nine fifteen. As she sprinted across the street to her office, she pulled out her cell phone and dialed Nina.

She picked up on the first ring. "I have minutes. What's up?"

"Is Dax in town?" Laney was hoping that Nina's little brother, Dax, who ran a plane charter business was up for a little night flying.

"Yes, ma'am. He landed a couple of hours ago, and I'm willing to bet that he's still at the Lakeway airport filling out paperwork. If there's one industry that's at least twenty years behind the times, it's airline travel."

"That inspires confidence." Laney said.

"Whatcha need from Dax? You have another patient who needs transport?" Nina was all business.

"Nope, just me. I need to get to Seattle as fast as possible. It can't wait until tomorrow." Laney smiled to herself. She was being impulsive and reckless and it felt damn good.

"Do I want to know why?" Nina asked.

"I have a bone to pick with a certain football player. I have the next two days off so why not do it in person?" Laney ran up the stairs two at a time to her office.

"Okey Dokey, one passenger for SEA. I'll give him a call and set it up. How soon do you want to leave?" Nina flicked some switches.

"ASAP. I need to run home, but I'd like to leave in an hour or so." Laney grabbed her purse and clomped back down the stairs. "Is that okay?"

"You bet. I'll have him call you back with the details. Gotta go." Nina hung up.

Sweet Louise was right. They did get a second chance and that was something extraordinary.

Chapter 17

Several hours later, Devon was fit to be tied. He couldn't reach Laney. He paced the tiny cage of a hotel room and tunneled his fingers through his hair. His mother had called and said that Laney knew the truth. He stopped at the bed, picked up his phone, which he'd thrown there not two minutes ago after the last time he'd dialed Laney's number. He hit redial.

"This is doctor Laney Nixon, if you have a life-threatening medical emergency, please hang up and dial nine-one-one. Otherwise, please leave me a message or press two to be connected to the medical exchange for the on-call doctor. Thank you." It was the same message he'd listened to a hundred times in the last two hours.

The doctor on call was no help. In fact, Dr. Ambrose or Anderson or whatever his name, had threatened him with all kinds of violence and legal action if he didn't stop waking him up in the middle of the night for something that wasn't a medical emergency.

Something was wrong. Laney wasn't the type to avoid conflict, if anything she'd face it head on. She wouldn't hide and not take his calls so that meant that she was in danger.

Where was she? He glanced at the clock on the nightstand. It was eleven-thirty here so it was one-thirty in Austin. He'd checked the Internet for car crashes in and around Austin and no cars matching either the Mustang or her Volvo had been in an accident.

Still, he couldn't shake the sinking feeling that something terrible had happened to her.

What if some strung-out junkie had car-jacked her and forced her to write him a prescription for painkillers? It wouldn't necessarily be on the news yet if she was tied up in her trunk. Did he really have to wait twenty-four hours to file a missing persons report? That's what the cops always said on TV. If only he knew some tech guru who could tap into traffic and security cameras all over Austin. Was that even possible?

Probably not.

But he could check with all of the twenty-four hour pharmacies. He sat at the tiny desk by the window and opened the lid of his laptop and Googled twenty-four hour pharmacies Austin.

Light knocking came from the direction of his door.

"Go away, I'm sleeping." Some of his teammates had been trying to get him to go clubbing, but that hadn't been his thing since his rookie days. He was too old to stay up all night and then go directly to practice. Partying was a young man's game.

"It's me." The voice was female.

Laney.

He actually heard his heart start beating again.

She was here?

He was at the door in less than a second. He threw it open and pulled her into a bear hug. Relief washed over him in a tidal wave of love. She was okay. He thought it was a real possibility that he might die of happiness. Or kill her for making him worry.

"Ouch, you're hurting me." Laney didn't struggle against him but she didn't hug him back either.

"Sorry. I was sure you'd been in a car wreck or kidnapped by a drug addict. But you're here." Relief was close to making his eyes water. He loosened his grip and stepped back a half step. She was here, in front of him, standing right here.

"You have a very active imagination." She had a bland look on her face so he couldn't tell whether she was angry or not. She was here though, and that had to mean something.

"Not usually. But I couldn't get in touch with you so my mind went down a negative rabbit hole." He closed the door and stepped out of her way. "Welcome to my gilded cage. As jail cells come, it isn't bad. Room service twenty-four hours a day and a view of downtown. Make yourself at home." His nerves were starting to kick in. The BLT he'd had for dinner rumbled around in his stomach. He gestured to the bed and then thought about it. That was too suggestive especially since she was probably here to strangle him. He glanced at her delicate hands. They knew their way around a scalpel, but what about a garrote?

"Why are you staring at my hands?"

"Judging whether they're capable of strangling me. My money's on yes." He chewed on the inside of his cheek and wished that it were tomorrow so they could be past the fight and were well into the making up portion.

"Don't be ridiculous. Most women don't have the upper body strength for that. Only five percent of homicides committed by woman are strangulation. On the whole, we like guns and knives." One corner of her mouth curled up. "Then again, I'm pretty fit."

"That's what I'm afraid of." He pointed to an overstuffed chair in the corner opposite the desk. "Have a seat."

"And you have a really big neck." She studied him. "I'm not sure I could get my hands around it."

"Thank God for small favors." He was sweating a lot. With his sleeve, he wiped his forehead. Nerves were a terrible thing. If she didn't start yelling at him soon and get it over with, he'd work himself up into a frenzy.

Her stomach rumbled so loudly that he heard it from across the tiny room. "Let me guess, you haven't eaten today."

"That's not true, I had some pig at the Luau block party but that was hours ago." She put a hand on her stomach. "I've traveled many miles since then."

If he didn't take care of her who would? For someone who was so physically active, she should remember to eat. He sure as hell had never forgotten to eat.

He picked up the hotel phone and hit the room service button. Stalling might not be the manliest thing he'd ever done, but it was as good of a coping mechanism as any. He grabbed the menu from off the desk and flipped through it. Taking care of her brought out the caveman in him—he wanted to beat on his chest and tell the world that she was his. But, after tonight, he wasn't sure she would be his.

"Room service." It was a male voice on the line. "How may I help you?"

"I'd like one of everything on page five and add a New York strip to that cooked ..." he glanced at Laney.

"Medium rare." She nodded.

God he loved that woman. She loved meat and liked her steak cooked just the way the Good Lord had intended.

"Medium rare and absolutely no knives on the tray." Devon winked at Laney.

"Playing it safe?" She smiled sweetly.

Devon used his hand to cover the phone. "I have a highly developed sense of self-preservation."

"Okay. I'll get that going. Have a good evening." The man hung up.

The best thing about hotel employees is that they rarely asked questions.

Slowly, Devon lowered the phone. Now what? She hadn't started yelling. Was he supposed to start the groveling process before or after she yelled at him? With his mother, he let her rant her fill and then apologized, but he wasn't sure with Laney. No other girlfriend had prepared him for this because when he'd made one mad, he didn't care enough to stick around. It wasn't like any of those women had been the one—no, *the one* was sitting across the room, her cool Caribbean blue eyes watching his every move.

He dried his palms on his thighs and sat on the edge of the bed.

She opened the purse in her lap, dug around in it, and pulled something out.

"I think this belongs to you." She opened her hand and sitting directly in the center of her palm was the brown leather bracelet he'd made for her. The leather was faded and worn like she'd handled it thousands of times. So she hadn't stuck it in a drawer and forgotten about it, she'd taken it out, touched it, held it, and remembered him.

That was the courage boost he needed.

"I should have told you. I wanted to, but I kept thinking that you'd remember me. I recognized you right off, so when you didn't recognize me, I thought spending time together would do it. But we kept seeing each other and you still didn't put it together." He took a deep breath and let it out on a sigh. The fact that she hadn't recognized him still hurt.

"You should have told me." She set her purse on the small table on her right. "I confided in you about … you. Do you know how stupid that makes me feel?"

He tunneled his fingers through his hair again. "I didn't think of that. I should have thought of that."

In hindsight there were so many things he should have worked out before jumping into the deep end with her, but damn it, she'd just walked back into his life, and he hadn't been ready. Well he was ready to see her, but he hadn't been prepared for her not recognizing him.

"When I planned the moment we'd meet again in my mind, it never occurred to me that you wouldn't know me. Yes, I should have handled it differently, but part of me wanted for you to remember on your own." He crossed and uncrossed his legs in an effort to make himself more comfortable, but the truth was he wouldn't be comfortable until she forgave him. "I know it was prideful, but I wanted you to remember me because I guess it meant that you'd still have feelings for me."

All along he'd thought she was at a disadvantage because she didn't know they had a past, but now he saw that he was the one with the handicap because he was ready to pick up where things had left off, but she was at square one, starting over.

She mulled that over and finally nodded. "Just because I didn't know you right off, doesn't mean that some part of me didn't recognize you. From the moment I saw you at the stadium, I felt like I'd known you forever." She shook her head. "For me, that's saying a lot. I don't usually feel close to people that quickly ... or ever."

"Could you come sit over here?" He patted a spot on the bed next to him. He needed to touch her ... to have her close.

"Why?" She looked skeptical. "Are we finally going to have sex?"

"Not until we finish talking, but it's good to know that you're open to having angry sex." He smiled to himself. "I want you to come over here, because we both can't fit on that chair, and I need to touch you. Even if it's just to hold your hand."

She stood and walked the four steps to the bed and sat. "Now what."

He put his arm around her and with the other hand drew up the bracelet she'd made for him so long ago from his front trouser pocket. "I carry it with me always—well not on the field because there aren't any pockets in my uniform."

He handed her the well-worn green leather bracelet.

"What happened to it?" Gingerly she took the battered green-turned almost gray with time circlet of leather.

"I might have left it in my pants pocket once or twice and it went through the wash." The green had faded into more than one pair of jeans.

"The one you gave me stays in my wallet. It's always the first thing I move over when I buy a new wallet." She was sentimental, she just didn't know it.

His heart rate calmed a bit. Knowing that she always had his bracelet with her like he did with hers meant something.

"I love you." Those three words weren't anywhere close to enough to explain the vastness of his feelings for her.

"Okay, I sort of get you not telling me … sort of. I should have recognized you. I feel bad about that." She ran her thumb over the worn greenish leather. "I came all this way to throw yours in your face, but now I want to keep it." She didn't sound sad so much as thoughtful—like this was a revelation that just occurred to her. "So what do we do now?"

"We pick up where we left off all those years ago, and we get to know each other for the people we are today." It hadn't escaped his notice that she hadn't said that she loved him back. Doubt pricked his heart. If the reciprocal words weren't automatic, it probably wasn't forthcoming. She'd said that she was falling in love with him, but not in love yet. It would do for now, but it wasn't enough—not nearly enough.

She stood and climbed in his lap. "Do you know how many times I've wanted to do this since I met you fourteen years ago?" She wrapped her arms around him. "We have so much time to make up for." She kissed him hard and hungrily on the mouth. She leaned back just a bit. "I'm staying the weekend. Grace called her husband and smoothed it over. We can spend the weekend together, when you're not working."

He couldn't believe his luck. Not ten minutes ago he was worried that she was hurt, and here she was sitting on his lap.

Abruptly she straightened and looked at him. "That's okay, right? You're not mad or have other plans."

"Are you kidding? I can't believe how lucky I am." He pulled her closer. She fit against him nicely—she fit into his life nicely.

"You know, The Emerald City Comic Con is this weekend." She tried to sound nonchalant.

"Is it?" He grinned at her.

"Can we go, can we go, can we go?" She bounced up and down on his lap.

"I have practice tomorrow morning and one in the evening, but in-between … you bet." He loved everything about her. There was nothing he would change. She made his life bright and colorful.

"Good, because I already bought us tickets." She was so excited that she sounded like she was all of ten years old.

So she'd bought tickets for them even while being mad at him. She hadn't come to break up with him? She might only be falling in love with him, but she did see a future for them—even if only for this weekend.

Chapter 18

It seemed odd that Laney should be this nervous over something as basic as sex, but here she was hiding in the bathroom trying to decide if she had the courage to open the door and show Devon the sexy black lace teddy that hours ago she'd thought was a good idea. She studied herself in the mirror.

Her nipples poked out through the somewhat itchy lace, and the front was basically a halter-top split from navel to breast with a tiny little piece of lace holding it together. The matching black lace panties were little more than a string and a swatch of fabric.

It was hard to feel sexy when the damn thing itched and the fluorescent lighting turned her skin to a sickly shade of green. Still, some men liked lingerie, and hopefully she wouldn't have to wear it long.

Picking up her hairbrush, she swiped it through her hair a couple of times and then brushed her teeth. She was stalling, but she couldn't help it. For the last fourteen years, her life had been leading up to this moment. She'd built it up so much in her mind that the pressure was getting to her.

What had started fourteen years ago was about to finally happen. She wasn't a virgin—she knew what was about to happen, it's just it felt different knowing she was about to do it with Devon. He meant something—this meant something. It wasn't just two bodies coming together to fill physical needs. This was love.

As scary as it was for her, Devon was her future. The practical side of her brain said that they shouldn't have made it this far. Two teenagers meet one summer and are both so affected by it they still remember each other fourteen years later. Logically, they both should have moved on, but they loved each other—that defied logic.

Nerves tied her stomach up in knots. She pushed the medical explanation out of the way and simply enjoyed the quivers caused by a mix of anticipation and self-consciousness.

She should be exhausted. She checked her watch. In Austin it was three o'clock in the morning, but she was running on adrenaline.

Should she put on some red lipstick? That seemed like a waste, and it would probably get all over the sheets. She needed to put on her big-girl pants and get out there.

After one more pass with her hairbrush, she pulled open the bathroom door.

Devon lay on his back, his left arm flung high above him. She stepped into the darkened room. He didn't move. As she got closer to the bed, she heard light snoring.

He was passed out.

After years and years of anticipation, this is what she got. She snorted in a very unladylike way.

She glanced down at her nighty. Well hell, if he wasn't going to see it, she wasn't going to wear it. She slid the panties down and then pulled off the top.

"Wow." He mumbled.

She jumped back startled. "I thought you were asleep."

Her clothes were on the floor and it was too late to pull them back on so she just stood there.

"Just resting my eyes." He scooted over and threw back the comforter, his eyes never leaving her body. What she saw there was nothing short of awe. His gaze worshipped her body. "Come here."

She'd never felt more loved...cherished. She put one knee on the bed and he stilled her.

"Wait, I want to look at you. I've waited a long time for this." His hand started at her knee, slid up her thigh, resting there.

"Me too." She leaned down and pressed a kiss on his shoulder, right above his scar. With his covers pulled back, she had an excellent view of his body ... well most of it. "You're wearing boxers, it doesn't seem fair."

"I didn't want to be presumptuous." A slow sexy smile worked its way across his face. "I could be persuaded to remove them ... if properly incentivized."

"I love it when you talk like a stockbroker." She kissed her way to his nipple. "What's it going to cost me?"

His fingers slid to her opening. "A massage ... I get to give you a massage. I plan on memorizing every square inch of you."

"But it's late. Aren't you tired?" Not that she wanted to rush things, but he did have practice in the morning. He needed to get some sleep.

"I have all the time in the world. Lay face down." He pushed the comforter down to the end of the bed and rolled to the side. The front of his boxers gaped open and she saw that he was already properly incentivized.

"Your wish is my command." She purred. It was strange, she'd never thought of herself as a sexual person until now, but tonight, it buzzed through her. Instead of lying on the bed, she pressed her body to his and laid face down on top of him.

"This isn't what I had in mind." His voice was high and squeaky.

"It's exactly what I've had in mind for the last fourteen years." She kissed him hard on the mouth. With her palms on the bed on either side of his head, she pushed back and looked down at him. "You're nicely made." Her eyes roamed down his body. "Very nicely made."

His hand slid down her back to her butt and pulled her down more firmly on top of him. "I like the way you feel against me." He rolled her under him. "But I like the way you feel under me too."

Arousal heated her from head to toe. She yanked his boxers down to his knees, and then used her foot to work them the rest of the way down. Her gaze roamed down to his waist and then lower. "Wow. You like me a lot."

"Please tell me you brought condoms." He bit his upper lip. "I don't have any. It's not like I was anticipating sex this weekend."

"In my purse." She pointed to the small table by the overstuffed chair.

Devon was up and grabbing her purse in the blink of an eye. He upended it in the chair, sifted through the contents, and picked up the two condoms boxes she'd stopped and bought at Walgreens.

"Two boxes. You are confident." He waggled the boxes in her direction.

"You're a manly man. I wanted to be prepared." She patted a spot on the bed next to her. "I'm getting cold."

He was at her side before she'd finished her sentence. He rolled on a condom and snuggled up next to her. "How about that massage?"

"Absolutely," she gently pushed him down on the bed. "Lay back. I'm pretty sure that I can relax you."

"That's not what I meant." His eyes turn huge. "I want to do you."

"Me too." She laughed and sat back on her knees. "Close your eyes."

She straddled him at the waist, nothing sexual, she merely needed the proper position to massage his shoulders. She started at his shoulders and worked her way down his right arm—kneading and massaging the muscles until they were tender.

His eyes were closed but he breathed heavily. "I can feel how warm and wet you are."

"I don't know what you're talking about. This is a therapeutic message." She pressed herself harder against him.

"Stop that." He opened one eye and slipped a hand up her torso and cupped her right breast.

"Sorry." She knelt over him, taking all of her weight on her knees. Reaching behind her, she gently encircled him, stroking lightly. "Is that better?"

"Yes." His breathing turned rapid. "This is the best massage I've ever had."

"We aim to please." She used the tip of him to massage the cleft above her opening, and then slowly slid him inside of her. She lowered herself onto him and then rocked back on her knees coming up, and then lowered herself again.

"Definitely the best massage I've ever had." Both of his hands cupped her breasts and teased her nipples.

She rocked back and forth teasing him ... and herself. His hands left her breasts, grabbed her hips, and set her firmly on top of him. He jerked her hips up and pulled her down hard against him. Over and over, he jerked her hips up and pulled her down hard. She caught the rhythm and thrust hard against him. His hands slid up her back and fisted in her hair urging her head down.

He didn't take her mouth as she'd expected but his tongue laved one nipple while his hand cupped her other breast. His hips thrust faster against hers, and she rode him for all she was worth.

The laving turned to sucking as the pace increased.

His body stroked her higher and higher. The first twinges of orgasm tingled through her. She thrust harder and harder chasing the pleasure that was just out of her grasp. He shifted his hips and rocked hard against her. The orgasm shattered through her in a hailstorm of muscle spasm.

He rolled her onto her back and thrust deep inside her before gently rolling off of her.

Laney didn't know she could be both this tired and this relaxed. "That was definitely gorilla sex."

"I told you that you'd know it when you had it." He pulled her to him and snuggled up against her.

"Can we do it again … soon?" Sex had always been fun, but this was fireworks blasting, eat-her-weight in birthday cake good. "I like it. It was interesting."

"Interesting?" His voice was close to her ear. "You nearly killed me and it was just interesting."

"Interesting good … not interesting boring. I've never you know …" She shouldn't be blushing but she could feel her face heat. "Had an orgasm that wasn't due to clitoral stimulation. I was nice … very nice."

She couldn't help but analyze her body. That's who she was. And the human body was an amazing machine.

Gently, he rolled her on her back and spread her legs. He kissed his way up her inner thigh.

"What are you doing?" She tried to sit up, but he lightly pushed her back down.

"Giving you some reference data. You can't make an educated guess unless you have all of the facts." His tongue found its target.

Devon got her and loved her anyway. He was her other half.

Chapter 19

The next morning, as Laney ran laps on the track of the Seattle Seahawks CenturyLink stadium, she couldn't help but be enthralled by the barbaric ballet that was football. Being closer to a football game than she'd ever have imagined, she noticed that there was a lot more grunting and moaning than most people probably realized. The Lone Star's offense was playing the defense, and from what she could tell, they were trying to kill each other.

And this was only a practice.

She glanced down at her Garmin Forerunner GPS watch, which was helpfully counting the miles for her and noticed that she was almost to twenty. She'd only intended to do fifteen, but she'd been so captivated by the bone-crushing battle taking place on the field that she'd lost track of her laps. She slowed to a walk and let her muscles cool down.

From what she could see happening on the field, whoever had the football was a target, and it was open season. Football players were either the bravest or the stupidest people she'd ever seen. If a six-foot man weighing in at over three hundred pounds ran after her, she'd throw down whatever he wanted and run the other way. Devon's job seemed to be to kill anyone who got near the quarterback. He was sort of a quarterback bodyguard. He had the size for it, but truly she'd never met such a gentle soul.

She smiled to herself. Those hands could be rough when she wanted them to be. This morning he'd showed her the finer points of morning sex.

Coach Robbins blew his whistle, and the action on the field halted.

A blonde girl of about seventeen dressed in Lone Stars sweats, walked toward Laney on the track. She caught up to Laney and walked beside her.

"So you're Laney." The accusation wasn't even veiled.

"Guilty." Laney had the urge to put her hands up like she was under arrest. "And you're CoCo, Coach Robbins' daughter."

All Laney received in answer was a curt nod. Laney had no idea what she'd done to piss off the teenager, but clearly there was something.

"So what's the deal with you and Devon? Are you still mad about the car?" CoCo had the tone and bearing of an FBI interrogator.

In light of more recent events, Laney had forgotten about the Mustang. "No, we worked it out." She smiled hoping to defuse the situation. "He's off the hook."

All the tension and animosity left the teenager. "Good. He meant well, but sometimes I can't figure out what's going on in his head." CoCo shook her head and sighed like the overwrought parent of an ADHD kid. "Sometimes, he just doesn't think about the consequences."

Laney bit back a smile. CoCo was more grown-up than Laney. "How'd you know about the car?"

"He was babysitting the boys while Dad and Grace had a date night. I helped him write the apology. He was worried that you'd dump him over that." CoCo clearly didn't think that Devon had been there to watch her too.

"He's off the hook. He meant well, but it was too soon for such a grand gesture." Although now that she knew he was DJ, the gesture didn't feel so sudden.

CoCo nodded. "Thanks for that. I'm trying to get him to see the big picture, but sometimes he gets carried away. I swear, these men …" She gestured in the direction of the field. "It's like babysitting adult-sized toddlers."

"Your burden is great." Laney nodded. "Don't give up on them, they can use your guidance."

Laney decided that she liked this intense girl. She clearly loved the players in an older-sister kind of way.

"He's really into you." CoCo pointed to Devon who was watching as Coach Robbins gestured grandly toward the yellow goal post. "Don't take this the wrong way, but if you hurt him, Grace and I are prepared to kill you in some really gross way."

Was there a right way to take that? Laney bit the inside of her cheek to keep from laughing.

"Okay, I promise to do my best not to hurt him. It says a lot about him that the women in his life are so concerned about him." With all the women in his life threatening Laney, more than likely she'd end up in a shallow grave.

"He's a good guy. Trust me, you can't say that about all the guys on the team." CoCo's cynicism should belong to a forty-year-old woman with two divorces under her belt. "For example, if I could just get Big Billy Gains to see more than a girl's cup size, maybe he'd finally have a grown-up relationship." She shook her head. "Don't tell him I said it, but he's not too sharp. I don't like to talk bad about any of my guys, but the truth is the truth. What can you do?"

"Sounds like raising football players is tougher than it looks." Laney bit down even harder to keep the laughter out of her voice.

"You have no idea." CoCo was dead serious. "How far did you run?"

"By the time I finish cooling down, it will be twenty miles." Laney said. She wondered if CoCo knew how proud her stepmother, Grace was of her. "Did you know that Grace talks about you all of the time? She calls you her island of estrogen in her world full of testosterone."

There was nothing Grace seemed to love more than motherhood. Maybe one day, Laney would know what it was like to be a mother. Did Devon still want four kids like he had fourteen years ago? That might be problematic.

"Yeah, Grace is okay." But the tone of CoCo's voice made it seem that Grace was better than just okay.

"So how did you get to come to Seattle and not your brothers?" Being an only child, Laney was always interested in siblings. Houses with more than one child seemed noisy and chaotic, but in a good way. She'd always been a little bit jealous.

"Dad has started taking one of us with him on away games. He rotates between me and my brothers … well not the baby until he gets a little older."

"That sounds fun. My parents only took me to medical conferences." Now that Laney said it out loud, it sounded worse than it was.

"I'm sorry. That sounds bad." CoCo's eyes turned sympathetic.

Was Laney about to fall under CoCo's protection?

"I'm not going to lie, it was dull." All she'd done was sat in the hotel room waiting for her parents to return. They'd always promised to take her somewhere fun, but never did.

CoCo thought for a minute and then said. "We're all going to Elliot's Oyster House after this. I hope you and Devon can come."

"Thanks, I'd love to, but I need to check with Devon." Laney's stomach rumbled. "I'm hungry and fresh oysters sound wonderful."

"They have the best. And they serve them however you want. I like on the half-shell with lots of lemon." CoCo's intensity was fading and a genuine warmth was taking over.

"That's my favorite way to eat oysters too." Her stomach rumbled again. "That sounds really good."

Two hours later, Laney pushed back from her seventieth tray of fresh oysters and stared down Big Billy Gains. "Want to keep going? I can do this all day."

Big Billy was looking a little green. He'd challenged her to an eating contest and he was losing … and not gracefully.

"I would have never believed it if I hadn't seen it with my own two eyes." Coach Robbins had acquired his current amazed look right around tray number ten. "She's a tray ahead of Big Billy and doesn't show any signs of slowing down."

"That's a real woman who can eat like that." An African American football player named Keshaun smiled and his gold front teeth winked in the fluorescent light. "When you get tired of white bread over there, give me a call."

Devon put his arm around Laney. "Coach is it okay if I kill him? Sure, he's a pretty good running back, but we have like six more."

"Nah, I like him. He gives great Secret Santa gifts." Coach Robbins clapped Keshaun on the shoulder. "Besides, Grace gets mad when she has to wash blood out of my clothes."

"Uh oh." Laney pointed to Big Billy. "Someone grab him, he's about to lose his oysters."

A couple of the offensive line sprang into action and helped Big Billy up and over to the closest bathroom, she hoped. They were in the Elliot Bay private dining room to keep them away from the very vocal Seattle Seahawk fans. Devon had explained that it was okay to do things as a team in Seattle before the game as long as they did it private, but after they beat the crap out of the Seahawks, it wasn't healthy to be seen out in public.

That kind of made sense.

Devon pulled Laney in for a half hug and then kept his arm around her. "I'm going to keep her. I'm thinking of putting her picture up at my restaurant with a big sign saying that whoever can out eat her gets their meal for free."

"You'll never have to give anything away. That's a safe bet." Coach Robbins nodded. "Truly amazing."

"I know." Clint, Summer's husband, still looked stunned. "I can't wait to tell Summer. She's going to show up at your house with food. My Summer is a feeder. She likes cooking for others, and now that she has someone who can really eat, she's going to see that as a challenge."

"Summer likes to bake." Devon added helpfully.

"I look forward to the challenge." Laney snagged Big Billy's uneaten tray from the other side of the table and pulled it over. "I love food."

She picked up the closest oyster and downed it.

"Amazing." Coach Robbins couldn't move past the amount of food she could put away.

"I remember Big Billy being tougher than that." A large man two tables over who Laney thought might be on the defensive line shook his head. "We're going to have to call him Hurl from now on."

"I still don't know where she puts it." Said an African American man at the same table. "What do you weigh like one-ten soaking wet?"

"It's a gift." Devon patted her slightly pooching stomach. He was so proud.

Laney smiled to herself. It was nice to finally have a boyfriend who appreciated everything about her.

"How about dessert?" Devon picked up the dessert menu. "I'm thinking the Fried Chocolate Truffle Sundae."

"Ooooo. Now you're speaking my language. That sounds good." Laney finished off Big Billy's oysters.

"And she's going to eat more." Clint pulled out his smartphone and clicked a photo of Laney. "Sorry, just had to capture this moment."

"I bet she's fun at an all-you-can-eat buffet." Coach Robbins grinned at her.

"After the first thirty minutes, they usually offer to give it to me for free if I agree to leave. I've been banned from Buffet Palace for life. My picture's on the podium up front, and the hostess knows to not let me in. Apparently the all-you-can-eat snow crab legs do have a limit." Laney used to be embarrassed by that, but it appeared amongst the football community she was a rock star.

"That's my girl." Devon slid his hand down her back and absently rubbed her lower back. It felt fantastic.

"You're so lucky." Keshaun sulked. "My girlfriend won't eat carbs, or protein, or salad dressing, or dessert. On our last date, all she ate were green peas. She spent most of the night chasing them around the plate with her fork."

CoCo sat next to him. "That's because your girlfriend is a skanky gold digger who only wants your money. You need to date someone with more substance."

"She wants me to buy her a Mercedes Benz roadster." He studied his shoes.

"Dump her." CoCo rolled her eyes. "You better not buy her that car. If you do, I'll never speak to you again."

"Okay." He blushed, well would have blushed if his skin hadn't been a lovely shade of tobacco brown. "Where do you meet the good ones?"

"We've talked about this. Meeting women at a strip club is not a good idea." CoCo's voice was very put-upon. "The grocery store is good, or have a friend set you up. Ask Grace or Laney."

Laney sifted through her mind for a single someone for Keshaun. None of her teammates would do for him. "There is a nurse who works in recovery who would be perfect for you. Her name is Krystal."

His whole face lit up. "Really? Maybe you could give me her number, or I'll give you mine."

He reached into his pocket and pulled out a business card. He turned his huge brown puppy dog eyes on Laney. "Here's my card. It has all of my numbers. Maybe you could give it to her … and tell her that I'm a good guy?"

"Sure." Never in a million years would Laney have thought she'd be fixing up football players with her coworkers. Devon brought so much to her life and had included her one hundred percent in his. Things were working out nicely.

Chapter 20

Two weeks later, Lara slipped into a coma. The end was near. As Laney sat holding one of Lara's sweet little hands with Sweet Louise holding the other, Laney racked her brain for a treatment that she hadn't tried. Maybe there was something new—a new drug, anything, but she knew there wasn't. She'd tried everything and had failed. She felt this failure all the way down to her soul.

For the first time in a long time, Laney embraced the tears and let them flow. Devon held her and patted her back—words weren't necessary. It was nice to be held and comforted—to let someone else shoulder the pain for just a bit. Not too long ago, she'd thought that showing emotion was a sign of weakness, now she just accepted it as part of who she was. Crying did offer some relief, if only a temporary one.

The aching emptiness and finality of death left a gaping hole in Laney's heart. One day soon, she would have to say goodbye to Lara forever. No longer would she be able to see this beautiful little girl, or hear her voice, or see her smile. Lara wouldn't ever go trick-or-treating again, or fail a math test or fall in love, or kiss her puppy, or get married, or have a family of her own. It was a waste of a perfectly lovely soul. Right now, she wanted to punch God right in the face for giving her this precious little girl and then taking her away. It wasn't fair or right—there was no justice in it. No amount of planning had prepared her for losing Lara. Death was nothing new to Laney, but right now she wanted to knee him right in the balls.

"Do you believe in heaven?" Laney glanced up at nothing in particular. "She asked me that a couple of weeks ago. I told her that I didn't know, but that I hoped there was a heaven. I want there to be one…for her."

"I know that when the time comes, her soul will find peace and love in heaven. I know it." Sweet Louise wiped her own tears and looked down at Lara with a heart breaking love that was so intense and beautiful that it would span years and lifetimes.

It was like looking in a mirror. That's how Laney felt about Lara. Death couldn't stop what she felt for Lara and no amount of time would change it. Laney's soul would love Lara forever.

The concept of soul had always fascinated Laney. As an analytical person, she'd never quite wrapped her head around the idea, but she knew that every person had one. "A twentieth century doctor named Duncan McDougall hypothesized that the soul weighed twenty-one ounces. He weighed people before and after death and found that one actually weighed three-quarters of an ounce less after death. He hypothesized that was the soul. Of course there are many other reasons that a person could weigh less."

"Of course it is child." Sweet Louise patted her hand.

"There's an Anesthesiologist in Arizona who has some interesting theories on the soul and a quantum consciousness. Using quantum physics to explain that an item can be in two places at once, he thinks that microtubules in the brain working independently of conscious thought are actually part of a quantum consciousness. When a person dies, those microtubules return to that quantum consciousness." Laney glanced up.

She wasn't sure what she was hoping to see … a universal consciousness floating around?

Was her soul still here or had it moved on?

"I prefer to think of it as heaven." Sweet Louise dried her eyes. "I need to believe in that so I'll go on thinking of her sweet face waiting for me when I get there."

Laney had never thought of it that way. What did she need to believe? Science had always spoken to her, but that was because she was able to make sense out of it. But did she believe it?

She needed to believe that Lara would be safe and happy and healthy. She needed to believe that there would be someone looking out for the little girl. She needed to believe that she'd see Lara again healthy and whole. But more than anything, right now, she wanted to tell Lara how much she loved her. It was important. The part of her that had stayed numb to death could no longer hide from it. She cared and loved her patients. Separating it was just an illusion.

The evidence was pretty overwhelming that coma patients could understand what was going on around them.

Leaning down close to Lara's ear, Laney swallowed back the flood of tears clogging her throat, "I love you little one … always."

It struck her that she never remembered saying 'I love you' to anyone. Surely she'd told her parents when she was young. But as she'd gotten older, sentiment had not only been shunned but not tolerated at home. She'd been taught that tears were useless and that emotion equaled weakness.

Her cell buzzed with a new text. She wiped her face with her sleeve and pulled out the phone. "ER—STAT!" Glowed in white letters against the blue background. "I have to go. I have a patient in trouble."

"Can't someone else take this one?" Devon loosened his arms but didn't let go. "You need a moment to gather yourself."

"There is no one else. I'm the doctor on call. This is my job." No time to think—onto the next emergency. She wanted to run away—curl up in a ball on her office floor and hide, but that wasn't an option. And she didn't hide from anything.

She shook off Devon's arms and rose. "I have to go."

She sifted through her current sick patient list and the only name that came to mind was Lincoln Lafferty—a twelve year-old-boy fighting like hell with Leukemia. He had horned-rimmed glasses and Harry Potter hair. Her arms ached to hug him and tell him that everything would be okay.

The message buzzed again. "Sorry."

She took off at a run, hit the stairs, and took them to the first floor. She just wanted a day—one day when she didn't have to face down death. That was selfish—her patients didn't get a day off. Still, she desperately wanted one day when it didn't weigh heavily on her mind. This was the life she had chosen or rather, the life that had chosen her. Medicine—especially pediatrics—was a calling that she hadn't been able to ignore.

She put the tears away and tried to don her professional armor … but there were holes in it now. Big, glaring holes that let love in. She was so damned tired … tired of pretending that she didn't care. Maybe caring was the key to fixing the broken bodies? If so, it was a small price to pay for saving a life.

She made it to the Emergency wing out of breath and rattled. He was in room six.

Lincoln sat up eating a chocolate pudding cup and bleeding from the central line right under his clavicle.

"He yanked it playing football." Michael the nurse in charge rolled his eyes up to Laney's as he blotted blood with four-by-four gauze squares.

"Football … FOOTBALL. Are you kidding me?" She threw her hands up. Here she was fighting tooth and nail to save him while he was doing everything he could to get sicker. This was not happening.

She turned to his parents sitting in the chairs to the right of the hospital bed.

"What possessed you to let him play football?" Her voice was controlled and tight. She was done watching what she said around patients—professionalism wasn't working so now she'd try a little real world. If they weren't behind their son's recovery, she might as well throw up her hands and walk away … only she wasn't a throw in the towel kind of person.

"He was feeling better. We were just throwing the ball around in the front yard, and then some of the neighborhood boys showed up. It turned into a game. Linc was doing fine until he took that hit." Mr. Lafferty wouldn't make eye contact.

"Someone tackled him?" Mrs. Lafferty's voice was high and squeaky. She brought up her elbow and nailed him hard in the upper arm. "I go to the grocery store for one hour, and you have him playing football."

Usually the hospital had a zero tolerance policy for violence, but Mr. Lafferty had it coming so Laney pretended that she hadn't seen anything.

"He was feeling fine." Mr. Lafferty rubbed his arm. "I don't see what the big deal is."

Mrs. Lafferty's eyes turned the size of grapefruits and she reared back for another elbow. "Are you kidding me? That's the dumbest thing I've ever heard."

Laney stepped in. "Mr. Lafferty, may I see you in the hall … NOW." She pointed to the open doorway.

Slowly, like a kid dragging his feet to the principal's office, Mr. Lafferty made his way out in the hall.

"Do you know what that central line does?" Laney worked really hard on not wringing his neck. The calm, controlled demeanor under which she'd formerly operated, was completely gone now. Emotion made her so mad she could hardly see straight. "It's where we give him his medicine, chemotherapy, and any liquids that may be necessary. These are the things that are fighting the cancer. If this central line doesn't work, we have to install a new one. Because of his compromised health, we don't have a lot of veins to choose from. I can't treat him without a central line—do you know what that means?"

"I didn't realize." He chewed on his upper lip and fiddled with the dirty gimme baseball cap on his head.

"Without treatment, his chances of a recovery are very slim." She didn't want to come right on out and say that his child would die, but hopefully this man could read between the lines.

"Okay, okay. I'm beginning to see that football wasn't such a good idea." He took the cap off, smoothed his hair, and them replaced it.

Were men the champions of understatement? "It was a very bad idea. From now on, he needs to rest. I will determine when he's recovered enough for contact sports. Are we clear?"

"Crystal." Lafferty had the good sense to look embarrassed.

A strong, familiar hand pressed lightly at the small of her back. "Is everything okay?"

Devon was so close that she could feel his breath tickle her hair.

"You're Devon Harding." Mr. Lafferty seemed to have forgotten all about his sick child. "I'm a huge fan."

She was getting the idea that Lafferty was a bit of an ass. Her sympathy for Mrs. Lafferty doubled.

Devon ignored Mr. Lafferty and pressed Laney closer to him. "Is everything okay?"

"It is now. I was just explaining to Mr. Lafferty that football isn't a good choice for his son who is on chemotherapy." Laney couldn't help the reproach in her voice. At least she hadn't resorted to calling the man names. Dumbass came to mind along with idiot and imbecile.

"Yes, I can see how that would be a bad idea." Devon chewed on the inside of his cheek probably to keep from laughing.

"I can't believe I'm standing here talking to you. You're the best offensive tackle in the league. Think you could give my boy some tips?" Mr. Lafferty was dead serious.

Laney almost lost it.

Devon must have sensed her near-murderous intentions because he snaked his arm around her waist and pulled her back a good foot from Lafferty. "Why don't you go over to the computer and order something or type in your notes or whatever medical people do when sitting at computers? I'm going to have a little chat with your patient's father."

Laney glared at Lafferty but allowed Devon to lead her over to the nurse's station. "I do need to order a sterile tray and a new catheter."

She sat behind the computer and logged into the medical program. She typed her notes and placed the orders. After some deep breathing to get her pulse and temper under control, she stood and walked back to room six.

She went directly to her patient. "Linc, we're going to need to take out the old line and install a new one. I'm going to numb you up like before, but it may hurt."

When dealing with patients, she always told them the truth. Kids knew when adults were lying, and once they detected a lie, their trust was gone.

"Okay." He picked up another chocolate pudding cup. "I guess you have to."

"Only if you want to get better. That's our goal, right? To get better." Laney turned to Michael who was still mopping up a tiny stream of blood. "Is it salvageable?"

Michael shook his head. "I don't think so. The vein's compromised."

She shook her head. Not that she would take the advice of all of the nurses, but Michael was really good—one of the best she'd ever worked with.

"Can you grab me a sterile tray and new catheter? I've already noted it on his chart." She grabbed a pair of gloves from the box by the door.

Michael waited for her to take over with the gauze, and then he headed out of the room.

"Okay kiddo, let me look at the damage." Gently, she pulled the gauze back and checked the line. It had stripped the vein. She needed to remove it and stitch up the hole. "Yep, you're definitely getting a new line today."

"I promise not to play football ever again." Linc sounded completely forlorn.

"Let's not be too hasty. I think you should play football and whatever sports you want, but not until after I give you the okay. I know that some days you don't feel as sick as others, but you are sick. Your body is fighting hard to fix itself, and it needs all your strength and energy. I'm not saying you can't ever play football. Just give it a little while." Laney worked the line out and applied pressure to the bleeding wound.

Linc hadn't even winced. She set the small tube down on the bed next to him and used both hands to apply pressure. "You need a couple of stitches."

Michael rolled in a cart complete with the sterile tray and a new catheter wrapped in plastic.

"You want to stitch that up first and then move on?" Michael pulled a new pair of gloves out of the box by the door and slipped them on.

"You read my mind." She dabbed at the open wound. "The bleeding has almost stopped. Hand me the—"

He placed the syringe of anesthetic in her hand before she even had time to finish her sentence. Michael was an exceptional nurse.

Laney injected the anesthetic near the wound, waited for it to take effect, and then made two tiny stitches in the skin closing the wound. Michael took the needle from her and handed her a sterile dressing. Michael would be a huge help in the operating room, but he preferred the emergency room.

Linc shifted. "You're Devon Harding. Wow."

Laney didn't need to look over her left shoulder to know that Devon was in the room. He had a presence, and people always recognized him.

"Keep still, I need to numb the new site, and then I'm going to insert the new catheter." Laney scoped out a good vein and made a mark with a pen of where she would enter the vein. She swiped the area with antiseptic and injected the numbing agent.

Without turning around, she spoke to Devon. "Why don't you explain to Linc, here how football isn't the best choice of pastimes when he's on chemotherapy?"

"Well now …" Devon sounded unsure of himself. She'd forgotten, he didn't like hospitals even though he spent a lot of time in them these days. "I think football is fine as long as he's a spectator."

"That hit you took last week against the Dolphins looked brutal. How's your back?" Linc said between bites of chocolate pudding. This kid really loved his chocolate pudding.

"You have no idea. My back is black and blue." Tentatively, Devon moved to the edge of the bed. "Maybe you and your family would like to come to practice tomorrow? I'd be happy to arrange it. I'm sure the guys would love to meet you."

"Seriously?" Linc nodded. "That would be awesome."

"Hold still." Laney put a hand on his chest while Michael walked around the other side of the bed and pressed lightly on Linc's shoulder.

Michael nodded to her that he was holding the patient in position. She popped in the line and taped it down. She got it in on the first try.

"Good job, Dr. Laney." Michael nodded.

"Thanks." She added tape to the edges and stepped back. "Can't even feel it, can you?"

Linc looked down a little surprised to find a new IV port in his chest. "Nope, I didn't even realize you'd started."

"That's my girl. She's the best." Devon nodded.

"He's your boyfriend?" Linc was very impressed.

Devon was more than her boyfriend, she was in love with him.

Chapter 21

All along Devon had known Laney was a doctor, but he'd never seen her in action until today. As he suited up for practice, he still couldn't believe how she'd been able to perform minor surgery so effortlessly. She was amazing.

He wanted to do so much for her, but all she wanted from him was him. He smiled to himself. While that was pretty awesome, he wanted to show her how much he cared. But, she wasn't into big, expensive gifts.

He needed to do something small, personal—something meaningful that would ease her heart. Lara's dying was killing Laney, but she always kept her head held high even as her heart was breaking. It was hard for Devon to watch.

As he grabbed his helmet, Keshaun smacked him on the back. "Thank Laney for me. Krystal is fantastic. She doesn't let me get away with anything, makes me open the door for her, and she eats steak. I'm in love."

"That's good." He tucked his helmet under his arm. "One of her patients will be coming to practice tomorrow. Think you can sign some autographs?"

"Anything for Laney." Keshaun grinned. "Maybe we could tailgate again at the hospital. I could rack up some nice points with Krystal."

"Such a humanitarian." Devon punched him in the shoulder.

"You know it." Keshaun cocked his head to the right. "I'm one step away from being Mother Theresa.

"Wait up." Clint caught up to them. He had his helmet hooked into the crook of his arm, and he carried a huge plastic box with a handle. "Summer made five dozen cinnamon rolls for Laney. She says that if Laney can eat them in less than thirty minutes, she can get in the Guinness Book of World records for the most cinnamon rolls eaten in one sitting."

Judging by the incredible smell wafting up from the box, it was full of cinnamon rolls.

"Are those the ones she made last Christmas with the cream cheese icing and the little bits of orange zest?" Devon's stomach sat back on its heels and begged like a dog for a treat.

"Yes." Clint eyed him suspiciously. "But they're for you to take to Laney."

Devon and Keshaun exchanged a look.

Keshaun crossed his arms. "Think we can take this skinny-assed white boy?"

"With my eyes closed and one hand tied behind my back." Devon nodded. "Hand over the cinnamon rolls, and no one gets hurt."

"They're for Laney. Summer made that very clear." Clint took a step backward.

"It's not like we're going to eat them all. We might save a few for Laney." Keshaun stopped in front of Clint. "I'd hate for you to suffer a career ending injury over some baked goods."

Clint looked at Devon. "It's come down to this … you taking food out of your own girlfriend's mouth. I knew you were self-centered, but this is a new low."

Clint tried to say it with a straight face but he couldn't keep the laughter out of his voice.

"She's not here and besides, I'm not taking all of them out of her mouth, just a dozen or so." Devon took the box. "Crap, they're still warm."

"Fine, but y'all are going to be in trouble. I'm telling Summer." Clint folded his arms against his chest. "She's going to be pissed. See if she ever makes your favorite cheesecake brownies again for your birthday."

As threats went, that one was downright mean.

"Why you gotta go and hurt my feelings?" Devon reached into the box and pulled out a cinnamon roll. Cream cheese icing oozed down the side. He bit into it and cinnamon-orangey goodness swirled around his tongue.

"Harding, are you eating before my practice?" Coach Robbins yelled from the locker room door.

Devon popped the rest into his mouth and said around the cinnamon roll. "No, coach."

"You know the rules. No eating right before practice unless you want to clean your own puke off my field." Coach Robbins headed toward them. "I smell cinnamon."

"Must be air freshener." Keshaun stepped between Coach and the cinnamon rolls. He popped a whole one in his mouth.

"Are those cinnamon rolls?" Coach Robbins was nobody's fool. He grabbed the box. "Damn, they're still hot."

He took a deep drag of cinnamon. "It's a crying shame that I'm going to have to confiscate these. No food in the locker room."

"What? That's not a rule." Devon grabbed for the box, but Robbins turned away.

"Yep, it's brand new. Just went into effect a half second ago." Robbins took another hit of cinnamon. "I'm going to need more coffee to pair with these lovelies."

"Damn, you'd think Grace kept you in baked goods so you wouldn't need to steal other peoples." Devon shook his head. He'd only gotten one and the chances of getting more were slim to none.

"There's always room for cinnamon rolls." Coach Robbins carted them out of the locker room.

"That was just mean. I'm going to have to call Grace and tell her that Coach is cheating on her coconut pie with Summer's cinnamon rolls." Devon shook his head. "How am I going to break it to Laney that she almost got to eat her bodyweight in cinnamon rolls? She's going to be so disappointed."

"There are some things women just don't need to know." Clint nodded.

"I hear you." Devon agreed. Laney sure could use some cheering up today and cinnamon rolls would have gone a long way to put a smile on her face. He wanted to do something special for her—something meaningful that would help her get through losing Lara. His eyes strung with tears at the thought. He was going to miss that little girl more than he'd ever thought possible. He needed to do something for Laney and for himself.

Devon smiled to himself. The beginnings of a plan were coming together. He needed to enlist his mother's help and maybe the front desk lady at Laney's office too. What had her name been? Heather ... no Helen. She was the Chief Smile Officer—well she was about to earn her title. Laney needed reminding of all of the lives she'd saved because those are the numbers she should be focusing on.

Six hours later, Devon looking over his right and then his left shoulder like he was making sure he wasn't being followed, opened the front door to Laney's office. Laney was in surgery and wasn't there, but he couldn't take any chances.

Once he'd explained his plan, his mother had arranged a private and secret meeting with Helen.

Helen was waiting for him with a huge smile on her face.

He knew exactly what he wanted to do for Laney.

"Is there any way to contact some or all of the patients that Laney has saved?" Devon pulled a folded letter out of his left breast pocket. "I'd like to send them a letter."

"I don't understand." Helen's smile turned skeptical. "I don't know if I can give you that info—HIPPA reasons."

"I was thinking that Laney needs a Wall of Fame. My letter asks for them to send a recent picture of her former patient along with a quick note of what they are doing now. I was thinking we could make a display or something." He could see it in his mind—what he wanted, but he wasn't sure he was explaining it correctly.

Helen's upper lip quivered and tears gathered in her eyes. "That's the sweetest thing I've ever heard. She's having a hard time with Lara's death. She thinks I don't know, but I see that she's suffering."

He could see it now, Helen was more than just an employee she was Lara's friend. "Think you could manage to get me that list?"

"I can't give you patient info, but I can compile it and send out the letters myself. Hand it over, and I'll get started right now." She held her hand out.

Devon handed her the letter.

"I've worked for doctors for the better part of thirty years, and Dr. Laney is the best one I've ever seen. She cares so deeply about her patients and truly wants to help them. She has a gift." She unfolded the letter and skimmed it. "Nice. I'll take care of everything."

"Helen, you're a good woman." Devon nodded.

"That's what all three of my ex-husbands said right before they left me." She laughed to herself.

"Clearly they were all crazy." Devon liked her. Helen was kind and just a little bit feisty.

"That's what I said right after I told them not to let the door hit them on the butt on the way out." She winked.

He could see this woman hanging out with is mother. They would get into some serious trouble. Maybe he shouldn't mention it to either of them.

"And mum's the word on this. I want it to be a surprise." Devon just wanted to make sure they were on the same page.

With her right hand, Helen zipped her lips shut and threw away the key. She was like the crazy aunt he'd always wished he'd had.

Laney was going to be so surprised and happy. She'd been focusing too much on her losses and not enough on her wins. A Wall of Fame was just what she needed.

Chapter 22

A week later, Laney sat at her desk pouring over Lara's file, looking for something she'd missed. She rubbed her eyes and continued to stare at the computer screen. The lab results hadn't changed in the five minutes that she'd been staring at them, but she needed to do something.

Lately, her personal life was wonderful, but her professional life felt like it was falling apart.

Lara hadn't woken from the coma and the analytical side of Laney's brain told her that it wasn't likely that she would, but her heart was breaking. She closed her eyes, and then opened them again in the hopes that some new idea would pop into her head. There had to be a way to save Lara. Just because things looked bleak, she wasn't giving up. She couldn't. Lara had to get better. There was so much she—they—hadn't done together.

Losing any child was a pot-shot to the chest, but Lara, that was a kick to the soul. Children should be protected and loved, not stabbed with needles and poisoned with radiation. Why had she ever thought she could do this?

She picked up the nearest stack of papers and hurled them against the wall. She was pissed … at herself and at whatever Supreme Being who thought childhood leukemia was a good idea. Babies should be born with a little expiration date tattooed on the bottom of their left foot. That way, the rest of the world could be ready when the time came. Life was precious and perfect and came to an end. Nothing lasted forever … except heartache.

She picked up a stapler and chunked it against her closed office door. It was childish and destructive and felt wonderful. Next, she threw the penholder and then the tape dispenser, and then her wooden 'inbox' full of mail. She kept on going until the only thing on her desk was the phone and her laptop.

Now that the rage was dying down, she felt mildly better. Allowing herself to give into her feelings was hard, but it was also freeing. Keeping everything bottled up had led to headaches and sometimes even esophageal spasms. Now her office was a mess, but her head was clear. Most of the gnawing anxiety that she'd missed something was gone.

She needed to either start yoga or kick boxing—something to relieve the stress. Running usually did it, but now it wasn't enough.

Her door burst open, and January stood there in all her sun-tanned glory. "Redecorating?"

"Something like that." Laney was embarrassed at having been caught during a weak moment.

"I like it. It's sort of a destructive meets *Hoarders Buried Alive* thing." She shook her head. "But you really need some stacks of dirty dishes and mountains of Beanie Babies to really pull it off."

Laney laughed. "Thanks, I'll keep that in mind."

"So you're probably wondering why I'm here." January's smile faltered. She'd never been one to beat around the bush.

"I haven't gotten there yet. I was still pondering the Beanie Babies." Laney felt a thousand times better. Having a friend to distract her from her troubles was just what she needed. "Have a seat."

Laney pointed to an overturned chair in front of her desk. "What can I do for you?"

January righted the chair, sat, took a deep breath, and made eye contact. "I'm pregnant, and I need a birthing coach."

It took a full minute for the words to penetrate Laney's brain. "I'm sorry, did you say pregnant?"

"Yes, I'm knocked up. The father is an asshole and won't be in the picture. I need your help. You're the only one I trust to get me through this." Her shoulders slumped and her voice shook. "I loved him, and I thought he loved me, but I just told him about the baby and he hung up on me." Short sobs rattled out of her. "I don't know what to do. Well besides blocking his number so he can't ever call me again … the prick."

Laney was up and pulling her friend into her arms, before she'd even given it a thought. "Hush now, we'll get through this together. You're going to be a wonderful mother, and your baby will have four doting aunts. Who needs men?"

"They suck. He sucks. I feel like such a fool." Tears rolled down her cheeks.

In all the years she'd known January, she'd never seen her cry. January was strong and sarcastic and the most independent woman she'd ever met.

"I knew you were seeing someone new, but you don't talk about him much." Laney stroked her back like Sweet Louise had done when she was hurting.

"He's quite a bit older than me. We were keeping things quiet." She shook her head. "I don't know what to do now."

"Have you had a blood or urine test to confirm it?" Laney went into doctor mode.

"No, just a couple of those home pregnancy test thingys." January wiped her eyes. "I was hoping he'd come to the doctor with me, but it looks like he's out of the picture. I have terrible taste in men."

Laney didn't want to agree with her, but it was kind of true. "Well, you're better off without him. Who needs him anyway? You have us, and pretty soon you'll have a beautiful baby. Men come and go, but best friends are with you no matter what."

"Thanks." The sobs started up again.

"Let's get you an appointment with your OBGYN and then go from there. I know it feels like the end of the world now, but I'm excited at the prospect of a baby. I get to spoil him or her, and I plan on babysitting a lot." She continued to stroke her friend's back. "Devon's going to be so excited at being an uncle."

Laney wasn't sure why that had popped into her head. Her future was with Devon—it was so clear to her now. She'd never really thought about it before, but she wanted to be with him forever. It should scare her, but the idea was comforting … like coming home after a really long trip and knowing that her life was waiting for her.

"I can tell by the look on your face that something really important just happened." January shook her head. "You really have the worst poker face in the world."

"No I don't." Laney laughed, but she did. It was time to admit it.

"So what new earth-shattering conclusion have you just come to? I need something to take my mind off my own earth-shattering conclusion." January put her hand on her flat belly as if she needed an explanation.

"I just realized that not only am I in love with Devon, but that I want to spend the rest of my life with him." It sounded so strange coming from her lips. Usually such large life decisions took years to figure out.

"Wow, that's big." January nodded. "But you two fit together. It's not apparent at first, but when you're together you complete each other." She rolled her eyes. "That was the corniest thing I've ever said. I think the pregnancy hormones are screwing with my head." She bit her bottom lip. "But it's kind of true. When y'all are in a large group of people, you seemed to gravitate toward each other—not because either of you aren't comfortable in groups, but because you genuinely like to be together. It's nice to see two people who enjoy each other's company so much that they don't need anyone else. I hope that doesn't change."

Laney had never really thought about it. When she was with Devon it felt natural, like they should always be together. He liked that she wasn't perfect, and that awkward side of her was completely okay with him. Likewise, she loved everything about him too. More than anything, she wanted them to always be together.

"So now that you and Devon are officially a couple, you should ask him to marry you." January was completely serious.

"What?" That was preposterous. She couldn't ask him to marry her … could she?

"Why not? I happen to know a thing or two about men. In today's world, the woman can ask as easily as the man. Don't let him get away. He's one of the good ones—I should know. I seem to only pick the bad ones." She sighed dramatically. "He wants you … you want him. Why shouldn't you be together?"

January sounded so tired. It must have been a rough day for her.

"Tell me about your mystery man." It didn't really matter if he was going to be there for January because Laney and the rest of the Tough Ladies would be.

"Not much to tell. Like I said, he's older and apparently doesn't want kids … or me. I'm so good at the falling in love part, it sucks that I'm not so good at inspiring the same in men. Falling in love alone—the one-sided love affair—seems to be my specialty. Why is that?" January sounded like she wanted an honest answer.

"There's nothing wrong with you—it's them. The men you pick aren't always emotionally available." Laney was trying to be nice. The men January picked weren't always physically available either. Sometimes they were married. Was this what happened?

"No, he's not married. That only happened once, and I didn't know he was married when I met him. That little bombshell came weeks later." January wasn't defensive as much as self-effacing. She was tougher on herself than she was on other people. "My baby-daddy isn't married if that's what you think. He's just an asshole. Can you believe that he hung up on me when I told him about the baby?" She shook her head. "I can't believe that I actually thought I loved him."

"He's sounds like a complete dickhead." Laney agreed. Anyone who hung up on their girlfriend when she clearly was in trouble deserved to die a thousand deaths at the hands of January's friends. Friends could always dream up much better torture than the actual person who'd been wronged. It was a Universal Law.

"If anyone knows what he's like, it's you." January said under her breath.

Laney had no idea what she was talking about so she let it go. January was dealing with some major stress right now, so possibly talking about the absentee father was a bad idea.

"Okay, so I've been chosen to be the birthing coach." Laney smiled proudly.

"The others are going to be so jealous."

"Yeah, well before you crow too loudly, just know that you're the logical choice. Nina travels too much, Susie would seriously freak out, and Charisma would probably make me do push-ups during the delivery. You're the only sane one among us." January grinned. "You won by default."

"Wow. That's so incredibly un-flattering. I don't know whether to hug you or punch you." It was Laney's turn to roll her eyes.

"Just keeping it real, Lanes." January stood. "I have an appointment with a new OBGYN tomorrow at nine-thirty. Think you can sneak away and come with me?"

Laney pulled up her calendar. Her first patient wasn't until noon. She blocked the morning and sent a quick email to Helen letting her know that she'd be out of the office. "Okay. Tomorrow morning, I'm all yours."

"Goody." January did her best Marsha Brady impersonation. Sadly, it was the only impersonation she did.

"New OBGYN? What's wrong with Dr. Martinez? Why change now?" Laney just caught that fact. She and January used the same OB.

"Because my ex knows Dr. Martinez pretty well. They're offices are in the same building and they see each other all the time. She knows I was dating him." January sounded a little worried.

It hit Laney. "She offices out of the Seton Professional Buildings. All those offices are for doctors. Do I know him?"

"Yep, and I'm not going to tell you who he is. It would make things weird … really weird." January took a deep breath and let it out slowly.

"It's not Dr. Dick is it?" Laney glanced down at January's feet. That would be weird.

"Are you kidding me? That's just gross." She shifted her weight. "No, Dr. Dick and I haven't mingled DNA or anything else."

"Thank God." Laney was truly relieved. She'd always be there for her friend, but knowing that January was having a freaky-foot-fathered baby was hard to take.

January waved. "I'll see you tomorrow. I'll text you the address. Love ya' man."

And January was gone.

Now Laney had a puzzle to figure out. So she knew January's ex-boyfriend. Did she know him well or was he merely a casual acquaintance? She had something to occupy her mind in addition to Devon and her patients. She picked up her cell phone meaning to call Nina, but she didn't know if January had told her yet about the baby so she put the phone down.

Instead, she pulled up the Seton Professional Buildings website. They had over a hundred doctors' offices in three different buildings. And she knew most of the providers. Her father's offices were in Building One.

Holy crap—had January been dating her father? Laney threw up a little bit in the back of her throat. That was just disgusting. Her father didn't date. She shook her head. That was ridiculous. Elvis Presley would have a greater chance of being January's baby-daddy.

Clearly January was hurting, maybe Laney could help by talking with the baby's father?

That's what friends did for each other, they smoothed the way. January would do the same for her. Laney started at the top of the list and worked her way down.

Chapter 23

Devon stood in Laney's office doorframe and just watched her. Would he always get that little zing when he saw her? Would he always have that little stomach flip-flop at the prospect of seeing her? Would he always feel the need to primp just a little bit right before he was supposed to see her?

He hoped so. Having lost her and then finally found her again, he hoped to never take her for granted. Being in love made him feel all of seventeen again—it was nice.

"You're staring." Slowly Laney's eyes rolled up to meet his.

"I didn't want to disturb you." And he just liked watching her. Everything she did was efficient and graceful.

She leaned back in her office chair. "So, dinner and a movie? I need to change first." She pointed to her scrubs. "Sorry, I haven't had time yet."

"Feel up for dinner and a movie in the parking lot? I brought over the big smoker, and Keshaun's rented an outdoor movie screen and projector. He's out to impress Krystal by giving the kids a movie night. I think he has two screens going—one with *Aladdin* for the younger kids and one with *Twilight* for the older ones. Most of the players are coming and bringing food too." He sat in the chair across from her desk.

A bright smile worked its way across her face. "That's the nicest offer I've had all day. I love *Aladdin* and *Twilight*. Thank you and your friends for doing so many wonderful things for the patients. Since you've come into my life, you've brought so much happiness."

Devon thought he might explode with pride or at the very least walk on water. "It's nothing."

"It's not nothing and you know it. You're blushing, it's adorable." Laney grinned.

"I'm not adorable, I'm manly." He flexed his arm muscles. "See. Manly."

"Put those away. There's so much testosterone wafting through the air that I feel hair growing on my upper lip." Laney laughed.

It was corny and stupid, but God, he loved making her laugh. It was a shame that her smile would be short-lived. They had some pretty tough subjects to cover this afternoon.

He took a deep breath and dove in. "We need to talk about Lara."

All the cheer drained from her face—it was like a punch to the gut. He hated hurting her, but there wasn't any way to pretty this subject up.

"We need to talk about her final wishes." The fact that a five-year-old had final wishes was the saddest part of this whole discussion. He'd promised himself that he'd face this head on and not get choked up in the details. He had to be strong for Lara, his mother, and for Laney. He wanted to shoulder as much of the burden as his strong women would let him.

"Before she went into a coma, Lara made me promise to write down her final wishes. I guess she and my mom have been discussing it." He pulled out the folded piece of notebook paper where he'd written down everything Lara wanted. Carefully, he unfolded it. He could feel the tears gathering in his eyes, but he soldiered on. "She would like to be an organ donor."

His voice cracked. "I don't know if that's possible considering her illness, but she was adamant about it."

The grim reality of what happened next for Lara hung in the air like a damp blanket snuffing out all brightness in the room.

"That is so like her. Wanting to help others—thinking of them when she should be thinking of herself." Laney grabbed a handful of tissues from the box on the left corner of her desk and dapped at her eyes. "I hate crying. I've cried more in the last two weeks than I have since babyhood."

He wanted to go to her, scoop her up, and tell her everything was going to be okay, but he needed to get through this first. "I don't know the procedure after organ donation, but if we can, mom and I would like to have her buried in our family plot in Dallas along side my father. She's our family, and we'd like for her to be with us." Tears were unmanly, but he couldn't have stopped them if he tried so he grabbed a bunch of tissues and swiped at them. "We were going to surprise Lara, but it's too late. A few weeks ago, my mother filed papers to formally adopt her. I know we should have asked you first, but we wanted her to have our last name. Because all parental rights had been signed away a long time ago and she's dying, I was able to fast-track it. The paperwork should come through next week. I'd like to bury her with our last name, if you don't mind."

Laney's lower lips wobbled as tears streamed down her face. She opened her mouth, closed it, and then nodded.

"There's just one more thing." He took a deep breath and let it out slowly. "Lara doesn't want a church funeral or in her words something sad. She wants a circus themed party in her honor right here in the parking lot so all the kids can have fun. We're to have clowns, zebras, a circus tent, and …" he could barely make out his notes through his own tears, "trapeze artists. She requests that we serve cherry Kool-Aid, vanilla ice cream, chocolate cake, cotton candy, and popcorn—there are to be no vegetables or iced tea. She was very particular on this point. And no one is allowed to wear black or feel sad."

He just couldn't go on. There was absolutely nothing worse in the world than a dying child and he wasn't sure he would survive this. He bowed his head and gave into the grief. If he couldn't show the woman he loved that he was vulnerable, then he didn't deserve her.

All of a sudden, Laney was there, pulling him into her arms. She cradled his head against her shoulder and finger combed his hair. "All Lara ever wanted was a family, and you gave that to her. I can't thank you enough. You're an amazing person."

"You're the amazing one. You gave her to us." Devon clung to her. She was here for him and he for her.

"Wow, listen to us. We're each other's cheering section. We're so cute, I want to punch us in the face … repeatedly." Her chest shook with laughter. "I never thought of myself as the lovey-dovey type, but look at us. It's both cute and disgusting."

He smiled. She was so good for him. "How's it feel?"

She shrugged. "It's not bad … I'm getting used to it. Though, sometimes I feel like I should do a glucose blood test because I'm turning so sweet." She continued to finger comb his hair. It was so soothing. "But I draw the line at cutesy nicknames."

"Damn, I was just about to burst out with Sweetie-kins Cuppy Cake." Devon nuzzled her cheek.

"That just makes me hungry. If you're going to go with a nickname, you're going to have to do something that's not food related." She bit her top lip thinking. "How about Snuggle Bear?"

He let it settle on him and then shook his head. "No can do. That makes me think of that fabric softener bear.

He is not sexy." Devon kissed her jaw. "How about Sweet Buns?"

"Nope, food related." Her stomach rumbled. "Makes me think of cinnamon rolls."

Devon froze. "Speaking of cinnamon rolls, there's something I should tell you."

Laney leaned back and eyed him suspiciously. "I was wondering when you were going to bring up the five dozen cinnamon rolls. Summer texted me yesterday that they'd been confiscated by Coach Robbins. FYI-Grace isn't speaking to him, and he never gets her famous Chicken Parmesan again. I'm told there was weeping and begging, but Grace was unmoved."

"Thank God, justice has been served." It was wrong for Devon to be happy because Coach had gotten in trouble, but he didn't care. Summer's cinnamon rolls were fantastic, and there should be some punishment for taking them away. "I can't wait for you to have Grace's Chicken Parmesan. She makes it for my birthday, and it's crazy good." He kissed his way to her ear and whispered, "Want to babysit the Robbins kids with me tonight? We could make out on their couch after all the kids go to bed."

"It's so cute that you babysit." She kissed his cheek.

"Not cute, it's manly ... remember?" He flexed his left again.

"Sorry, I forgot. Manly ... right." Laney licked the underside of his jaw. "I love you."

Devon's world shifted and those words tattooed themselves on his soul. "It's about time you admitted it. Say it again."

"What do you mean it's about time?" She punched him in the arm. "I love you."

He closed his eyes and let the words wash over him. "It's taken you long enough. I've been in love with you since I was seventeen. You have some serious catching up to do."

238

"Excuse me? I fell in love with you back then, I just … lost my way so technically, I fell in love with you first." Laney nodded. "You know it's true."

"Hello, love at first sight." He pointed to himself. "I saw you first. You were getting out of your father's car. I had to knock like five other guys out of the way so I could help you with your bag. Don't you remember the kid with the bloody nose screaming like a girl?"

Devon had done a lot of things he wasn't particularly proud of, but popping a boy who'd stood between him and Laney and who had refused to move, wasn't one of them.

"What boy?" Her eyes squinted like she was deep in thought. "You mean that girl?"

"No, it was a dude. I remember punching him because he wouldn't move out of the way. He had a full-on mustache and five-o'clock shadow at noon." Maybe they were talking about two different people. He didn't remember giving two people bloody-noses though.

"Her name was Natalie, and she had a deeper voice than you do. She was in my cabin and had a serious crush on me. She kept bringing me wild flowers and extra cookies from the canteen." Laney nodded.

"That explains the pink tennis shoes. I just thought he was color blind." He shook his head. "Are you sure he was a girl?"

"Yep. She sends me a Christmas card every year. She's Natalie the Bone Crusher—"

"From the WWE? She's awesome." Devon couldn't believe that he'd punched a girl. That was bad, he felt horrible. His mother was going to kill him. "I should apologize."

"I wouldn't. She holds a grudge. I'm pretty sure she can wrap you into a pretzel if she wanted to." Laney was completely serious. "Back then, I had to keep talking her out of killing you. I'd let sleeping dogs lie."

"I feel bad." He'd never hit a girl and only fought to protect himself these days.

"Don't. I'm pretty sure she can take you." Laney wasn't saying it to be mean, just stating a fact.

Devon shook his head. "Manly … why is that so hard for you to remember?"

"Don't get your panties in a wad, you're the manliest man I know." She patted his cheek, "except for Natalie."

Laney giggled … actually giggled. Like it was a surprise to her also, she clamped a hand over her mouth.

The sound went straight to his heart. She loved him. Laney-Elaine Janece Nixon … EJ—loved him. He'd known it forever, but it was good to hear it again.

Chapter 24

Two days later, at exactly ten fifteen in the morning Laney's lovely little world collapsed. As she walked out of exam room one, her phone beeped with a text from Sweet Louise. "She's gone. I held her hand as she slipped away. It was peaceful. So sorry."

Laney took off in a dead run, she hit the stairs, and was out of the building and crossing the street before she'd realized that she was still holding her phone. By the time she made it to Lara's room, they had wheeled her body out. Sweet Louise sat by the window looking down at nothing. The grief on her face was deeper than tears. It was the look of total loss and utter heartbreak that she'd seen on too many parent's faces after the death of a child.

Laney put her hand on Sweet Louise's shoulder.

"I knew this day was coming, but …" Sweet Louise shook her head. "It still snuck up on me. I thought I was ready, but I'm not."

Laney knew she was supposed to say all the comforting things like 'she's in a better place' and 'she didn't suffer' but she couldn't get the words out. Trite, generic words of consolation felt like a betrayal of a little girl whose personality and soul that was so beautiful and expansive and generous. Without her, the world had lost some of its brightness.

"Even when she fell into a coma, I kept thinking that she would wake up. I kept hoping for a miracle ... praying. My mind knew she would die, but my heart kept up hope. I still can't believe it." Sweet Louise continued to stare at nothing, her voice distant and hollow. "My mother always said there was hope. But sometimes there isn't."

For the first time, Laney could see the situation so clearly and for what it was. Lara had given her so many things, but the most precious was hope.

"Until recently, I thought I didn't believe in hope." Laney's voice was scratchy and sounded like it came from far away. "I told myself that patients were just broken machines that needed fixing. I told myself that I didn't believe in hope or miracles. But I do. Up until the very end, I kept combing through Lara's medical records looking for something I'd missed. I was hoping to find something I could use to fix her." Her voice broke. "Lara showed me that hope is what drives me to do better and that I'm surrounded by miracles every day. I see that now. Life isn't the miracle—love is." She smiled. "A miracle is a lovely little girl who only wanted a family and finally got one. Another is, a sweet lady who saw a dying, lonely child and loved her anyway. And then there's a man who found the love of his life at seventeen and never stopped looking for her. They may not be flashy—be healed—miracles, but they still qualify."

Sweet Louise covered her hand with hers. "Hon, I don't know how you do it. You see some of the worst things humanity has to offer and you manage to see the good. That takes a special person." She laughed quietly. "You're a better person than me. I'm so sad and mad right now, I just want to punch someone."

Laney took a step back and then grinned. "I'd offer myself up, but I'm not that into pain."

"Hon, you're so skinny that my fist would go right through you. Since that would leave a gaping hole, and my son's in love with you, I'm thinking he'd be mad. I'd rather punch a stranger." Sweet Louise's tone was warming. She was coming back to herself.

"Now that you mention it, I do feel like punching someone. I need to do something violent. I'm thinking of taking Krav Maga. I hear you get to punch and kick people. That's sounds pretty good right about now." Why didn't the hospital have a punching bag around for all of the grieving parents to work out on? Maybe she'd install one.

"Since I can't punch a stranger, I like to picture Minnie Davidson. She made my elementary school years a living hell. When I hit middle school and grew these," Sweet Louise pointed to her boobs, "all the boys paid attention to me and wouldn't let her tease me anymore. Now that I look back on it, I should have punched her." She shook her head. "Missed opportunity."

"We could track her down." Laney put her arm around the older woman. "I think we should."

"She died." Sweet Louise shrugged. "Damn it."

Laney busted out laughing. Her nerves were raw and it didn't make sense, but she laughed until her eyes watered. It shouldn't be funny, but at the moment, it was absolutely hilarious.

"Who would you punch if you could?" Sweet Louise wiped the tears of laughter out of her own eyes.

"I don't know." Laney dried her eyes. "Let me think."

"Honey, I don't mean to be rude, but you sure are a goody-two-shoes. At any given time, I can produce a list of at least ten people I'd like to punch. Do you want it in alphabetical, order of appearance, or level of hatred?" Sweet Louise punched her playfully on the arm. "FYI— you're not on the list."

"Thank God." Laney sifted through her mind. "I guess I'd like to punch Jackie Merksion because she was the head mean girl at my high school. She'd be my top pick, but after her, maybe … Caligula because he seems like an ass."

Sweet Louise nodded. "You're going old school. People to punch throughout history. I like it. I'm with you on Caligula, and I'll add Nero and Adolph Hitler. Also, that pink Energizer bunny really pisses me off. I'd like to run over that thing with my Caddy."

"I hear you on the bunny. He's just so damn cheerful." Laney's shoulders shook with laughter. They were deflecting the tragic with the ridiculous. She'd seen it a hundred times. Sooner or later, they needed to get back to the business at hand. Since she wasn't one to ignore things, it might as well be now. "Have you told Devon?"

Sweet Louise glanced at the empty space where the hospital bed had been.

Laney noticed that Kisses had curled up in a ball right where the bed had been. She wasn't sleeping, she just lay there dazed. That's exactly how Laney felt.

Sweet Louise shook her head. "No. You're the only one I've notified. I wanted some time with you to digest things. You know—two women who loved her comforting each other. We women bare things most men couldn't handle on their best day. I needed just a moment to wallow in my own misery and commiserate with another strong woman because I had to comfort someone else. Devon's going to be so shaken up by this…we'll need to be strong for him. I guess I needed to be weak for just a little bit before I have to put on that damn brave face that all mothers wear when we don't have any choice. It's funny. We're supposed to be the weaker sex, but when it comes to life, we do all of the heavy lifting."

Laney pulled her into a hug. "I've often wondered how much further society would be if women had been in charge."

"The world would be a different place. Summit meetings would involve a covered dish luncheon, Spanx would be out-lawed, and PMS days would be considered paid sick time. I'm pretty sure that chocolate would be the national food and anyone wearing socks with sandals would be shot on sight. It would be estrogen utopia."

"I like your version of the world. Too bad it's not reality. This morning, I saw a man in the lobby wearing white tube socks pulled all the way up to his knees with his black sandals. It was painful." Laney knew they were talking around the subject of Lara, but she couldn't help it.

"Your retinas should take a sick day." Sweet Louise patted her on the back. "Now you're going to have to watch hours of kitten and puppy video on YouTube to counter act it."

"That sounds pretty painful too." They needed to head back to Lara. "Do you need me to make the funeral arrangements?"

"No, I've got it handled. I just wish the adoption had gone through before she died." Sweet Louise seemed so much older than she had not two seconds ago. "I wanted her to know that she belonged to me."

"She did know. She was the happiest that I've ever seen her. She told me that now that she had a family, she'd have someone to look down on from heaven. I know that you made her life better and gave her comfort when she was so scared of dying. You made her feel loved and important and wanted. That's all she ever wanted." Laney didn't have the words to thank Sweet Louise for what she'd done.

"I hope so. All children should feel loved. That's one of the reasons that I've decided to become a foster mother. I'm going to build me a big ole house and fill it with kids who need love. It was Lara's idea. She didn't want me to be lonely after she was gone. Always looking out for others—that's one of the things that makes," she caught herself, "made her special."

Tears rolled down Sweet Louise's cheeks. There were no racking sobs just a steady stream of sorrow that ran so deep that it was palpable.

"I think that's lovely. I can see it now. Huge, loud family dinners with smiling kids chattering away. I can't wait." Laney realized that she wanted this too. She wanted Sweet Louise to build her house close to her and Devon so they could see each other every day. She loved kids so much and wanted a house full of them. "Does Devon know what you're planning?"

Sweet Louise wiped her nose. "He threatened to buy me the lot next to his."

Laney smiled all the way down to her toes. "That's perfect. We could watch the kids when you need to go out. We could all barbecue in the backyard. How wonderful will that be?"

Sweet Louise looked her up and down. "So you're planning a future with my boy?"

Laney chewed on her upper lip. "I guess I am. Is that okay?"

The older woman hugged her tight. "I'm so happy for you. Has he asked you to marry him?"

Laney realized that she was getting ahead of herself. "Um … no."

Devon had told her that he loved her, but they'd never really talked about the future. When had their relationship moved from new to together forever? She took a deep breath and finger combed her hands through her hair. It had been moving toward forever since she was sixteen.

"I can see that this is hard for you—realizing what the future holds." Sweet Louise patted her shoulder. "Some things can't be planned or even figured out, they just are. Devon is your other half—not everyone gets to find theirs. Don't analyze it, just live it."

"I'm working on it. He's just so confident that everything will work out." Sometimes Laney liked that about him and other times it was so annoying.

"Once my boy makes up his mind, there's no turning back. But you're probably the only person who has the power to shake that confidence. On the night of your first date, do you know that he practically emptied his closet trying to find the perfect outfit? He was worse than any girl I've ever known. I laughed my ass off, but he was nervous, and he's never nervous. It was sweet. He's never really had to try around women, because there were always so many around, but with you he has to try ... wants to try. That will keep him on his toes." Sweet Louise had become a mother figure to her.

"I want to do the same for him, but I didn't have the example of love he had growing up. And there is some pretty astounding data that suggests nurture is way more important that nature. I'm going to try really hard, but love isn't as easy for me as it is for him." Only right now, she felt like she was drowning in love for Lara.

Sweet Louse touched her cheek. "I think you've told yourself that for so long that you actually believe it. I've never seen anyone who loves so much as you. Each child you treat takes root in your heart. You worry and fuss over them just like they were your own. I've seen it ... the nurses have seen it. Do you know that there's not a nurse here who wouldn't bend over backward for you? Not because they have to, but because they want to. They see how much you care and they want to help. Over the years, you and Devon will hurt each other's feelings—that's part of life—but the love will always be there. Some days you will wake up in a bad mood, look over at him, and think, 'I don't need this shit today', but then he'll do something sweet and you'll remember that your life together is so much better than life apart. Love isn't short-lived it lasts forever. In your heart you know that because you love deeply."

247

So the nurses had noticed how much she cared about her patients? They did smile and offer to do whatever she wanted. Laney had noticed that they didn't treat other doctors that way.

Sweet Louise pulled her into a hug. "I gather your father wasn't the nicest role model. Just because you grew up with him doesn't mean that you're going to be like him. You are your own person. You do things differently—react to things to differently. You are not your father."

She was her own person. Most of her life she'd gone out of her way to do exactly the opposite of her father. Maybe it hadn't always been rebellion and perhaps some of it had been because she knew her own mind. That made more sense because Laney had never really thought of herself as rebellious.

"I'll tell Devon. You have enough to worry about." She checked her watch. Three more hours of practice. "I'll drive over to the stadium and tell him in person."

It would be the hardest thing she'd ever done.

Sweet Louise pulled back. "You're a good child. I'll take care of all of the funeral arrangements. Most are already done, but there are some details that need to be ironed out."

Laney's phone buzzed in the front pocket of her white lab coat. She released Sweet Louise and pulled it out. A text from Helen flashed on the screen, "Patients waiting … are you planning on seeing them, or should I reschedule?"

"Crap." Laney shook her head. She'd run out on her patients. This was bad. "I've got to go." She gave Sweet Louise a quick hug. "I left my patients. Don't worry, I'll tell Devon. You stay here. We'll be back as soon as we can."

Laney was out the door and running down the halls. It seems that she was always running from place to place. Sweet Louise didn't think that Laney was anything like her father. She'd never really thought about it, but she wasn't. Since he always treated his patients like broken machines that needed fixing, she thought that was the way it was supposed to be done. But she had her own way. It involved caring and hope. That's what drove her—not fame or recognition or even money—it was love.

Chapter 25

Devon knew something was wrong the moment he saw Laney's face. She stood next to his car in the parking lot. The Mustang that she now drove exclusively was parked next to his Dodge Viper. She'd finally accepted him and the car he'd bought for her. That made him smile.

She took one breath and fat tears rolled down her face. A loud honking sob drowned out the words she was trying to get out. Lara was gone, he could feel it in his soul.

He gathered her in his arms and just held her as his own tears flowed down his face. They would get through this together.

They rocked each other back and forth for several minutes.

Devon felt a huge hand on his back. He glanced over his left shoulder to find Keshaun.

"Krystal just called. I'm so sorry about Lara." Keshaun scooped them both up in a huge hug.

"Lara? What happened to Lara?" Clint Grayson was there.

Keshaun whispered, "She died."

Clint nodded. "I'll text Summer. I know the ladies have been planning for this day. Grace has been cooking and freezing meals, and Summer's been baking up a storm."

Keshaun let them go. "I'm so sorry. What can I do?"

The big man who was known as one of the meanest defensive lineman in the country was all sappy sadness.

Laney wiped her face with the sleeve of her lab coat. "I don't think there is anything to be done. But thank you."

She looked overwhelmed that Keshaun would care.

Clint's phone buzzed. "Okay, we're all going over to the hospital for a sort-of wake. Grace and Summer are rounding up the food and will set up in the parking lot. They would like to give a staff-appreciation dinner for all of the people who helped Lara. Keshaun, can you get those movie screens again? Summer has put together a memorial for Lara, and then after they can show the kids a movie."

The thought tore at his heart. Lara was gone, but would never be forgotten. And his teammates were rallying around him and Laney and his mother because they wanted to help.

"Wow. I don't know what to say." Laney was truly awestruck. "Y'all are doing exactly what Lara wanted … turning this day into a party. She would be so happy."

"That's what family does." Devon let her go, but kept his arm around her. "These guys are my family and Lara is my family … now you're family."

Laney looked so pleased to be included. He'd never given it much thought, but her family kind of sucked. Of course she would want to be part of a loving family. At camp, she'd been so curious about his family and had loved listening to stories about all the things they'd done together.

"I can't believe y'all can put this together so quickly." Laney shook her head.

"Are you kidding? Summer, Grace, and Sweet Louise could run the world blindfolded and with one hand tied behind their backs. If those three ever turned evil, the world would be in serious trouble." Coach Robbins kissed her cheek. "I'm so sorry for your loss."

"Thank you." Laney nodded.

"Even though it's October, my sons, Cart and HW, have already started decorating all of the trees in our backyard with Christmas ornaments so that Lara can see them from heaven." Coach Robbins smiled sadly. "Apparently when Grace took them to meet her, they promised that she would be able to see them from heaven."

"That's so nice. Lara would love it." One corner of Laney's mouth turned up. "She loved all things sparkly."

"Me too." Devon turned around to find Warren Daniver, team owner. "I'm a sucker for all things sparkly."

"Not something you hear very often coming from a man." Coach Robbins clapped Daniver on the back.

"I'm not your everyday guy." He grinned. Since Grace had walked into Coach's life, Daniver had become more than just the man in charge, he'd become a friend. "Grace called and told me everything."

He turned to Laney and held out his hand. "Warren Daniver."

"Laney Nixon." She shook his hand once and then dropped it.

"I missed you the other night. I was late to movie night." Daniver shoved his hands into his front trouser pockets. "Sweet Louise told me all about Lara and the Lone Stars would like to help. I heard Lara wanted to have a circus themed funeral. I propose we do it on Halloween. I think we should make it an annual thing. I've contacted Ringling Brothers, and they've agreed to host. The Lone Stars would be happy to pick up the tab."

Laney's mouth dropped open. "I don't know what to say … thank you doesn't seem like enough."

He shrugged. "I am in awe of what you chose to do for a living. My little sister, Leah, died at the age of nine from leukemia. The fact that you've chosen to help sick children makes you an angel. Whatever you need, I'm here."

Laney hugged Daniver. The gesture seemed to take him by surprise. "I'm so sorry for your loss. I bet Leah was a joy."

Daniver's eyes filled with tears. "She was a handful."

Laney let him go and stepped back. "I think a yearly circus is the perfect way to remember Lara. Thank you very much."

"I hear we're tailgating at the hospital. There's talk of Grace's cinnamon bread." Daniver closed his eyes and savored the thought of cinnamon bread.

Grace's cinnamon bread was savor worthy. "Wait until you taste it. If heaven had a taste that would be it."

Laney still looked a little overwhelmed. "Here I was thinking that this evening would be one of the hardest of my life and y'all swoop in and make me smile. I don't know what to say."

Coach Robbins hugged her. "You're family."

Devon could tell that Laney was warming to the idea of a big, loud football family.

"That's right, Laney." Keshaun pointed to Devon. "If he doesn't treat you right, it will be my pleasure to beat the crap out of him."

"Nope, I'll do it." Big Billy Gains who'd finally accepted that Laney could out eat him, stepped up.

"Y'all will have to get behind me." Clint held up his hand.

"Please, I could whoop all y'all without even breaking a sweat." Devon pulled Laney closer. "Don't listen to them. They're all crazy. I'm a great guy. Just ask my mom."

Clint threw back his head and laughed. "Your mother is a bigger threat than all of us put together. Remember what she did to Debra?"

"Who's Debra?" Laney glanced at Devon.

How did he call her the team whore without making it sound really bad? "She … um … well—"

"She's my ex-girlfriend—sort of, and while I didn't know this at the time, she tried to sleep with everyone on the team." Coach Robbins scratched the back of his neck and didn't make eye contact. "She's kind of a groupie."

Devon noticed that the color drained from Daniver's face and then he turned around and Devon couldn't tell if it got worse. Maybe he wasn't feeling well.

"I don't understand … groupie … like teenager girls who follow rock stars around?" Laney sounded confused.

"That's exactly it. Only she doesn't come around anymore." Devon still couldn't believe what his mother had done. "My mom got her a job at Safe Place—the battered woman's shelter. According to my mother, she's doing really well—"

"What?" Daniver's voice was a squeaky roar.

"Debra's working on the hotline, taking calls and counseling victims of domestic violence. She's doing a fantastic job." Devon wanted to put a hand on the man's arm to calm him, but he looked like a tiger ready to take on any challengers. So the team owner who was always calm, cool, and collected could lose it from time to time.

"No, that's not possible." Daniver dared Devon to dispute him.

"Yes, she's a phone counselor and doing a great job." Devon wanted to add that he was sorry that Debra wasn't as skanky as they'd originally thought, but it seemed rude.

"But she's …" Daniver's color was coming back, but he still looked like a caged animal ready to strike.

"I can get her number from my mom, if you'd like to give her a call and see for yourself." With his free hand, he pulled out his phone. "I'll text my mom."

"No, no…don't worry. I don't really care." Daniver's voice cracked telling everyone that he did care. Usually the king of cool, now he couldn't even pull off nonchalance. "It sounds like your mother has done a good thing."

"Damn straight." Keshaun nodded. "Sweet Louise gave Debra something other than the team to fixate on. Sweet Louise takes being the team mom to a whole new level."

Daniver looked like he just couldn't get his head around the idea that Debra was volunteering.

"Sorry the family's a little messed up." Devon whispered in Laney's ear. "But we all love you."

She looked around like a little kid on Christmas morning. "This is perfect."

Chapter 26

Laney looked out the window of her office onto a bright and cheerful Halloween day. Ringling Brothers was setting up three huge tents. The red and white striped monstrosities were an interesting contrast to the cloudless day. Every time she happened to look out the window there seemed to be a steady stream of people holding the reins to zebras, lions, poodles, and elephants. The air around the hospital buzzed with childhood excitement that made her smile until her cheeks hurt.

"This is all for you kiddo. This is your gift to the world." Laney said to the empty room. She could feel Lara with her—there was no explanation, but she could feel the little girl's excitement all around her.

Yesterday, they'd laid Lara to rest at Greenwood Cemetery in Dallas. Despite the fact that the cemetery bordered Central Expressway and McKinney Avenue, both traffic-laden streets, the cemetery was peaceful in a gothic sort of way. It had been a private ceremony with only Devon, Sweet Louise, and Laney in attendance. The hospital chaplain had driven up and performed the service. Laney smiled to herself. Right before the service started, a mariachi band that'd been playing at a funeral on the other side of the cemetery noticed their small party and wandered over. Seeing that the coffin was that of a child, they insisted on staying and playing until the casket was lowered into the ground. They'd refused money when Devon had offered it. The informal fiesta funeral had made every one laugh—just the way Lara wanted things. Nothing had been sad.

And today was no different. There was no way anyone could be sad with clowns running around. They'd taken over the hospital, roaming the halls, making everyone laugh.

"Yep, kiddo. This is all you."

A knock sounded at her closed door.

She turned around. "Come in."

The door opened and there stood Helen, smiling as always. "There are some people in the waiting room who want to see you."

Laney glanced at the clock on her computer. "I don't understand. We don't have any more patients to see. The last one left over and hour ago."

A mischievous gleam twinkled in Helen's eyes. "Still, our waiting room is overrun with folks. You need to get out there before they start rioting."

Laney felt her brow scrunch up. "It's not full of clowns or something?"

Because that wouldn't be creepy.

Helen moved out of the doorway. "I'm pretty sure none of them would be offended if you called them clowns. In fact, I bet they'd all be okay with you calling them whatever you want. You're kind of their hero."

"Huh?" Laney walked past Helen, pushed open the door that lead to the waiting room, and stopped short. It was full to bursting. She knew these people—recognized some faces, but couldn't put names to all of them. The woman standing right in front of her was Pam Scherrer, Teddy Scherrer's mother. Teddy had died early last year. His face she could recall with great clarity.

Pam threw her arms around Laney and pulled her in for a tight hug. "This is a thank you party."

She stepped back and Laney looked around trying to figure out why there was a 'thank you' party going on in her waiting room.

"I don't understand." Laney recognized the Leiman's, Bonnie and Chuck, along with their fifteen-year-old daughter Jena whose leukemia was in remission. Jena had been a patient earlier this year.

"This is a thank you party for you because you've done more for our children than we could have ever expected." Pam gestured to all of the folks milling around.

"But Teddy …" She didn't want to say died, but it hung in the air.

Pam smiled brightly. "You gave us two more years with our sweet boy—for that, we will forever be in your debt."

Laney didn't know what to say. She'd always counted the losses as well … losses. She'd never seen them as a win. But more time with Lara would have been a win, a huge win.

Pam pulled her into another hug. "Helen contacted us with the idea of making you a picture Wall of Fame, but we wanted to thank you in person. Pictures didn't seem like a big enough way of showing our appreciation."

Laney glanced back at Helen.

Helen shook her head. "Don't look at me. It was Devon's idea. He would be here right now if he could, but he had practice." She gestured to Pam. "She took over. I might have started the ball rolling, but she took it and ran with it."

Pam grinned. "That's right. This is the first annual Laney's Angels reunion. We're having one every year on Halloween to go along with the circus." Pam grabbed Laney's hand and pulled her farther into the room. "Do you realize that you've saved over a thousand children? They couldn't all be here today, but every single one has written you a letter, and most are coming to the circus tonight."

She pointed to a huge red, metal bucket full of letters in the corner.

"I don't know what to say." Laney was overwhelmed by the love that she felt in this room. These people were here to thank her. She tried to tell herself that she'd only been doing her job, but deep down, she knew that wasn't true. She'd loved every single child that had ever come through her practice ... and now, they were returning the favor. It was a sea of love pulling her along.

She went from person to person, faces clicking with names, and received hugs, kisses, and sometimes tears of joy from families she'd healed. She turned to her left and almost knocking Nina over. Laney looked around. All of her teammates were here ... in costume.

"Did you think we'd miss this?" Sweet Louise laughed. She was dressed as Glenda The Good Witch. "The girls and I have been chatting about your deplorable eating habits."

Laney hugged each lady in turn.

"I knew it was bad, but I didn't realize how bad." Charisma shook her head. She was dressed as a boxer complete with boxing gloves. The outfit really fit her personality. "I'm going to have to do some one-on-one coaching with you. Food is important."

"And here come the threats." January put her arm around Laney. January's nun's habit was complete with huge metal crucifixion. "I'm telling you, torture in the Dark Ages was nothing compared to a one-on-one session with baby Hitler over there. I'd run away from home if I were you."

"Don't be such a crabby pants." Susie was being extra Snow Whitey being that she was dressed as Snow White for Halloween.

"You would be so much more interesting if you'd cuss like a sailor while dressed as Snow White. That would be fun." January rolled her eyes. "Instead, you feel you must act like Snow White."

She straightened her own nun's costume. "Thank God I haven't taken on my costume's characteristics." She snorted. "I guess it's too late."

Charisma laughed.

"I don't know about y'all, but I feel a little over dressed." Nina shook the tailfin of her mermaid costume. "Someone could have mentioned that this wasn't a costume party."

Sweet Louise pulled her phone out of her cleavage to read a text. "Everything's ready."

"What's ready?" Laney looked around. There was more.

Nina took her hand and said, "Laney's Angels please follow us to the window. Laney's about to get more than she ever bargained for."

"I don't understand." Laney allowed Nina to lead her to the back of the waiting room—a wall of windows overlooking the hospital.

Sweet Louise pulled the brown cord and the wooden mini-blinds went up in a whoosh of dust and sunlight. "Hon, I'm going to need to speak personally with your cleaning company. They leave a lot to be desired."

Across the street, there were giant block letters in the windows of the hospital. Laney shaded her eyes from the sunlight and squinted to get a better view. Children of all shapes and sizes held up letters in the windows. She read the word on the top floor, "Mill? I don't understand."

The 'm' was turned upside down and became a 'w'. "Will…"

She moved to the next line, "you."

And then the next, "marry."

The breath caught in her throat as she moved to the floor below, "him?"

The next floor down had a huge arrow pointing down.

On the first floor, Devon stood with an arm full of yellow roses staring up at her.

"Will you marry him?" Someone read from behind her.

Laney stood there for a moment, just taking it all in. Devon had loved her for almost half of her life, had given her a family, and showed her that love was the only thing that mattered. There really wasn't much of a choice.

She beat on the glass and nodded, but the sun reflected off of the window and she could tell that Devon could no longer see her.

Frantically she beat harder.

"Honey, try this." Sweet Louise handed her a roll of silver duct tape. "I've always found it useful in a pinch."

Laney's heart was pounding a mile a minute. She made a huge 'y' in the window in front of her, an 'e' in the next window, and an 's' in the last window.

The kids in the hospital windows stopped jumping up and down and looked back and forth at one-another.

"You spelled 'sey'. For someone with such a huge brain, you missed something." January took the duct tape from Laney. "I'll fix it. Why don't you go tell him in person."

Laney couldn't help the deer in the headlights look she knew she had, and she didn't trust her voice. She nodded to everyone and took off in a dead run. She was down the stairs and running toward Devon in record time.

"Yes, yes, yes, a thousand times yes." She jumped into his arms and wrapped her legs around his waist. "It took you long enough."

His arms came around her.

She'd been waiting fourteen years for this day. It occurred to her that falling in love was reckless in a way.

She'd thought she needed to go skydiving to feel reckless when all she'd needed to do was find her soul mate.

"Give me some credit, it took me a while to find you." Tears rolled down his cheeks. "And this took some time to set up."

Happiness flooded Laney. "I love you."

She took the giant rose arrangement mashed between them and tossed it to the ground. "I love you."

She kissed him hard on the mouth.

The hospital and professional building erupting in hoots and hands beating on glass.

"I'd get down on one knee, but you're attached to my waist. I'm afraid I'd injure us both." The happiness radiating out from Devon was something she'd remember forever. "I got you a ring, but you just threw it on the ground."

Laney unwrapped herself from Devon, picked up the roses, and found the little black velvet box. She opened it, and her heart skipped a beat.

A thin braided gold band—like the bracelets they'd made for each other— held a huge, perfect princess cut diamond.

"Lara insisted that it be a princess cut. That kid knew diamonds. She helped me pick this one out." Devon held his hand out for her to hand him the box.

"Lara? You planned this with her?" Laney didn't think she still had the capacity to be overwhelmed, but she did.

"Of course, I had to ask her if it was okay to marry you." Devon laughed loudly. "She reluctantly gave her blessing, but she wanted to pick out the ring."

Laney felt her own tears of joy running down her cheeks.

Devon gently took the ring from her and held it out so she could see the engraving, DJ+EJ=4EVER.

"Just like the tree at camp." Her heart did another love flip-flop. "I hope it fits."

"I measured your finger when you were asleep. Do you think I'd leave anything to chance?" Devon slipped it on her finger.

It was a perfect fit.

"My life started the day I met you. I can't wait to see what our future holds." Devon kissed her lightly on the mouth.

Her life had begun the moment she'd met him too. He was her other half, her home, her family. They were soul mates.

"Damn, we're so sweet, I'd really like to punch us right now." Laney finally got her DJ forever.

Epilogue

One Year Later
"Are you sure you want to do this?" Devon clapped a hand on Big Billy Gain's shoulder. "She's eating for three now. Last Sunday I swear she ate an entire side of beef. It was a thing of beauty."

Devon beamed at his pregnant wife. She was sitting in the main dining room of First and Ten Barbecue directly under a huge picture of her complete, with a sign proclaiming that if you can out eat her, meal is free. They'd been open for three months and many had tried, but all had failed.

"I've got a rep to protect, and I've been training." Big Billy was trying for bravado, but his eyes showed fear.

"This is your last chance." Laney massaged the muscles of her lower back. "I haven't eaten all day. I'm telling you right now, it's going to be a blood bath."

Devon stepped behind his wife and took over massaging. He loved watching her body grow with his children. There was something inherently manly in having a pregnant wife. He'd gotten her that way, and the whole world knew it.

Laney rubbed her belly. "Lara and Lacey are starving. They love meat."

"It's your funeral." Devon pressed lightly right where he knew her back hurt. She melted back against him. Being married was the best thing ever. He got to wake up next to her and fall asleep right beside her. In between, he got to look at her.

"I can't watch." His mother took the hand of a four-year-old girl named Hannah who was her third foster child. "Come on baby girl, I've got a change purse full of quarters, and that coin-operated carousel on the playground outback isn't going to ride itself."

Hannah clung to his mother's leg like a life preserver. She'd come from a terrible home, but his mother would love her up. She'd be smiling and playing by herself in no time.

"I've got a hundred dollars that says Big Billy wins." Warren Daniver held up a hundred dollar bill.

Clint shook his head. "But she—"

"Make it five hundred and you've got yourself a deal." CoCo stood.

"Done." Daniver didn't bat an eye.

CoCo smiled sadly. "Since you missed the first beat down Big Billy took in Seattle, you might as well hand over the money and save yourself this disappointment."

"Of course all money won today will be donated to Project Hope so we can further the music lab at Dell Children's." Grace shot CoCo a look. "Otherwise it's gambling, and you're too young."

"Some people suck the fun out of everything." CoCo tried to pull off upset, but she leaned over and gave her stepmom a huge, wet kiss on the cheek.

Even though he'd given up football earlier this year, shortly after they'd won the Super Bowl again, his football family was still with him. Most of them hung out here, which was wonderful for business.

To save Big Billy from the humiliation he was about to face, they'd closed early so only friends and family were here to witness the shaming of Big Billy Gains.

"Choose your weapon." Devon looked to Big Billy. "Choose carefully, because if she really likes it, she's just going to eat more."

Big Billy nodded confidently. "Beef ribs. The only reason I lost in Seattle was because I don't like oysters."

"Keep telling yourself that, big guy." CoCo patted him on the shoulder. "Whatever it takes for you to sleep at night."

Devon grimaced. "Beef ribs, those are her favorite."

"I meant pork ribs." Big Billy's eyes darted around nervously.

"Sorry old friend. The rules are the rules. As the challenger, you get to pick the food, but you only get one choice." Devon signaled the waiter to bring over two platters of beef ribs.

He set the smaller one in front of Laney and the larger platter in front of Big Billy.

Laney switched the platters. "He's new."

Devon nodded to the waiter. "That's my wife. She's an eater. Why don't you have a seat and watch her out eat the meanest defensive tackle in the NFL." He turned back to Big Billy. "Laney has agreed to give you a ten rib handicap. On your mark, get set, eat."

This last year with Laney had been the best year of his life. All the waiting around to see her again had taught him to never waste a moment. He smiled to himself as he watched her. She was his, he still couldn't figure out how he'd pulled that off. What had started at summer camp would last forever because they were soul mates. He was the luckiest man alive.

About the Author

Katie Graykowski is an award winning author who likes sassy heroines, Mexican food, movies where lots of stuff gets blown up, and glitter nail polish. She lives on a hilltop outside of Austin, Texas where her home office has an excellent view of the Texas Hill Country. When she's not writing, she's scuba diving. Drop by her website www.katiegraykowski.com.